Praise f

"Anyone looking to escape into a classic 'who dun it' tale will like this book! Nell, the main character, is a likeable soul who is struggling with several aspects in her life—being recently widowed, being an 'emotional eater', and the fact that someone seems to want her dead! I enjoyed getting to know her and the other supporting characters in this book. I feel this is an excellent book to read on many levels, and a great way to spend a relaxing weekend!"

—K. C. Berg, Author of *Fallen Angel*

Advance Praise for Death Nosh:

"You can always count on Mary Grace Murphy turning out an excellent mystery, but she surpasses herself with her latest book, Death Nosh. *She goes about assembling all the ingredients in this who-done-it by making us care about her characters, her dogs, and her mouth-watering recipes. To make sure we're hooked, she employs the clever device of her murderer talking to us in a first person point of view, making us eager to learn who he or she is. You won't be able to stop reading."*

—Jean Thomas, Award-winning Author of *Too Good To Be True*

"In this third volume of Mary Grace Murphy's Noshes up North Culinary series, widowed Nell is once again involved in murder. However, her sleuthing skills are right on target (even if more than a little suspect themselves) and get her into a whole lot of trouble. The police chief is willing to work with her...but could it be he's interested in Nell more than her take on the murders? This fun read will keep you turning the pages."

—Nancy Sweetland, Author of *The Perfect Suspect*

Death Nosh

A Noshes Up North Culinary Mystery

Book 3

Mary Grace Murphy

WD PUBLISHING

Editing: Brittiany Koren
Cover art design and interior layout: Ed Vincent of ENC Graphic Secvices
Cover photographs © Shutterstock.com

Category: Cozy Culinary Mystery
Description: *Retired teacher and food blogger, Nell Bailey, searches for a killer in her Northeast Wisconsin hometown.*
Ebook ISBN: 978-0-9981673-2-9
Paperback ISBN: 978-0-9981673-1-2
Hardcover ISBN: 978-0-9981673-0-5

First Edition published by Written Dreams Publishing, September 2016.

PUBLISHING

Green Bay, WI 54311

Other books in A Noshes Up North Culinary Mystery series

Death Nell

Death Knock

Dedication

For my sister, Jeanne, the most determined person I know, whose strength and unshakable love always surrounds me.

For my brother, Jack, whose quick-witted sense of humor and constant reading of books served as models for me in my formative years.

When the three of us are together, the laughter never ends.

Chapter 1

The police car parked on the street sent a warning flare up in Nell's mind. She pulled in behind the cruiser, but hesitated before getting out of her vehicle. Why would an officer be *here*? One way to find out. Nell clutched the plastic tray of homemade peanut butter cookies in front of her as she rushed from her car. It was almost dark in the late afternoon, but the streetlights were twinkling and gave Nell a spotlight on the falling snow. She approached the large Victorian home where, the previous evening, she had been a guest. The outside still looked festive and inviting, except for that squad car casting suspicion in her mind. She rang the bell, uncertain if Yolanda would answer its call.

"Nell Bailey, what are *you* doing here?" Chief Vance, head of the Bayshore Police Department, stood tall in the doorway and did not step aside to allow her to enter.

"I want to pay my respects to Clayton's daughter and to offer some goodies so other visitors can have a bit of a nosh." Nell uncovered the tray and the aroma of the still warm cookies floated up to her nose. "Also, I attended the Christmas party here last night."

"I'll be damned." The chief shook his head. "How you are able to insinuate yourself into every case is beyond me. You've become Bayshore's answer to Jessica Fletcher."

"Case? Are you saying Clayton Dunbar was murdered?"

Chief Vance stepped aside and gestured into the room. "That's not what I'm saying, but come on in. There's no point in having you stand out in the cold." He closed the door behind her, but kept her standing in the foyer.

Nell wiped her feet on the rug then noticed Hazel Burton, Clayton's longtime housekeeper, hovering in the background. Nell walked over to give her a hug. "Hazel, I'm so sorry for your loss. I know you worked for Clayton for years so he must have been like a member of your own family."

"He was, Nell. Mr. Dunbar was such a kind, gentle man. I can't believe he's gone." Hazel's frail body shook as she wiped at her eyes. "I know he was old, in his nineties, but he was so healthy. You saw him last night. He was happy, bouncing around like a man twenty years younger."

She took the tray Nell offered and trudged back to the kitchen. As she watched, Nell realized Hazel was just as fragile as Clayton. How had she been able to care for this magnificent home on her own? Shaking that thought off, Nell walked back to the chief.

"Are you suspecting foul play, Chief?" Nell asked.

She returned the chief's stare until he answered, "The cause of death has yet to be determined. How did you know him?"

"We taught a couple of years at the middle school together. He was finishing up his career and I was starting mine. Clayton helped me learn the ropes my first year. After he retired, my late husband, Drew, and I used to run into his wife and him around town. Every year he always invited me to his Christmas party, like last night. I was so pleased that he kept having the parties even after Bernice died."

"Do you think you could make a list of the guests who attended last night? Hazel's too upset."

"I could, but I wasn't here the entire time. It was an open house type of party." Nell absently stroked the soft green velvet on the back of the settee in the gigantic foyer. "His daughter, Yolanda, might be a better person to ask. I think she's been visiting for a few days. She may have access to a guest list."

"According to Hazel, Yolanda Dunbar Nyland said her goodbyes to her father last night. She headed down to Milwaukee in her rental car early this morning to catch a plane back to Florida." The chief frowned then studied Nell. "I guess I'm asking for your help."

"Yes, I'll definitely make a list. I probably can name all of the guests. They arrived at different times, but most everyone stayed until the end." Nell's blue eyes shone and her voice went into high gear. "There are tons of other ways I can help, too. I'll do anything..."

"Don't get ahead of yourself, Jessica Fletcher, I'm only asking for a list of guests." He looked toward the kitchen. "I could ask Hazel to make the list."

"No, I'll do it. I thought so highly of Clayton; this will make me feel as if I'm helping."

"Okay. Bring it down to the station tomorrow morning." The chief opened the front door.

She took the hint and slipped outside.

Nell pulled her old tan Mercury into the garage, saying a silent prayer in thanks that the thirteen-year-old Sable still ran well. She opened the door to the kitchen to the delight of her feisty miniature schnauzer, George, and mischievous Maltese, Newman. They were named during a time when *Seinfeld*, even in reruns, was her favorite comedy show. Heck, it still was.

"Wanna go outside?" Nell walked to the sliding glass door in the living room and they ventured out onto the snowy patio. The boys trotted out to the yard to settle up some business. Newmie ran back to Nell, but George stood there. She knew he was waiting for her to throw the ball. Nell almost always played fetch when she came out with them.

"I hate to break it to you, George, but winter has arrived. Soon there will be deep snow out here and most of our outdoor time will be on our w-a-l-k." Nell spelled the word out as she didn't want to take them for a spin right now. She started toward the door with Newmie on her heels. "Come on, George. Time for a treat." He trotted toward her.

Once inside, Nell was true to her word and doled out treats. She then threw a few stuffed toys around in the living room to give the dogs a bit of exercise. She could only imagine what it would be like if she had two big dogs instead of little ones.

Next she grabbed a notebook and plopped in her easy chair. Her boys settled down on the floor as she clicked on the TV. Thoughts of her conversation with Chief Vance were foremost on her mind. Why would the police still be in the Dunbar home so long after a body was found? Could Clayton Dunbar have been murdered? Three hours ago the possibility hadn't even crossed her mind. Something must have made the chief suspicious. *But what?* Right now she had a little bit of an in with him. She needed to show the chief what an asset she could be. Police officers must need to bounce ideas off other people. Maybe their wives listened and offered opinions strictly off the record? But Chief Vance wasn't married...

As she was beginning to mull that fact over in her mind, the phone rang. Nell looked over on the end table and read the caller ID. It was Sam Ryan. Sam, the wonderful man who Nell had been seeing for several months. She felt a twinge of guilt.

"Hello, Sam," she said as she picked up the phone and held it to her ear.

"Ahh, Nell, how I look forward to our talks each day," Sam admitted in his deep, sexy voice that made her melt on the spot.

"Me, too. I hope your day has been without incident." Nell knew Sam was concerned about his restaurant and bar, Sam's Slam. Heidi, one of his best waitresses, had been having some personal problems recently and it had been affecting everyone on the premises.

"No more than usual. Just glad to go into my office for a bit and talk about something else."

"Oh. Then I guess it's time to bring up another topic." Nell ran her fingers through her silver hair and lowered her voice to a whisper. "I may be involved in another murder."

"What?" bellowed Sam. "That's not welcome news. What are you talking about?"

Too late Nell realized her statement wouldn't be met with excitement. "I guess I'm overstating my involvement. Remember I went to a Christmas party last night at the home of a former colleague, Clayton Dunbar?"

"I do," Sam said sounding somewhat apprehensive.

"This morning I saw on Facebook that he died. He was ninety-two, so I didn't think too much about it. I made some peanut butter cookies for his family and visitors. I took them over a couple hours ago and paid my respects to his housekeeper."

"Okay. Everything seems fine so far."

"The chief of police was there examining the scene and asked me to make a guest list from the party last night. He must be looking for suspects."

"Let me get this straight, Nell. The police were at the residence of someone who died in their home. I believe it's called proper procedure. I would imagine the police need to speak to those attending the event to ask if he was exhibiting signs of illness or distress. They would need a list of attendees. You've been asked to help. It sounds innocent to me. I don't see any reason for you to think there's been a murder." Sam gave a little chuckle. "I think you've exaggerated the situation this time, Nell."

"Maybe so." Nell heard a loud male voice in the background. "Who is yelling?"

"I don't know," he sighed, "but I better go check it out. Talk to you later."

Nell hung up her landline phone. Sam wasn't seeing Clayton's death and Chief Vance's request the way she was. Her explanation may have made Sam feel relief, but his reaction didn't please her. Nell adjusted her glasses and walked to the kitchen.

She needed carbs.

Chapter 2

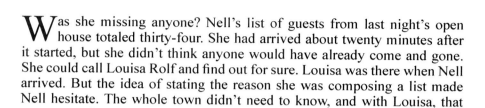

Was she missing anyone? Nell's list of guests from last night's open house totaled thirty-four. She had arrived about twenty minutes after it started, but she didn't think anyone would have already come and gone. She could call Louisa Rolf and find out for sure. Louisa was there when Nell arrived. But the idea of stating the reason she was composing a list made Nell hesitate. The whole town didn't need to know, and with Louisa, that was sure to happen.

In most cases, she could have waited for Yolanda to visit Bayshore to ask her, but Nell wasn't sure when Yolanda would come back. Besides, Yolanda had waited until the middle of the party to make a grand entrance down the staircase, as usual. The woman had to be pushing seventy. Her debutante performance was getting a little old.

Nell glanced at the end table next to her chair with regret. The flattened bag of semi-sweet chocolate chips advertised her weakness. It had only been half full, but she'd been saving it to make a batch of fudge to have on hand for Christmas visitors. She had already made several batches to donate to the library bake sale. Ahhh, who was she kidding? Not even herself. She would have made one more batch of fudge and eaten it all. Nell picked up the empty bag and took it to the trash.

It was difficult for her to maintain good eating habits over the holidays. And by holidays, she meant Halloween through Valentine's Day. These months were considered the height of candy and dessert season. She had worked hard through October and November this year with the help of the local Bulk Blasters' group meetings and working out at the Bayshore Fitness Center. She was able to control her eating habits enough so she hadn't gained any weight. She hadn't lost any either, but other years she gained at least ten pounds over those months and never lost it again. Now with Christmas coming, she was starting to fall back into the old pattern. Nell took a deep breath. The chocolate chips were gone and couldn't tempt her anymore. She must move on.

Her thoughts went back to her friend, Clayton. Why would anyone want to kill such a kind, old gentleman? It didn't make sense. Unless...unless something was up with Yolanda. Maybe she was in deep financial trouble and couldn't wait for him to die to get her inheritance. Good grief! The man was ninety-two. However, it wasn't unusual for someone to live a few years past one hundred and Clay had been in great physical shape. Waiting for money another ten years might not have fit in Yolanda's plans.

Nell rebuked herself for her thoughts. She was making the worst kind of assumptions in her mind. Yolanda had always seemed self-centered to Nell, but she also was a loving daughter. She couldn't be the one.

Her friend may not have been killed at all. *Chief Vance is doing his job and covering all the bases.* She should put the thought of murder right out of her head until she knew more. She looked back at her guest list and her mind went in a different direction. She'd call her good friend, Elena, and get her take on it. Nell picked up the phone.

"Hello," Elena rasped as she answered the phone on the fourth ring.

"Did I catch you at a bad time?" Nell inquired.

"I was out in the garage looking for the miniature Christmas tree to put on the front porch," Elena sighed. "I know I should let the machine pick up and return the call later. Somehow when the phone rings, I go to it, just like Pavlov's dog."

"Do you want to call me back later so you can continue searching?"

"No, it's fine. I'm here now. I hope you have some interesting news to share."

"I do. This is top secret, so don't tell anyone." Nell again scanned her list of guests.

"Who would I tell?" Elena laughed.

"When I dropped cookies off at Clayton's house today, Chief Vance was there." Nell held her breath. "There's a possibility he could have been killed."

Elena gasped. "He thinks Clayton Dunbar was murdered? The chief said that?"

"Not...*exactly* those words."

"What *were* his exact words?"

"He mentioned I insinuate myself into every 'case' and he compared me to Jessica Fletcher. If it isn't murder, what is the 'case'?" Nell rubbed her left eyebrow.

"Could have been a slip of the tongue."

"Yes, but the chief also asked me to make up a guest list. I think of it more as a list of suspects."

"Now that information interests me. Since you've called, am I right to assume that you plan to do some amateur sleuthing?"

"I'm noodling with the possibility." Nell smiled to herself.

"You know, partner in crime, if you need me, I'm available."

"Thanks, partner in crime-*solving*." Nell chuckled as she ended the call.

The branches of the trees were covered in snow-white crystals in Nell's backyard as the sun rose the next morning. As they raced out of the doggie door, George and Newman made fresh tracks in the snow. Last night's paw prints were covered with glittering cotton and Nell knew she would soon be shoveling out a path for them. But first, she'd enjoy a cup of coffee and then take the boys for a walk.

As she read the paper over her steaming cup of liquid energy, Nell considered taking the guest list from Clayton's open house down to the police station. She needed to come up with a way to make sure she could get into the chief's office and talk to him. The benefits of working *with* him instead of *against* him were tremendous. She didn't need to be the one to physically capture the killer. Nell had no desire to claim credit. But she did have some recent experience figuring out the identity of a murderer. If she and the chief put their heads together, the case would be solved sooner. How could she make Chief Vance see it her way?

Her chores completed, Nell drove down to the station on a mission. She would refuse to leave until she saw Chief Vance. Just that simple.

As she approached the door to the police station, it was opened for her by the chief.

"It's about time you got here. I've been waiting for that list you promised. I thought you'd be here first thing this morning," Vance snorted as he stood towering over her.

"It is first thing. It's only eight o'clock." Typical man, trying to throw her off by putting her on the defensive. "I wanted to speak with you and didn't know what time you rolled out of bed in the morning." Nell walked toward his office.

"Where do you think you're going? Give me the list and then our business is done." Vance's fingers combed through his thinning hair.

"Didn't you hear me when I mentioned I wanted to speak with you?" Nell glanced around the room at the members of his force. "Privately." She was willing to make a scene if he refused and was sure the look in her eye conveyed that message.

"All right, but make it quick."

Nell followed him to his office and accepted his offer of the visitor's chair. "What can I do for you? And don't even *think* about saying you want to help with the case."

"Is there a case?"

"Ah, Nell." He sat down behind the desk and shook his head. "I guess I'm not giving away any secrets by confirming it's true. I'm sure word is starting to spread even as we speak. Now how about that list you made?"

"Oh, yeah." Nell dug for it in her purse then handed it to him. "I came up with thirty-four guests, but now the word is out, so I want to check with a woman who arrived before I did. It's possible someone could have left before I got there."

"Thank you, Nell. I appreciate the list." The chief practically jumped up from his chair.

"Oh, no. I have questions. You're not hustling me out of here yet."

"In reference to what?" Vance's eyes squinted at her across the desk. "I told you, you're not getting anywhere near this investigation. Your *help* isn't needed."

"I already have helped you, and you thanked me. Remember?" Nell pulled her iPad mini out of her purse. "How was the murder committed? Please give me the details. As you said yourself, it's circulating in town. Isn't it better for me to hear it from you than the rumor mill?"

"All right fine, have it your way." Chief Vance gave an exaggerated sigh. "I gave the details to Clayton's daughter in Florida and shortly afterward received a phone call from the local paper with the exact information, so I gather Yolanda has contacted her local friends." He fumbled with a pen on his desk. "Dunbar was poisoned."

"Poisoned?" Nell repeated. "What was used? Did it happen at his party?"

"Without giving away too much, he *was* surrounded by a lot of food last night. I'd imagine he consumed more than he's accustomed to eating. Perhaps some dishes were unfamiliar to him and he wouldn't have noticed if they tasted funny." He stood up and headed to the door.

Nell put the iPad back in her purse and moved toward the chief. Her mind was full with the thoughts of poison, and she appreciated the chief being so forthcoming. She was about to thank him when he spoke up.

"I've heard that you're known in town for being somewhat of a foodie. Do you ever do any catering? Did you bring any food to the open house?"

Nell's head snapped back in order to give him a piece of her mind, but instead she saw twinkling eyes and a hint of upturned lips. "Very funny."

She walked out of the police station with a new appreciation for the chief. *There may be more to him than meets the eye.*

Chapter 3

When Nell got home, she was full of speculation about Clayton Dunbar's death and gave Elena a call. Ideas were flowing at a fast pace. The two old friends, who secretly thought of themselves as female versions of Sherlock Holmes and Dr. Watson, tried to come up with a feasible plan to assist the authorities in their hunt for the killer.

"You know," Nell admitted, "I didn't expect to learn Clay was murdered. I thought Chief Vance was being overly cautious, and that when I went to the station this morning, I'd find out Clayton died from a heart attack."

"Those were my thoughts initially, too," Elena agreed. "Who could be mean enough to kill that kind-hearted old guy? And for what possible reason?"

"We have to find out what happened. It's our mission, if we choose to accept it."

"Well, maybe we *shouldn't* choose to accept it. Not yet anyway. Give the police some time and if they can't find the killer, we'll step in to help."

"By then, some leads may have gone cold. We need to strike while the iron is hot." Nell snapped her fingers which made George jump to his feet from a resting position.

"If my memory serves, I believe you've been warned in the past about interfering with an investigation."

"The chief was never serious about charging me with anything. I'm not too concerned about it." Nell leaned over to pet George to calm him. "Before I phoned you, I made a quick call to Louisa Rolf. I wanted to make sure I hadn't missed any party guests on my list for the chief."

"Did she remember anyone else?"

"No, but now she'll talk about it all over town," complained Nell.

"Let it go. For most people, her gossip goes in one ear and out the other."

"That's true," Nell said. "It's time I give Sam a call, and then I'll start thinking about which of the finger foods may have held the poison last night. You know, Chief Vance's snarky comment asking if I brought any food to the party hit a little too close to home."

"Why's that?"

"I didn't take any food to the open house. The caterer had prepared everything so elegantly; there was no need for offerings from a home cook. But Clayton did try some of my food. We were having a nice chat in a small group when he leaned over and told me he wasn't going to eat any dessert. He said he had some of my fudge a friend had brought him from the library bake sale, and after everyone left, he was going to eat it. I was delighted because he was choosing my humble fudge instead of all of the elegant desserts offered. I hope he really did eat it later that night and went to bed with a good taste in his mouth."

"Mmmm. Everyone raves about that fudge. You should enter it in a contest or next year's fair. And you know, Nell, it had nothing to do with his death. I'll see if I can come up with any general information about poisons in food. Talk to you tomorrow."

Elena's kind words had helped, but Nell knew Sam didn't agree with her about searching for clues in a murder case. Still, she hit Sam's number on her cell phone, apprehension or not.

"Sam's Slam," Sam answered.

"Are you busy, Sam?"

"I can always spare some time for you, honey. How was your morning?"

"Very interesting. I took my list of guests from Clayton's open house down to the police early this morning."

"Good. You've helped now, so it's out of your system. When it turns out he died of natural causes, you'll be glad that you didn't waste your time and effort looking for clues."

"Clayton was poisoned," Nell's voice shook. "It was murder."

There was silence on the other end for a moment. "That surprises me. I'm sorry that your old friend died, but don't jump to conclusions. The elderly gentleman could have accidently swallowed something from the wrong bottle." Sam lowered his voice. "Either way, accident or murder, it has nothing to do with you."

"Of course it has something to do with me. I was at his house only a few hours before he was found dead. I could have eaten the same food that killed him. Moreover, he was my colleague and friend." Nell talked faster and faster with each sentence. "I've found key clues in other murder investigations. I have to lend my expertise to this case."

"The police have plenty of *expertise*, Nell." Sam's voice had risen to the point Nell needed to hold the phone away from her ear. "They don't need Nell Bailey to maneuver herself right into their way."

"Needed or not, I'm helping."

"No! You're not getting involved. I'm putting my foot down." Nell's cell phone almost throbbed.

Crickets could have been heard on the line.

Finally, Nell, in a calm voice, broke the silence. "Who are you to tell me what I can and can't do? I think we've talked enough for tonight."

"On that point, you're correct."

One trouble with cell phones was the absence of the physical pleasure of slamming the phone back in its cradle. Nell pressed the End button with vigor.

The more Nell thought about her conversation with Sam, the more irritated she became. No man had told her what to do since she was a young girl, and admittedly, that was when she needed direction from her dad. Drew shared his opinion about what she did, but never issued an order. She hadn't given him orders, either. They were adults and made up their own minds. If there were consequences from choosing poorly, they suffered them together.

As much as Sam's presence in her life had made it richer, she was unwilling to succumb to his commands. If Sam thought she would back down, he was mistaken. Where did he get the nerve?

In an effort to free her mind of negative thoughts, she pulled out the ingredients for a healthy salad for lunch. Crisp greens, cucumber slices, juicy tomato wedges, and chunks of leftover chicken breast filled the bill. She drizzled a bottled vinaigrette over it, and for a final touch, tossed on a few cashews for crunch. Her lunch was ready in less than ten minutes. The salad was tasty and filled her need for something healthy. Who knew what kind of temptations might be lurking, waiting to be given in to during the rest of the day?

Before she left for the police station, Nell had shoveled the light snow off her patio to allow the boys to get outside for some fresh air. Now George and Newmie were looking toward the backyard with purpose. She opened the sliding glass door and let them out. Once on the patio, they raced out to the backyard. There wasn't enough snow to stop them from giving a squirrel a good workout right up a tree. Eight wet paws returned to the house with the owners of those paws quite pleased with themselves for getting rid of a varmint on the premises. If only Nell's problems could be so easily solved.

Her relationship with Sam was in jeopardy. She had no plans of stopping her investigation because of a direct order from Sam Ryan. He was a stubborn man and she didn't imagine it would be easy for him to apologize. But, there was no way she was sorry she had stood up for herself. He wasn't about to receive an apology from her. A thought came to her mind, but she ignored it. *Don't go for the chocolate. Think about something else.*

Poison. She knew next to nothing about poison. She needed to do some research in that area. She could try to find books, but maybe the internet would be a faster and more thorough choice. She made a mental note to do an internet search later tonight.

The identity of the killer had her stumped. If she made a list, Yolanda would be on it, but who else? Yolanda probably stood to inherit the estate. Clayton had lived in an elegant old mansion, the former home of a United States senator, but Nell had no idea about his wealth. He'd taught school for close to forty years, but she couldn't remember his wife ever working. Pondering that thought for a while, she remembered something about Bernice being from the East Coast and coming from money. As far as Nell knew, they had only one child. Who, other than Yolanda, would benefit financially from Clayton's death?

Is there any way, *other* than financially, that someone could be rewarded by his demise? Could Clayton possibly have had some sort of information that someone didn't want to get out? Perhaps something was going to happen, or Clayton had pertinent knowledge. With him out of the way, the road could be clear for the culprit. Where this train of thought was taking her, Nell had no idea.

What about a possible theft? Had the killer taken something out of the house after delivering the poison? Could Clayton have owned some item that he didn't realize was worth a fortune? For some people, that's reason enough to kill.

No one else died from the food at the open house. Was the murderer present the night of the party and purposely handed Clayton the tainted bite? She thought back and recalled the guests chatting with their host pleasantly the whole time she was there. There'd been no animosity.

Way in the back of Nell's brain, an irritating little pebble of doubt gnawed. What if the poison wasn't delivered through the party food? Could Clayton have swallowed something hazardous without knowing it, as Sam had suggested? It would help to discover the kind of poison the killer used. Chief Vance chose to clam up when she asked him. However, he hinted at having a sense of humor as she left the police station. Maybe she could use that to her advantage.

Chapter 3.5

The fake bottom of the desk drawer stuck. I set the handful of items I wanted to hide down on the desk and used both hands to jimmy the latch. Finally it released, and I deposited copies of the official paperwork. The original documents were back in the briefcase. I needed to put a move on to position the briefcase in exactly the same spot as it had previously occupied. There. That looked right. He'll never be the wiser. This is almost too easy. What kind of loser takes his briefcase to the fitness center anyway?

I felt in my pocket for the round, hard shape that filled me with ecstasy. *Ahhh.* I unwrapped the butterscotch and stuffed it in my mouth.

Chapter 4

Nell walked to the scale at her Bulk Blasters meeting, hoping to have lost some weight. She would be satisfied with staying the same, but she didn't want to gain. Wearing her light clothes and removing her shoes, she stepped on the precision instrument that so easily could alter her mood.

Heather, the young and bouncy weight recorder, chirped happily, "A gain of half a pound. That's still good for this time of year, Nell."

"I'll take it, but I had my fingers crossed for a loss." Nell moved on so the next person could step on the scale. She hardly felt like staying for the meeting now, but these were the times she needed to stay.

Their leader usually had an encouraging message, so Nell settled herself into a chair next to Dottie Dumpling. What an unfortunate name for a woman who was chronically overweight! They had met shortly after Nell moved to Bayshore, a bustling community of five thousand residents, located thirty miles north of Green Bay. Nell had been driving out to the bay to look at the water. She had a flat tire, moved to the side of the road, and Dottie and her husband, Leo, stopped to help. Dottie was lively and full of fun and she kept Nell entertained while Leo changed the tire. The two had never become close confidantes, but they remained friendly. Nell had Dottie's daughter in class a few years later and, after that, taught her son, too.

Dottie joked ever since she accepted Leo's last name, a couple "dumplings" were added to her body every year and stuck to her like glue. She was never able to take off the baby weight, either. Several years older than Nell, Dottie had started to experience health problems which had made her realize she had to take charge. She had joined Bulk Blasters only last week.

"Dottie, it's so nice to see you again," Nell said. "How's life treating you?"

"Great." Dottie tossed her dark bangs and spread her hands in front of her protruding stomach. "Everything that is, except my increasing waistline."

"That's why I'm here. I started a couple months ago in order to gain some control over my compulsive eating and lose some weight." The two commiserated as they waited for the meeting to begin.

"I'm not mentioning this to everyone, but I've recently started using a CPAP machine at night while I sleep to help me breathe," Dottie confided. "It's uncomfortable and I have a hard time sleeping. I've decided to lose weight so I can dump the machine."

"I'm glad it's giving you motivation, but maybe the machine isn't fitted properly," Nell said. "Other people I know have told me having the CPAP has made a world of difference in their energy. They are able to sleep soundly at night and feel refreshed when they wake up."

"That's the theory, but I don't like the contraption over my nose and mouth." Dottie gave Nell a wink. "A bit of the romance disappears as soon as the mask goes on, too."

"Oh, dear! I hadn't considered that. I guess you do have a reason other than good health to lose some weight."

"I'm going to do it this time, Nell. Just wait and see."

That evening as Nell prepared her supper, she thought about how hard Dottie was working to lose weight. Maybe the two of them could pair up to walk together, or call back and forth if either of them were tempted. Being partners could be a wonderful benefit for both of them. Keeping those thoughts in mind, Nell's meal consisted of baked chicken, asparagus, and pickled beets. A simple meal, yet delicious and healthy. She put every thought of caramel or chocolate right out of her mind. If Dottie could lose weight, then so could she. They would need to make sure they encouraged each other to stay on target and not give themselves a treat. Partners walked a fine line between motivating each other toward success and giving each other permission to stray from the plan. Would the two of them be helpful to each other, or would they be willing accomplices on a food binge? She'd mull it over before giving Dottie a call.

Chapter 5

"Dad, what are you and Nell doing for your birthday?" Benita Ryan inquired as she walked from the kitchen to the bar at Sam's Slam. She perched on a barstool as she waited for an answer.

"Probably nothing," Sam mumbled as he busied himself moving beer into the cooler and avoided eye contact.

"Nothing? Why aren't you and Nell getting together?"

"I think I should stay visible here for week or so."

"Are you still worried Heidi's ex-husband will show up again and cause another commotion?" Benita took the band out of her long, dark hair and combed her fingers through it.

"Once I showed up, Al quieted right down."

"You set him right, Dad. He won't be back. Besides Heidi told me she and Al worked out their problem last night." Benita gave him a wink. "Why don't you take a couple days off? Go have a good time with Nell."

Sam shrugged his shoulders.

"Nell does know it's your birthday soon, doesn't she?"

Sam frowned.

"Well, I can take care of it pronto if she doesn't. I'm good at dropping big hints, so I'll give her a call right now." Benita pulled out her cell phone.

"Hold on there just a minute, Bean. I don't want you calling Nell." Sam flashed his blue eyes at his daughter.

Benita slid her phone back into her pocket and gave her dad the once over. "What's going on?"

Sam hung his head and rubbed his hands along the sides of his pants. "Not that it's any of your business, but Nell and I are taking a little break."

"Taking a little break? Dad!"

"Now don't go getting all in a huff. We've had a difference of opinion, that's all."

"What did you do?"

"Why do you think *I* did something?"

Benita drew in a loud breath. "Because you're my father and I know how stubborn you are. I advise you not to let this go on too long. The longer the separation goes on, the harder it will be to get back together. You and Nell make a great couple. A difference of opinion can be smoothed over if someone apologizes. Sometimes we all say we're sorry even if we think we're right."

"Yeah, well, I don't."

"Then take my advice as a chance to learn something new. Men and women are different, you know."

"You think you're sharing a new concept with me? I'd say a different species." Sam grabbed three beers in each hand and turned to set them in the cooler. One slipped out of his fingers and shattered on the floor, spreading broken glass and sticky liquid at his feet. "Damn!"

The Bean shook her head as she got off the barstool to return to her work in the kitchen. "Just think about what I said," she called as she pulled her shiny, black hair back in a ponytail and went through the doorway.

"I hope a difference of opinion is all it is," Sam muttered to himself as he started to clean up the mess, "and Nell isn't as stubborn as I am."

Chapter 6

Nell glanced at the caller ID on her landline, half hoping it was Sam, but was relieved when she saw it was her good friend and sleuthing buddy. "Hello, Elena. What are you up to this fine morning?"

"Nothing, and that's why I'm calling. I finished putting up all of my Christmas decorations and would love to go to lunch. Any chance you're free?"

"There's always a chance I'm free when going out to eat is the main event. I wanted to talk to you today, too," Nell said. She willed her eyes not to mist up, thinking of Sam. "Where do you want to go?"

"It doesn't matter much to me. Do you need more information for your foodie blog on any place in town?"

"Today I need to concentrate more on the conversation than on the food." Nell played with the gold necklace she always wore around her neck, an anniversary gift from her late husband.

"Is something wrong? The way you said that sounded ominous."

"I'm fine. Let's say Miner's Fish House at 12:30. Okay with you?"

"Perfect!" Elena agreed. "See you there."

As she walked into Miner's Fish House, Nell hung up her coat and then surveyed the tables in the bar area for her friend. A few tables and bar stools were occupied, but she didn't find Elena. She went to the dining room, appreciating the British themed pub that found a home in Bayshore. A waitress was leaning over a quiet corner table, setting down a Bloody Mary. Nell headed in that direction and caught the waitress, Lynn, before she left. "I'd like one of those, too. And please add extra hot sauce to mine and no lemon."

"Coming right up."

Elena looked good as always. Her highlighted hair was cut in a sassy new style and today her nails were colored Coral Kiss. She took a big sip of her drink and sighed. "That hit the spot."

"Yes, they do make a good Bloody Mary here. I love all the produce and other goodies that accompany it." Nell settled into her chair and picked up the menu on the place setting.

Elena whispered, "I had a horrible thought about the poisoning. What if it wasn't necessarily meant for Clayton Dunbar? What if someone put some contaminated food where anyone at the party had access to it?"

"What an awful thought! It could've killed numerous people. Someone who could do that would be truly evil."

"I know, and it would make it much harder to find a random killer." Elena stirred her drink.

"You've given me something to think about as we have our lunch. Have you decided what you're going to order?"

"No. Why don't we wait a while and enjoy our drinks. It'll give us a chance to catch up," Elena said. "I have a feeling you have something to discuss with me."

"It's really not that big of a deal." Nell drew in a deep breath and looked around. She then fixed her eyes on Elena. "I'm irritated with Sam and don't think we'll be going out for a while."

Elena's dark blue eyes widened as she stage whispered, "Not that big of a deal? What happened?"

Nell started going through the conversation she had with Sam.

Lynn came with her Bloody Mary just in time for Nell to fortify herself with a big gulp. The spicy drink burned going down her throat, but she managed to relate Sam's big finish to her friend. "Then he said I was not to continue with any investigating and, get this, he 'put his foot down.' Can you believe it?"

A gasp escaped from Elena. "He actually said 'he put his foot down'?" At Nell's nod, she continued, "He can't order you around. Who does he think he is, your father?"

Nell took a sip and adjusted her glasses. "My thoughts exactly. I don't need someone in my life who thinks he can tell me what to do."

"Do you think he said it without thinking how it sounded?" asked Elena. She tilted her head. "You know, Sam's a great guy. I'd hate to have seen the last of him. And you have been so happy. I'll bet he's sorry he ever uttered those words."

"I agree with most of what you just said, Elena. But I don't know if he's sorry. Sam is a stubborn man and he will have to admit he made a mistake. If he doesn't realize what he did was wrong, then I don't see any future with him." Nell took a big bite of her dill pickle.

The friends looked over the menus and made their decisions. They each ordered another Bloody Mary while discussing other news of the day.

"Your food should be up shortly," Lynn said as she placed their second round of drinks before them.

"Thanks," said Nell.

"I have a little news of my own to bring up." Elena's eyes twinkled as she looked at Nell. "But I kinda hate to mention it after hearing about your situation with Sam."

"Don't be silly. What's up?" Nell's eyebrows raised in anticipation.

"You'll never guess who called me... Herbert Caruthers!"

Nell paused, running through the imaginary rolodex in her mind. "Am I supposed to know who he is?"

"I must have mentioned him to you. I went out with him a few times in college. We didn't hit it off romantically, but he was a good guy." Elena was beaming.

"Well, I do declare, Elena May," Nell said in her best Southern accent, "I've never seen you quite so giddy. Could there be more to the romantic story here than you're revealing?"

"You know, you're horrible with accents and my middle name isn't May." Elena sniffed. "We liked each other, but it wasn't the right time. I met Tom, and Herb was dating Iris, the girl he later married. It wasn't meant to be."

"Why might he be calling you? Is something 'meant to be' now?"

"Don't be ridiculous, Nell. I shouldn't have told you. You make a joke out of everything. It's probably nothing."

"Why is it 'probably nothing'? I wasn't joking about anything. Maybe he is a widower or divorced, and you could relight the flame. You hear about those stories all the time where people meet again at a high school reunion and fall in love. It gives two people a second chance at having a relationship. I think it's very romantic."

"He's asked me to meet him for lunch tomorrow right here. I have to admit, I'm a bit excited."

A steaming hot pasty was set before Nell and a juicy cheeseburger and garlic fries were delivered to Elena. They practically swooned from the aroma.

"I'm happy to see this place is offering the choice of chili sauce, along with ketchup and gravy for a pasty now. It adds a southwestern Wisconsin touch to the entrée." Nell poured an equal pile of chili sauce and ketchup on her plate to alternately drag parts of the pasty through. She took a bite. "Hot. And delicious. Just the way I like it."

Elena started in on her burger and fries. "Yum. You know how much I like a good burger. And these fries are out of sight."

The next few minutes were quiet as they finished their meals. Nell made a point to only eat half of her pasty, so she could take the rest home for another meal. Soon they headed toward the door. "Why didn't you suggest some other place to go today if you're coming here tomorrow, Elena?"

"I like it here and so many choices are offered, I always find something tempting."

"I'll be waiting to hear all about your meeting with Herbert. I hope you have a lot of fun. You never know when something interesting will happen. But you might not want to order the garlic fries tomorrow," Nell said with a wink.

Chapter 7

George and Newman climbed over each other to get to Nell as she walked in the door. She bent to pet them and love them up a bit. "How are you doing, guys? Wanna go outside?" She walked out on the patio with them and waited while they scurried around and raised their legs. Once back inside, treats were handed out and then the threesome hit the couch. Nell was in the middle with a dog on each side. Petting her boys was soothing to them and gave Nell a chance to think about Clayton's death.

She gathered together her thoughts about the poisoning. First of all, the food had come from Brenda's Good Taste, a wonderful local catering company, owned and operated by former student, Brenda Goodwell. Nell had been to many events Brenda had catered and everything looked and tasted divine. She couldn't imagine anything harmful coming from her professional kitchen. Still, it had to remain on her list.

Second, a whole dish couldn't have been ruined or more people would have died or at least become ill. Could someone have slipped some poison into a separate appetizer or piece of dessert, and handed it to Clayton?

Or third, could the offending substance have been put in a random piece of food for anyone to eat as Elena suggested? And what about the drinks? Someone could have slipped a foreign substance into Clayton's cocktail.

She better delve into these thoughts a little deeper. Brenda's Good Taste was the place to call for catered parties and other events in town. Brenda had been at the open house, along with two young workers. The dining room table was made into a buffet which offered smoked salmon, oysters on the half shell, and a heaping platter of jumbo shrimp. All of the dishes were finger food, so fancy toothpicks were at every dish. The slices of luscious prime rib carved at the end of the table were paired with warm rolls. Trays of artisan cheeses, sausage stuffed mushrooms, and lobster wontons tempted the partygoers, as did the goat cheese and pecan stuffed dates wrapped in bacon.

Nell licked her lips at the thought. She hadn't nearly finished running through the hors d'oeuvres in her mind. Added to that, she hadn't begun listing the desserts. Nell's food cravings were kicking into high gear. She might be well served to stop thinking of the individual menu items and begin thinking of the mechanics of delivering the poison.

A vial of liquid poison could easily have been slipped into a drink before it was handed to Clayton. A tainted pill could have been pushed into a date, a roll, or a piece of caramel coffee cheesecake. However, it would mean someone attending the party wanted Clayton Dunbar dead. Elena had given her the suggestion that some individual item could have been poisoned, but it wasn't necessarily meant for Clay. It was a disturbing thought which made Nell remember the Tylenol poisonings in Chicago in 1982. Bottles of Tylenol were tampered with by dropping capsules laced with potassium cyanide into the containers. If she recalled correctly, the pills were taken by several innocent people who later died. These devastating incidents led to many reforms in the packaging of over-the-counter drugs.

Nell looked up potassium cyanide on her laptop and found it was a colorless crystalline salt, similar in appearance to sugar, highly soluble in water. This could work for capsules or liquids. It would be harder to disguise a capsule in a piece of food than it would be to pour some in a cocktail. By either preparing or delivering a drink, the killer most likely knew who he was targeting.

Feeling rather proud of her ideas, Nell gingerly moved up from the couch while trying not to waken the boys at her side. She crept out to the kitchen and slowly lifted the lid from the cookie jar. *Just one would take care of her cravings.* All of her caution was for naught though, as soon two little dogs were at her feet with hopeful eyes and wagging tails.

"Okay, George and Newmie," Nell said. "I'll have a cookie and split one between the two of you." She grabbed two cookies and headed back to the couch. Nell's mind refused to rest even as the three of them enjoyed their treat.

"Boys, I'm giving myself all kinds of credit, but I've only come up with one possible poison that fits. There are probably ten, fifty, or one hundred more." George put his paw on Nell's leg, seemingly to comfort her. "I'd like to discuss my findings with Chief Vance, but I have a pretty good idea he would shut me right down. How do I make him understand I can help in this investigation? If he would share his information with me, we would both benefit."

Night had come early as it did in Wisconsin during the winter. The darkness usually made Nell eager to fix her evening meal. Tonight was no exception. She turned the oven on and pulled her leftover pasty from the fridge. Tonight's supper would be simple. She made a quick coleslaw to go with her pasty. It wasn't long before the enticing aroma of beef, potatoes, onions, and crust started to fill the air. The boys' little noses were sniffing away. "I'll be sure to save some crust for you, George. And I would never forget you either, Newmie." Nell bent over to give each of them a belly rub.

After they had eaten, the threesome snuggled together on the couch. The dogs soon fell asleep, but Nell's mind was in overdrive. She chose not to turn on the television. No binge watching tonight. Finding Clayton Dunbar's murderer was all that interested her now.

Chapter 8

Nell had hardly made it out of the bathroom early the next morning when her phone rang. "Who'd call me this early?" she mumbled to herself. She noticed from the caller ID that it was Elena.

"Well, girlfriend. What's so exciting about today's lunch with Herbert you can't contain yourself?" Nell chuckled.

"I wish that was the reason. I can tell by your tone you haven't heard the news yet."

"Heard what news?" All silliness had disappeared as Nell sat down on the couch.

"I'm sorry to be the one to tell you because I know you were friends, but Dottie Dumpling died last night."

"No, that's not possible. I talked to her the day before yesterday at our meeting. She couldn't have died."

"I'm so sorry, Nell."

"Where did you hear this? What happened?" Nell started rubbing her left eyebrow as tears formed in her eyes.

"I was up early today as I couldn't sleep. I went on Facebook and read a post saying she died in her sleep."

Nell exhaled. "Dottie was quite a bit overweight which isn't healthy and I know she didn't exercise much. But that was all going to change. She had started at Bulk Blasters and was so excited to lose the weight and feel better. I had hoped we'd be able to encourage each other."

"It's always a shock when friends are here one day and gone the next. How old do you think she was?"

"I'd guess sixty-two or three, which isn't that much older than I am." Nell stood back up and let the boys outside. "I'll make a trip over to Leo's later today. I'll bet the poor guy is heartbroken."

"I'll let you go then."

"Thanks for calling, Elena. And have a good time with Herbert."

Nell set her phone down and put on the coffee. She walked to the door and let George and Newman back inside to go to their bowls of fresh food and water. "We never know what each day will bring, do we, boys?"

The death of two of her friends a couple of days apart was quite a coincidence. She didn't think it was anything more, as in the last few years more and more of the townspeople around her age had either come down with illnesses or died. The older a person got, the more people they know, hence the more people they lost.

Nell thought about what kind of food to bring to Leo's house. His and Dottie's two children, who would each now be around thirty with kids of their own, would probably come home to comfort him. She decided on a casserole. She had a good one similar to jambalaya. The recipe started with a packaged rice mix and then onions, peppers, andouille sausage, and shrimp were all added. She was relieved she had all the ingredients on hand, even frozen shrimp.

As she fixed the casserole, taking care not to add too much spice, her mind went back and forth between Dottie's natural death and Clayton's murder. Nell struggled with both situations. After letting her hot dish simmer for thirty minutes, she turned off the stove, but kept the cover on the skillet. Needing some fresh air, she put leashes on the dogs' collars and took them outside for a short walk.

The exercise and the air must have helped all three of them, she thought, as when they came back in, they all seemed a little more settled. Nell prepared her dish to make the trip across town. "George, Newmie, why don't you take a little nap? I'll be back before you know it." She knew as soon as she was out of sight, that's exactly what they'd do.

Several cars were parked directly in front of Leo's house, so Nell figured other neighbors and friends had the same idea. She parked behind the other cars and carefully carried her covered dish to the house. She was welcomed in by one of Dottie's good friends and walked with her to the kitchen to put down her casserole. Then Nell stopped to offer her condolences to Leo, who looked like he'd aged twenty years since she last saw him. His drawn face and tired eyes made her know he needed his friends around him.

"Leo, you have my deepest sympathy. Dottie was such a wonderful woman."

"I can't believe it, Nell. I never thought she would go before I did. I'm older and a man. Men usually die first. That's what I always heard." Leo looked from friend to friend and sobbed, "How can I go on without my little Dot?"

Nell patted his hand and stayed for another half hour, visiting with Leo and the others. The funeral arrangements had not been made as Leo was waiting for his son, Wayne, to arrive from Stoughton and his daughter, Tina, from Chippewa Falls. He wanted them all to make the decision together as a family. No matter what day or time, Nell knew she would attend the service.

As she walked out the door, another family was coming into the house. She heard one of the young men say, "Uncle Leo," and knew he had more people there to comfort him. Family and friends meant everything as she got older. Nell was thankful for hers every day, even though she rarely saw her son.

She understood the stress and heartache involved in an unexpected death. Nell's thoughts went back to a little over five years before when Drew died. She'd come back from a weekend shopping trip with the girls to find he had passed on at home, alone. The fact she hadn't been there caused a terrible strain in the relationship she had with their son, Judson. Jud blamed her for not being there to save his dad. Even though the coroner said the massive heart attack killed him instantly, Jud still couldn't let it go. After picking at her about it for days, Nell had finally lashed out, reminding Jud he had promised to spend the weekend with his dad. She had her weekend arranged and he had been the one who backed out. The tension between them after that exchange went on for years. Jud had even moved to Alaska to make a point of putting distance between them. Thankfully, during this last year their relationship was getting back to normal. Nell was looking forward to the day when she no longer felt a knot in her stomach every time she thought about her son. She hoped Leo was spared any undue family difficulties.

A new posting on her food review blog was needed, so Nell knew what she'd work on tonight. Several times she had eaten at The Alibi in Stiles, and it was high time to write her review. She settled herself in her comfortable old wing chair with her laptop. George and Newman had come to terms with the dreaded piece of technology. They didn't like it because when it was out, there was no room for them on the chair. They each curled up in a corner on the couch instead and were soon fast asleep.

Nell always took her iPad mini with her on restaurant visits so she could enter any notes that she wanted to mention in her blog. She flipped through the entries for information to jog her memory, gathered her thoughts, picked up her pen, and made a quick outline of the information. She then opened her blog and composed her entry.

Nell's Noshes Up North

The Alibi
Stiles, Wisconsin

If you are heading up north for some snowmobiling this winter, you can't go wrong by turning off the highway and stopping at The Alibi. This is an old-fashioned Wisconsin supper club at its finest. It's out in the country, has a big parking lot, and serves excellent food and strong drinks. A designated driver would be the thinking person's answer when choosing to imbibe at an establishment far from home.

When you first enter The Alibi, you'll notice the high ceiling with a gorgeous crystal chandelier and the large bar. There are plenty of stools and tables, if you'd like to visit before you go into the dining room to eat. My friend and I had a wonderful time sitting at a table and watching all the patrons. A friendly bunch frequent The Alibi and we were soon included in their conversations as if they had known us for years.

The atmosphere of the dining room was like a north woods' lodge. It was rustic with lots of dark wood and even the head of a twelve-point buck hung on the wall. It didn't seem to mesh with the chandelier in the other area, but it was still tasteful in its simplicity. The cleanliness of both rooms was apparent, so we were anxious to read the offerings on the menu. We were quite pleased with what we found. The choices went from hearty salads to craft sandwiches to surf and turf. It was difficult to make a decision.

I chose a 12 oz. New York Strip steak with mushrooms and butter in a reduced wine sauce. A choice of potato or other starch was included, and I selected the baked potato with butter and sour cream. My dining companion picked the blackened salmon also with a baked potato. A large soup and salad bar was on one end of the room and we helped ourselves.

I always enjoy a fresh salad bar and this ranked second to none. Crisp mixed greens and a separate bowl of dark green spinach leaves started the line rolling. We walked down the row seeing every imaginable ingredient for a salad. There were the usual tomatoes, cucumbers, olives, shredded cheese, green peppers, and mushrooms, but also peas, beets, baby corn, hot peppers, both pickled and creamed herring, and feta cheese. And those were just the items I chose; there were many more. Salads could be dressed with ten different toppings. A number of cold salads such as red potato, pizza macaroni, and coleslaw were also on the salad bar. Moving to the soups, we were delighted to see clam chowder, chicken gumbo, and beef barley.

We brought our selections back to the table to find warm rolls with herb-seasoned butter. Not wanting to rush the experience, we ate at a leisurely pace. I had already decided I was enjoying my salad so much I'd take most of the entrée home. *One special note about the soup. Often I find soup when dining out to be over salted. I especially come across this with beef barley. I'm pleased to announce this beef barley soup was seasoned to perfection.*

The moment arrived when my entrée appeared. Even though I had already eaten enough, the tantalizing aroma of steak, topped with a butter and wine reduction, tempted me past the point of reason. I succumbed. It took all of my willpower to stop eating after three bites.

My friend said her blackened salmon was seasoned perfectly and wasn't fishy at all, which is sometimes the case. She happily offered to dine with me at The Alibi again.

I don't think I need to write down my opinion of this eating establishment. If you aren't going up north snowmobiling this winter, then next summer, stop here on your way north to go camping. Not doing that either? Make a special trip. It's only a short drive from Green Bay.

A true nosh or truly nauseous? —You Decide!

Chapter 9

Memories of Dottie filled Nell's mind, but it was the thoughts of Clay's murder which wouldn't let Nell rest that night as she tossed and turned in bed. She rose early and tried to busy herself with mundane chores. Nothing could get rid of her constant thoughts of the murder. Why did the police even suspect poison so quickly? There hadn't been time yet for an autopsy to be performed. Was there something about the body that had sent up a red flag? Nell didn't know enough about poison to be familiar with any of the signs. A thought entered her mind. She finished dusting, let the dogs outside, and walked to her office. She retrieved the phone book from her desk and whispered a prayer.

"Bingo," she murmured as she let the boys back in the house. "Just as I thought, guys. People of a certain age still have landlines with numbers listed in the book." George and Newmie looked at her with questioning eyes.

Pulling her cell from a pocket, Nell punched in the number.

She was about to give up after several rings when finally a weak voice whispered, "Hello."

"Hazel? This is Nell Bailey. I hope this isn't too early to call. How are you doing?"

"All right, I guess. I've been up for hours. I'm afraid Mr. Dunbar's death has taken its toll on me. I don't know what to do with myself. I'm sitting here in my house wondering if there was anything I could have done to save him."

Nell could hear Hazel's sniffles, and her heart went out to her. "This isn't your fault. Don't even think anything about it." Nell felt a pang of guilt, but had to continue. "Hazel, could I come over to visit you for a little bit? Would that be okay?"

"Why, yes, that would be lovely. Are you coming now? I can make some tea." Hazel's voice already had more spark.

"I'll be right there, but don't bother yourself with tea."

"It's no bother. See you soon."

Nell grabbed a few peanut butter cookies from the jar and put them on a paper plate, covering them with plastic wrap. She planted a kiss on top of each dog's head and walked toward the garage. True to form, George and Newman saw where she was heading or maybe smelled the cookies and followed her to the door. She doubled back, took another cookie out of the jar, broke it in half, and gave them the treat. "That's the last cookie you're getting from me today. If I keep this up, you'll both be round as a cookie. I won't be gone long."

Walking up the sidewalk of Hazel's lovingly cared for small home, Nell was glad she was visiting, even if she didn't learn any information. Was caring for Clayton's home such a part of Hazel's life that she no longer felt needed? Did she now have concerns about her own mortality? Nell knew she would help Hazel in any way possible.

Nell was met at the door before she had a chance to ring the bell. "Come in, Nell. I have the kettle on and soon we'll have tea."

"I brought some cookies for you. I hope you like peanut butter." Nell heard a small intake of breath and realized these were the same kind of cookie she brought over to Clayton's house when she heard of his death.

"I do. Please sit down." Hazel waved her arm toward the couch, so Nell started to walk to it. "Let me take your coat."

"That's all right. I'll take it off and set it down here by me." Nell wasn't intentionally trying to make Hazel feel worse, but she was, and hadn't even started on her questions. She considered staying for a chat and nothing else. But that wouldn't do. Time was of the essence and she needed answers.

"What flavor of tea would you like, dear? I have chamomile, peppermint, and orange blossom."

"Chamomile sounds wonderful. Thank you so much."

Hazel faltered toward her kitchen, leaving Nell alone to think about how she was going to initiate her questioning of this sweet lady. *I am really a despicable wretch.*

Before Nell had a chance to dwell too much on herself, Hazel appeared with a silver tray holding two antique china cups and a plate of cookies. Nell got up to help.

"Sit down, Nell. This is what I do...or did. I served Mr. Dunbar ever since the missus died."

Nell sat back down, accepted the tea, declined the cookie, and waited for Hazel to sit down, too.

Hazel positioned herself in a delicate, green Queen Anne chair and primly took a sip of tea. "Now, Nell. It is nice of you to visit an old lady, but I'm not a fool. I know what goes on in this town. I know you fancy yourself to be some sort of Miss Marple and I know you were a good friend to Mr. Dunbar. So tell me. What can I do to help you find his murderer?"

It took Nell a moment to recover from her surprise. "Hazel, I should have known you would be able to see right through me." Nell took the teabag out of her cup and set it on the saucer. "I do want to find out who killed our good friend, Clayton," she said and sipped the tea.

"I don't know what I'll be able to tell you that I haven't already told the police, but I'm going to give it my best try," Hazel said, clenching her small hands into fists.

"That's all I'm asking, and I appreciate anything you have to say. Here's my theory," Nell shared. "If the police were able to pinpoint it to poison immediately, there must have been some outward signs. Were you the one to find Clayton's body?"

"Yes, but the coroner came shortly after the police arrived and I don't know who actually announced it was poison."

As gently as she could, Nell inquired, "I realize this will be difficult for you, but what was the appearance of the body? Did he look any different to you?"

"You mean other than being dead?"

Nell reached her hand upward and automatically rubbed her left eyebrow. "I'm so sorry to have to ask you these questions." She took a deep breath and continued, "Yes, was there anything different about his body that made you realize he wasn't sleeping?"

"Oh, I knew he was gone the minute I saw him. He was pale, not his normal color at all. Even worse was the blood around his nose. It looked like he'd had a bloody nose in his sleep because he hadn't gotten up to wash it off." Hazel looked away. "I hate talking about Mr. Dunbar like this. He was such a good man. Always fair to me."

"If there's more, please tell me. Remember, I'm trying to find his killer."

Hazel lifted her chin and said, "I rushed over to him and saw all the bruising on his body. He had complained the last week or so about having bruises, but I hadn't noticed them under all of his winter clothes. With only his pajamas on, I could see them. Also, there was vomit on the bed beside him."

"Will you bear with me a little longer? I'd like to do some checking on the symptoms you've mentioned."

At Hazel's nod, Nell pulled her iPhone out of her purse and did a quick search. "Did Clayton take any blood thinners? Warfarin or Coumadin?"

"I don't know what he took. The coroner looked at all his medications and took some notes."

"Are his medications still at his house?"

"I would imagine so. What thoughts are going through that mind of yours, Nell?"

"If you still have a key to Clayton's house, I'd like to get in there and take a look at his pills." Nell looked at Hazel with raised eyebrows.

"The police want the house kept locked up, but I have the key. I'm still taking care of his home and have a lot of personal belongings there. The chief unofficially has allowed me to come and go as needed." Hazel frowned as she looked at Nell over the top of her glasses. "I'm not sure I should bring anyone else in the house, though."

"Truthfully, Chief Vance probably wouldn't like it if he knew I was in the house. But, as the saying goes 'what he doesn't know, won't hurt him' and I believe it. Besides, we're all working for the same cause." Nell tilted her head. "What do you say?"

"We'll do it for Mr. Dunbar. Anyway, I don't suppose the cops would put me in jail at my age. Do you?"

"Oh, no. You wouldn't be the one getting into trouble," Nell sighed as she finished her tea.

Nell parked her car on a side street down a ways from the Dunbar house. There was no point in parking in front of the house on Main Street and calling attention to the fact that she was inside it. She and Hazel walked to the back door of the house and entered the kitchen with as little fanfare as possible.

"Mr. Dunbar kept his pills in the cabinet in the bathroom."

"Was this the bathroom everyone used the night of the party? If it was murder, any of his guests could have come in and added more warfarin to the bottle or even aspirin for that matter." At Hazel's quizzical look, Nell explained, "I read a bit about warfarin when I looked up Clayton's symptoms. Aspirin also thins the blood. People on warfarin shouldn't take aspirin."

"Quite a few years ago, the butler's pantry was turned into a master bath. There's a half bath for guests off the foyer. That is the one that was used the night of the open house. Follow me."

They entered the master bath and Hazel went to the cabinet and opened it up. The quantity of bottles was astounding to Nell. She noticed many were over-the-counter supplements. Still, it was a large number to swallow every day.

"Is this where Clayton took his pills morning and night? I think it would be difficult to remember what to take when—there are a lot of bottles here."

"Oh, no. Mr. Dunbar had morning and night pill dispensers just like I do. You fix them up for a week or two in advance. That's how I manage anyway."

"Bingo! Here it is: warfarin sodium 3 mg tablet, one a day," Nell said, doing a little dance and shaking the bottle.

"What does that mean?"

She stopped dancing. "I'm not sure what it means." Nell opened the bottle of warfarin and took a look at the tablets. Once again her new phone made her life easier. "Here we go. The color for 3 mg is almost a café au lait color like the pills in this bottle."

"I don't know what that color even looks like," Hazel grumbled.

"It's like coffee with cream." Nell shook a pill out of the bottle to show her. "See the little number 3 on one side of it?"

At Hazel's nod, Nell said, "The 3 stands for milligrams. Clay used this blood thinner, so it's possible he received too big of a dose." Nell fingered her gold necklace. "He may have accidentally given it to himself. Where did he keep his pill dispensers?"

"In the top drawer by the sink."

Hazel found two pill dispensers in a drawer and handed them to Nell. There was one for morning and one for night, just as she had mentioned. Each was about half empty. "Did the police or coroner look at these dispensers?"

"No. They only asked to see the pills. I didn't think to mention the dispensers." Hazel's voice was hardly above a whisper.

Nell flipped open the individual containers for the next night and saw the 3 mg warfarin tablet with the night pills. She opened the plastic containers for the rest of the week. Nothing looked out of the ordinary. She had to be missing something, but what?

Chapter 9.5

How closely does an old man watch his medications? I'm thinking not closely enough. It was a cinch to talk my way in to Dunbar's house. Of course, I own several sets of burglary tools I've used through the years. No need for them on this particular caper. Caper? Kill is a more descriptive word and I tingle at the thought of it. The master bathroom led me to his pill supply. Once I realized the type of medication I was going to use, I realized it didn't matter whether it looked like an overdose or an accidental poisoning. It made no difference. All I needed to do then was wait for another chance to get in his house and make the exchange. Everything fell into place. The world will be better off without that geezer. Or at least I will be better off. Much better off.

Chapter 10

By the time Nell came home, all the water in the dogs' bowls was gone. She immediately cleaned the bowls and put in fresh water. "There you go, George and Newmie. I was gone much longer than I intended." As her dogs made a beeline to their bowls, Nell reviewed her afternoon. She had driven Hazel home and spent more time with her. The idea of Clayton being poisoned was upsetting to both of them. They discussed the open house and the guests. Neither of them knew of any reason to be suspicious of anyone in particular. Hazel was put out that Yolanda hadn't made the funeral arrangements, but Nell wondered if the holdup was because of the police not releasing his body. Perhaps there was an autopsy scheduled.

As Nell's brain was churning, her thoughts went to Sam and how a few months ago he would have been the one she'd have called when she had something on her mind. Not anymore. He'd been only too quick to state his opinion on her involvement in any murders. The words "put his foot down" still stuck in her craw.

She wanted to talk to someone, though, and called Elena to find out about her lunch date with Herbert. Nell was relieved to hear the pleasant greeting of her friend after the second ring. Elena filled her in on some of the details of lunch, but finally Nell had to ask the question burning inside her soul. "Has the flame been rekindled?"

"Goodness," Elena laughed. "This was two old friends catching up. That's all. We talked and laughed most of the afternoon. I'd forgotten how much fun he can be."

"Sounds like you had a wonderful time. Anyone who can make a person laugh is a good friend to have," Nell said. "I hope you meet with him again. There's no such thing as having too many friends."

"Even if we don't get together again, I'll remember the laughs from today for a long time." Elena's voice deepened. "Did you go see Leo yesterday?"

"Yes," Nell sighed. "He's broken up, as you can imagine. Maybe once his kids and grandchildren get home it will help. Leo's a good man and has always openly shown his love for Dottie."

"Her death hits us closer to home, while Clayton Dunbar's murder, even though horrendous, is the passing of an old man. He had a long, prosperous life."

"I know, but they both hit me hard. And speaking of Clayton, I visited his housekeeper, Hazel, today. She and I went over to Clayton's house."

"You're kidding. I'm surprised the police allowed it. You did contact them first, didn't you?" asked Elena.

"Of course not. Chief Vance would hit the roof if I even asked such a thing. And as I told Hazel, what he doesn't know won't hurt him."

"Only you would do such a thing. Why did you go to Clayton's house, anyway?"

"While speaking to Hazel, I thought of some things I wanted to check." Nell went through all she had learned from Hazel about Clayton's excess bruising, how he looked when she found him, and finding the warfarin tablets. "Someone could have slipped him additional warfarin or aspirin. Yep, I definitely think Clay was murdered. How about you?"

"What I think, Nell, is that you should get your butt right down to the police station and tell them everything you know. This is serious."

"Not yet. I know I can find out more info on my own." Nell glanced out the sliding glass doors and saw the light covering of sparkling snow. "I need a little more time."

"Not this again. Let's say you're able to uncover more clues. Will that be enough? My educated guess would be 'no' and you won't be willing to stop until you have the whole case solved and tied up with a pretty bow!"

"So you're telling me you aren't willing to help me this time, Watson?"

"I didn't necessarily say *that*, Sherlock."

The next morning, after walking the boys, having coffee, and reading the paper, Nell had another question she needed answered. She remembered Hazel was up early each day and gave her a call.

"Good morning, Hazel. This is Nell Bailey."

"Oh, hello, dear. Have you figured out who killed Mr. Dunbar yet?"

"Well, no. Murders don't usually get solved that fast, but I do have a question I'd like to ask you."

"Go ahead. I'll try to help."

"I've given this a lot of thought," Nell began, "and I'm wondering if there's anyone who has access to Clayton's house. You know, someone who could go in and out without raising suspicions. Do you know of anyone?"

"Let me think." Nell could hear a sipping sound. Hazel was probably having tea. "Mr. Dunbar believed in drinking milk for strong bones. He had a glass quart bottle of whole milk brought in every day."

"Would that be from Gellman's Dairy?"

"I think so. It was usually delivered before I arrived each day."

"As far as I know, they're the only dairy that still delivers glass bottles in the area." Nell took some notes on the back of her cell phone bill. "Wasn't the milk left outside the door?"

"Oh no, he let the milkman come in the house and put it in the refrigerator."

Nell sat up straighter in her chair. "Hazel, do you know if the milkman had a key to the house?"

"He didn't need a key. Mr. Dunbar never locked his doors. The only reason I'm using the key now is because it's a directive from the police."

Nell slumped back down. The milkman could be a possibility, but so could any number of people who may have crept in the house and switched the pills. "Is there anyone else who comes in the house regularly?"

"The Colsen boy who runs errands for Mr. Dunbar," Hazel replied.

"Do you mean Zane Colsen?"

"Yes, that's his name. He lives across the street and comes over two or three times a week."

"Okay, this helps. I have some thinking to do. Can I call you again if I have more questions?"

"Please do. I want to see whoever committed this horrible act brought to justice."

Once off the phone, Nell gathered her thoughts. She glanced over at her couch and noticed George and Newman fast asleep. She'd like her life to be so carefree! Instead, her mind burned with activity. She knew of two people who were in Clayton's house on a regular basis. But anyone with evil intent could have walked in the house and accomplished the mission at any time. Why didn't he lock his doors? That left a welcome mat out for thieves to walk right in and help themselves. Many precious antiques were displayed all through his lovely home. She stroked her gold necklace again.

Much as she dreaded the thought, Nell decided to go to the Bayshore Fitness Center and work on her excess bulk. It would have the added benefit of getting rid of some of her nervous energy. She changed into her workout clothes—gray sweatpants and a pink tee shirt—and went to the garage. The facility was only a few blocks away and she probably should walk there and back. But it was cold outside and the roads were slippery. She chose not to get ahead of herself and risk overdoing it. She'd only recently joined and was still dreadfully out of shape. Luckily Bayshore Community Hospital was right next door, so if there was an emergency she was in the right place.

The gal at the desk greeted Nell as she turned to go into the treadmill area. This spot was the most comfortable for her. She could set the machine to go slowly and not set any incline. She planned to improve and get a few sessions with a personal trainer to get her on the right track. Maybe she'd even go in the weight room someday.

Nell picked out a magazine from the rack, found a treadmill, and started to walk. She knew she'd feel good when she was all done.

Nell soon felt confident of her chosen pace and opened her magazine. It was all about food, her usual fare. She loved the recipes and articles about fancy restaurants. How ironic to read this magazine as she worked to rid herself of extra weight from eating delicious foods made from good recipes in wonderful restaurants! Time to pay the fiddler.

A couple of retired men walked in, chatting with each other as Nell was finishing her walk. They both went to the exercise bikes and she heard their conversation as she cleaned off her machine.

"Sure is a shame about Scott Marshall," the first man said.

"What's that? I haven't heard anything about him."

"He died this morning at the breakfast table. Keeled over right into his eggs. Bad heart."

"I'll be damned. I've known him since I was a kid. He's a couple years older, but my brother used to hang around with him." The man rubbed sweat off his forehead. "Wasn't it weird how he'd bring his briefcase in to the fitness center with him and lock it up?"

The second man shook his head. "He usually came from an appointment because he'd have good clothes on and change into his workout clothes in the locker room." He blew air out of his mouth. "I guess I'm in the right place. Maybe I'll go an extra twenty minutes on the ol' bike today."

Nell knew Scott Marshall as a nodding acquaintance. He was a mover and shaker in town, active in local government, and on the board of several local civic societies. She left the center, pondering the fragility of life and realizing she had another family to keep in her prayers.

George and Newmie pounced, jumped, and carried on as usual when she walked in the door. Nell let them outside and had treats ready when they returned. She hopped in the shower and lathered up with her new salted caramel shower gel. What a mistake! Now all she could think about was salted caramel and how delicious it would be to have some right now.

No. There would be no treat for her. She was made of stronger stuff. At least today she was, but who knew what tomorrow would bring?

After changing into clean, dark blue jeans and a warm periwinkle sweatshirt with Door County written on the front, she looked at the clock. Good. School was out. She'd been killing time for the last few hours, waiting until she could call her former middle school student, Zane Colsen. Nell had his number from a few times he'd done chores for her. She had several light bulbs on the garage ceiling he could change and then she could ask him some questions.

Nell picked up her phone and called Zane's cell phone.

"Hey, Mrs. B. Do you have some chores for me to do?"

"As a matter of fact, I do. Would you be able to come over here yet tonight?"

"No can do. I'm not even home. A group of us left after school for a conference in Green Lake. We're a little past Abrams right now."

"Good for you. What kind of conference is it?"

"Public speaking. I want to improve in forensics. Maybe even go to state some year."

"What a wonderful opportunity, Zane!"

"Yeah, so the conference will last several days. Do you want me to come over when I get back?"

"Give me a call first. The chores can wait. Have a good time!"

Nell pondered this temporary dead end, but soon had another thought. She'd head to Gellman's Dairy and inquire about their delivery method to

Clayton Dunbar. She got behind the wheel of her car, buckled the seatbelt, and backed out of her garage. The deliveryman may be more interested in speaking with her in person rather than a faceless voice on the phone.

Gellman's Dairy had a small cheese shop attached, so Nell headed there. She loved to purchase many of their different kinds of cheese and fresh curds. Whenever she played hostess, she bought her cheese from Gellman's. Nell walked in, asked the counter girl if she could speak to the owner, and was surprised when she was escorted to a small office. Nell sat down and after noticing the messy desk, chuckled to herself. *It's the sign of a hard worker who doesn't have much time for paperwork.*

"Mrs. Bailey! What can I do to help you?" A good-looking, brown-haired man of about thirty sat down behind the desk.

"Good grief, Mark. I thought I'd be talking to your dad."

"He's slowly turning the reins of control over to me. Are you still teaching? I remember the mythology skits we did in your class." Mark struck a pose and laughed.

"I took early retirement a few years ago. I remember assigning a lot of hard work, doing a lot of fun activities, but even more I remember so many great kids. Now it's my joy to see them grown up and being good citizens in Bayshore."

Mark smiled and asked, "What brings you here today, Mrs. Bailey?"

"Please, you're old enough to call me Nell now." She took a deep breath. "Did you know Clayton Dunbar, who lived in the senator's mansion?"

"I didn't know him personally, but Dad had him as a teacher in school." Mark tilted his head at an angle. "Why?"

Nell explained the situation and made sure he realized she wasn't accusing anyone at the dairy of anything.

Mark said, "I think the driver for that route is in the processing room. Excuse me while I check."

He left the room and Nell started to wonder what exactly she needed to know. She hoped her mind didn't go blank.

After five minutes, Mark walked back in with another man. Introductions were made and hands shaken.

"What would you like to know?" the deliveryman asked.

"Maybe you could take me through a typical delivery to Clayton Dunbar's house." Nell had a pen and notebook out to take notes.

"Sure. I'd park the delivery truck on the side street and go in the back door. It was left open for me to bring in his quart of milk and put it in the refrigerator. I would then leave and go on to my next customer."

"Is this a regular thing with customers? I mean, do you have other people who leave their house unlocked for you to take their purchases to their fridge?"

"A few. Not many. Mostly only in the summer where it might spoil if left outside too long."

"Okay." Nell thought for a moment. "Did anything unusual ever happen?

43

Did you see anyone strange by the house, perhaps skulking around?"

"Can't say that I have, but when I'm working I'm focused on getting the job done." He glanced over at his boss. "I'm not looking for anyone."

"I think that takes care of it. Thanks so much for your time. Both of you." Nell closed her notebook and put it back in her purse.

"Thanks, Jim. You can go on back to the dairy." Mark gave him a pat on the back as he left the office.

He turned to Nell with a chuckle. "Really? Skulking around? I've never seen anyone *skulk* in my whole life."

"I'm sorry. Your life must be so boring." She started for the office door, turned with a smile, and said in her best teacher voice, "But if we're going to play hardball, it's way past time for you to clean off that desk, young man!"

Nell found her way to the shop and could still hear Mark laughing as she left the building.

In the evening, as Nell sat on the couch with a dog on each side, she reminisced about Mark and what a good kid he had been. Now he'd become a fine adult with a good sense of humor. She was delighted she'd stayed in Bayshore all these years. Now she knew the satisfaction of seeing her former students as successful adults.

She wondered if the time had come for her to have a conversation with Chief Charles Vance. Nell knew she'd need to prepare for a fight because Vance wanted no part of her in his investigation. Why didn't he see the benefits of her help? She couldn't understand. She wouldn't do it on the phone, either. She had to go to the Bayshore Police Station and talk to him face to face. She'd better go over her notes and develop a plan of how she was going to present her information and get him on her side. Maybe she'd have to pull out the charm.

Nell drew in her breath, then slowly released it. What charm? If she had one bit of charm, Sam would have called her by now or been down here pounding at her door. She hadn't heard a peep out of him. So much for charm.

Thinking it over she realized it wasn't her lack of charm which was holding Sam Ryan back. It was his inability to admit he'd made a mistake and apologize. *No one could be as stubborn as an Irishman.*

Chapter 11

"Is there some kind of law in the 'How to be Irish' handbook that stipulates that every Irish male adult has to be as stubborn as an old goat?" Benita railed. She walked from the kitchen and sat on a barstool near Sam, who was standing behind the bar. "Dad, today is your birthday and instead of going out somewhere with Nell, you're going to tend bar all night. Why haven't you called her and straightened everything out?"

"Never you mind, little missy," Sam shot back, his blue eyes flashing at her. "I'll take care of my own affairs. This is none of your business."

"You *are* my business. I've been taking care of you since I was a tiny girl."

"I think it should be the other way around. I've tended to you your whole life."

"You know what I mean, Dad. We've always watched out for each other, and that's all I'm doing now." Benita's voice softened. "I love you and can see you're unhappy. Once Nell came into your life, you were a different man. Why can't you bring yourself to call her and make up?"

Sam looked at the wildlife clock on the wall. "Look, I have a lot of work to do here to get ready for the supper crowd. How about we discuss this later?"

"If you promise you really will talk to me about it."

Sam slowly nodded his head.

Nell sat up in bed in a cold sweat. Something had bothered her as she tried to get to sleep, but she couldn't put her finger on it. Her memory hit her hard in the night. Both Dottie Dumpling and Scott Marshall were guests at Clayton Dunbar's party, which wouldn't be unusual in a place the size of Bayshore. But now the host and two guests were dead in a matter of days after the doings. Could that fact be more than a coincidence? Nell knew she now had even more information to discuss with the police chief tomorrow. She hoped she could get back to sleep in the meantime.

After a few hours of fitful sleep, Nell sneaked out of bed without waking George and Newmie. She turned the TV on very low to a local news channel and watched until it started to get light out when she could take the boys for an early morning stroll. As the news, weather, and sports droned on, Nell worked on her plan to attain the chief's permission to help on the case. She had to be forceful without being argumentative. She wanted to present herself as a valuable asset, not a pain in the butt. Would Chief Charles Vance see things her way?

Nell had called ahead of time and made an appointment with Vance's administrative assistant to meet with him. Extra care had been taken with her clothes and makeup before heading downtown to see the chief. She'd been delighted when she stepped on the scale earlier and saw a three pound weight loss. The loss gave her the added boost in confidence she needed. Saying no to the caramel had worked and she'd take the small victory. Now dressed in slimming black jeans and a fuzzy baby blue sweater that made her eyes sparkle, Nell set out, knowing she looked good.

"Hello, Mrs. Bailey." The hazel-eyed, blond admin assistant gave Nell a big smile. "Please follow me back to the chief's office."

"Thanks," Nell said as she wondered if this twenty-something woman had been a former student whom she couldn't place offhand. The plaque on her desk said Judy Schurz. The last name didn't ring any bells, but it could be a married name. She followed Judy down the hall to Vance's office.

"Chief, Mrs. Bailey is here." Judy then turned and whispered, "Good luck," and Nell heard her heels clicking on the tile floor as she walked down the hall.

Without looking up from the work on his desk, Chief Vance said, "What can I help you with, Mrs. Bailey?"

"Please, call me Nell."

Vance looked up, did a quick double take, and said, "Okay, Nell. How can I help you?"

"It is I who can help you," Nell smiled.

"Here we go," he muttered.

"Wait...before you blow me off. I have news."

"You've got my full attention. What is it?"

Nell took a deep breath and said, "Dottie Dumpling and Scott Marshall were both at Clayton's open house."

"I know that." Chief Vance searched his desk, then held up and waved the handwritten list of names Nell had given him a few days before.

"Now they're dead, too. Doesn't it seem suspicious to you?"

"I know who dies in my town, Nell, but Dottie had health issues and Scott was seeing a cardiologist for years. Have you ever heard of coincidence?"

"May I sit down?"

Nell thought she detected Vance stopping himself midway into making a face, but he graciously said, "Yes, of course." He stood up and gestured toward a chair.

After they were both seated, Nell replied, "I have heard of coincidences, but I've also heard of patterns. This could be the pattern of a killer."

The chief rubbed his hands down his face and when he looked at her, Nell noticed his tired eyes and how strained he looked in general. "What do you want from me, Nell?"

"I want to help. If we pool our resources, I know we can find Clayton's killer, who may have committed all three murders."

"Don't get carried away. There aren't three murders. There is one case of poisoning that may be accidental." The chief shook his head and said, "I hope you realize I can't officially share police information with you. But if you unofficially want to put some feelers out or do some harmless nosing around, I won't reprimand you. And, if you find anything you think is important, you come to me. No more of this trying to find the culprit on your own. I've had enough of your Lone Ranger tactics. And whatever you do, don't bother anyone. I don't want to get a complaint about you from any of the citizenry."

"It's a deal." Nell reached over and shook Charles Vance's hand. "Can I call you Chief Chuck?"

Vance raised one eyebrow and gave Nell the fisheye. "I suppose it wouldn't hurt."

"Good. Now, Chief Chuck, I have a little more info to share with you." Nell was on the alert for any signs of spontaneous combustion as she related her interview of the milk deliveryman, her visit with Hazel, and her trip to Clayton's house.

Chapter 12

"I'm telling you, Elena, I thought the top of Chuck's head was gonna blow." Nell chuckled as she helped herself to a decorated sugar cookie in the shape of a star from the plate Elena offered.

"Oh, so it's Chuck now, is it?" Elena said with a wink as she poured them each a cup of coffee. "I'm glad you popped over as I was going to give you a call later."

Nell paused and looked at her friend with raised eyebrows.

"Herb called this morning and asked me out again. This time it seems a little more like a date. Can you believe it? I haven't gone out with a man in so long I don't know how to act."

"He must be an exceptional person. Your lack of dates hasn't been because of a shortage of invitations." Nell gave Elena a big hug. "I can't wait to meet this guy. Tell me more."

"He's taking me to The Wharf in Menominee, Michigan, just across the bridge from Marinette tomorrow night. I've been trying to decide on the right outfit to wear. I've even modeled a few in front of my mirror."

"I'm delighted to see you so happy," Nell said. "I can tell you have bigger fish to fry than being my partner-in-crime for this latest wave of murders in Bayshore."

"Wave of murders? What are you talking about? I guess I jumped in with my story before you finished telling me what happened in Chief Vance's office."

The last bite of Nell's cookie crunched, but she declined a second treat.

"No, I told you about Dottie and Scott Marshall both being at Clayton's house. Chuck doesn't think they're related."

Elena opened and then closed her mouth. Finally she said, "I have to agree with the chief. Those deaths seem like a coincidence to me, too."

"Ah, come on, Elena. There were just over thirty people at that party and in less than two weeks one tenth of them are dead?"

"I don't want to ask this, Nell, but would you *prefer* the deaths to be murder?"

"No, but I'm willing to open my mind to every possibility. The best part of my conversation with Chief Chuck is," she paused with a smile, "he's given me free rein to investigate to my heart's content."

"Free rein?" Elena tilted her head and asked, "Are you sure he said 'free rein'?"

"Maybe not in so many words, but he gave me an inch so I'm going to take a mile."

Nell chuckled to herself as she entered her home. Talking to the chief had gone much easier than she had hoped. Almost too easy. He offered no resistance at all. She bent down to pet George and Newman amid wagging tails and playful yips. "Just let me get in the door, boys."

On second thought, what had Chuck really given her? He was willing to listen to what she knew, but wouldn't share official police information. Nell understood there would be legal ramifications if a civilian was privy to sensitive info, but that was the sort of thing she needed to know. The one allowance Chief Vance made was giving her the go ahead for investigating. He wouldn't block her from gathering clues on her own. *Better than nothing,* she thought, *and now her foot was in the door.* Who knew what she'd be allowed to do next?

Nell stood outside on the patio while the boys went to a favorite tree in the backyard. George and Newmie came running and they all went in the house. As she put fresh water in their bowls and food in their dishes, Nell started to consider her own supper. She pulled shrimp out of the freezer, put them in a colander, and let cold water run over them. She grabbed butter and lemon from the fridge, and bread crumbs, olive oil, canned artichoke hearts, garlic, and red pepper flakes from the cupboard. The burning question was whether to make pasta or rice to go with the delicious shrimp dish. Instead, she chose cabbage. Back to the fridge for a bag of precut cabbage and she grabbed an onion from the basket in her pantry. Sometimes sautéed cabbage with onion was a nice change in place of grains or when she was on a low-carb diet.

As she was putting the simple meal together, Nell was plotting her next line of attack. If she thought Dottie had been murdered, she probably should go speak to Leo. Would he be receptive? It was difficult to say whether Leo would want her death looked into or decide doing so wouldn't bring her back. He didn't seem the type of man who would be uncooperative. They were friends, but that didn't mean Leo would do whatever Nell asked. Dottie's funeral was tomorrow. Did she dare interview Leo after the service? Good manners were telling her "no." However, the longer the questions went unanswered, the wider the path for the killer became.

As for Scott Marshall, Nell didn't have a clue how she'd approach his wife with questions, or even what to ask. The major inquiry would have to be: how were Clayton Dunbar, Dottie Dumpling, and Scott Marshall connected? When she uncovered the answer, she might be able to find out the identity of the killer.

Chapter 13

Nell took a giant breath and opened the heavy door of the First Christian Church. She had arrived early in order to check out the mourners, in addition to being a mourner herself. She wasn't so wrapped up in the investigation to lose sight of her grief. She had lost a friend and Bayshore had lost an upstanding member of the community. It was for that very reason, losing two friends who were good citizens, that Nell wanted to find the perpetrator of these horrible murders. The town wouldn't be safe until the culprit was behind bars.

Apparently Nell wasn't as early as she had thought as there was a line down the aisle heading toward Leo and his family, and the coffin. She took her place at the end and said a silent prayer.

"Good Lord, have you ever seen so many flowers?"

Nell recognized the voice and cringed. If only she had arrived a few minutes earlier or later. She chose not to turn around and hoped she wouldn't be caught.

"Nell Bailey, is that you?" The sound of a voice which could guide a ship on a foggy night dashed Nell's hopes.

"Yes, Louisa. I can't say it's wonderful to see you when we're meeting for such a sad occasion."

"I know. It was a little over a week ago when we were both celebrating at Clayton's house. Seems like people have been swatted down like flies ever since." Louisa Rolf hooked her arm through Nell's as though they were best friends.

Pulling her arm back from Louisa's grasp, Nell said, "You do have a way with words."

"I tell it like it is, as we used to say in the 1970s." Louisa paused for a response, but not receiving one from Nell, continued, "Have you heard what the holdup is on Clayton's funeral? Is Yolanda too cheap to come back and make arrangements? You know she'll inherit the entire estate, so she can afford it. Why doesn't she put him to rest before winter freezes the ground? Then the body will have to be held over until spring."

Not wanting to engage Louisa in conversation, but needing an answer, Nell whispered, "What makes you think Yolanda is the sole beneficiary?"

"She's an only child." Louisa's head waved from side to side. Her brassy, blond, tightly curled perm looked like the top of a spring dandelion and her tall skinny body its stem. "Okay, I see the look on your face, Nell. Before you spout off about any foundations or charities receiving bequests, Yolanda told me herself at the open house."

"Yolanda told you last week, out of the blue, before her father had died that she would inherit it all?"

"That's what I said."

"I know that's what *you* said, but is it what *Yolanda* said?"

Louisa pursed her lips and squinted her eyes at Nell's implication.

"Excuse me." Nell left her place before Louisa had a chance to reply and headed to the rest room. Louisa's announcement made her a little sick, as did even standing next to the walking billboard. This way she'd be able to get at the back of the line and away from the biggest gossip in town.

If Yolanda is the sole beneficiary, she'd be the one with the most to gain if something happened to her father. The trouble was, Nell was positive Clayton had mentioned two places he planned to help after his death. She recalled the Bayshore Area Humane Society and the hospital in town were at the top of his list. Both institutions needed upgrading and could benefit from a large donation. What would make him change his will and testament?

Although, it was entirely possible this was all gossip to Louisa. She loved to be in the know and sometimes made statements to make herself look as if she knew more than she did. Nell washed her hands and headed to the sanctuary.

She noticed Louisa was far ahead of her in line now and gave herself a mental pat on the back for executing her escape. The mourners moved slowly as everyone offered their sympathy to Leo and his children. When it was finally Nell's turn, she gave Leo a big hug. She realized she didn't have the heart to try to ask him questions about Dottie's death today. "I'll come over and visit again soon. Would that be all right, Leo?"

"Yes, yes, Nell. I know I'm in for a rough patch and am thankful for so many good friends. I miss her so much."

The line of people behind her was growing, so she moved over to talk with Wayne and Tina, his children and both former students of hers. Nell took a final look at the closed casket with the lovely picture of Dottie and the beautiful flower arrangement draping down, then scanned the church for a spot to sit for the service. She saw a place next to Louisa, but quickly glanced away.

She walked across the aisle to a different pew. A little bit of Louisa went a long way.

After the touching service where Pastor Gene memorialized Dottie's life and uplifted those who had gathered, there was a funeral lunch. The congregation and townspeople brought in all kinds of delicious food to be shared and made the eating together a celebration of the life of Dottie Dumpling.

Nell filled her plate with portions of casseroles, salads, and one of the famous egg salad sandwiches which was a particular specialty of the First Christian Church. She had been trying to avoid desserts, but backslid and took a chocolate and caramel bar she knew she'd savor and a lemon bar. She glanced at the tables around the room and saw Joyce Kerns waving her over.

Nell carried her plate over to the table occupied by the retired teacher who had worked with her at the middle school. "So good to see you, Joyce. How's your world?"

"No personal complaints," Joyce said, "but Bayshore has lost some of our best citizens lately. Although it gives Yolanda a reason to come home and see Vern." Joyce stirred her coffee while peering at Nell out of the corner of her eye. "Not that she ever needed an excuse."

"Vern who? What are you saying?"

"Don't tell me you haven't heard this nugget?" Joyce bent closer to Nell. "Vern Rolf and Yolanda are meeting on the sly."

"It must not be too much on the sly if you know all about it. Besides, I don't believe it could be true because Louisa hardly ever lets him out of her sight." Nell chuckled.

"Vern and Yolanda are the *entire* reunion committee for their high school class. Since Louisa isn't a graduate of the high school, she isn't allowed to help. Neither are any of the hometown graduates," Joyce smirked. "They meet alone every time she comes home. Once a reunion has passed, they start working on the next one right away. The funny part of the whole thing is, they throw the exact same party every five years. Same location, same food."

"How do you know so much about it?"

"My husband graduated with the two of them," Joyce said. "Toby spilled they were a big item in high school. When Yolanda went away to college, Vern went into the service. Weren't the citizens of Bayshore fortunate that he came home with Louisa by his side?"

"She is a piece of work, all right." Changing the subject, Nell tilted her head toward Leo. "He's in for a long haul."

"I know. I feel bad about Dottie. Remember how much she supported the school when her kids were there? You could always count on her to be a field trip chaperone or staple papers together for Tuesday envelopes going home, especially when other parents couldn't take off from work."

Nell nodded and stared at her lunch. She made a mental note Louisa was not the only woman in Bayshore who liked to spread stories around. Could the connection between Clayton and Dottie have something to do with school? Clayton had long been retired, but he used to teach at the middle school. How did Scott Marshall fit in with this theory? And should she spend any time at all on the rumored affair between Yolanda and Vern?

That evening at home, once again with a dog snuggled on each side of her, Nell tried to come up with any sort of relationship Scott Marshall could have had with the school. Nothing came to mind. It was possible Clay and Scott were longtime friends. She knew Clayton grew up in Bayshore and the man at the fitness center mentioned knowing Scott since he was a kid. Still, Scott was almost thirty years younger than Clayton, according to the obituary on Facebook this morning. Same age as Dottie. *Same age as Dottie?*

Dottie grew up in Bayshore, too. Maybe that was the connection. Nell rubbed her left eyebrow, thinking about what the chief's reaction would be if she told him the murderer was after people who grew up in Bayshore. *Wait, Nell.* There had to be something more.

Closing her eyes for a moment, Nell's thoughts went to Sam. She had expected him to come to his senses and call her. If this was the kind of person he was, it was a good thing she found out sooner rather than later. This whole deal with him made her glad she had waited five years after her husband had died before getting into another relationship. She knew she could handle whatever life threw at her on her own. Still, she had to admit to herself she'd like to hear his opinion on all that was happening, but she'd figure it out.

She felt the vibration of the phone in her pocket. Nell pulled it out and checked the caller ID. Speak of the devil. "Hello."

"Nell."

Sam's voice was so low, Nell couldn't resist. "Hello? Anyone there?"

Speaking louder this time, Sam said, "Nell, it's me."

"Hello, Sam."

"I've missed you, honey."

His deep sexy voice got to her every time and she caved in. "Ah, Sam. I've missed you, too."

"I'm so happy to hear those words. I hope we can get back to the way things were."

Nell's internal alert system began to hum. "Well, isn't there something you want to say to me?"

There was an uncomfortable pause before Sam muttered, "I was hoping we could forget about the harsh words we had and move on."

"I don't think so," she said. "I need to hear something from you."

"Okay. If this is how you want it, then I need to hear something from you, too. And that something is you've given up the foolish plan of looking into Clayton Dunbar's death."

The steam burned as it came out of her ears. "Really? That's how you see it? The entire concept of your controlling personality has missed you completely. You thought you could forbid me from doing something as if I'm a five year old and I'd happily comply? The fact a week has gone by and you still don't understand my objections, Sam Ryan, tells me there is no hope for us as a couple."

She hit the End button and if her iPhone hadn't cost so much, she would have thrown it against the wall. *Men!*

Chapter 13.5

The invitation to Dottie's house came sooner than I expected. I prefer to attend social events with a large crowd, making it easier to use the master bathroom. Not to say that being the sole guest has ever stopped me from completing my mission. I've accomplished that on several occasions in the past. There's so much information in the medicine cabinets and cupboards. A psychopath's dream. It's such an easy game, really.

I enter a bathroom and search for as many ways as possible to snuff out the host's life. Hmm, dump most the water out and exchange it for a different liquid. This time was easier than expected. My personal best, from a few years ago, was when I entered while another guest waited outside the door. I found nine ways to commit a clandestine murder from substances in the cabinet in under a minute. I only chose pills one time out of the nine. There are many ways other than medications to poison someone, and many ways to kill other than poison. Six different methods I've used so far, and some multiple times. Picks up my spirit.

The only problem I've experienced with using poison is I'm not around when the victim expires. I miss out on the death throes, which I've come to appreciate in my other kills. Or the look of shock on their dying faces as they realize I am the killer.

Life is good. At least my life. Ha, ha.

Chapter 14

The garage doors were shut and there was only one car in front of Leo's house the next morning. Nell parked her old Sable in the driveway and walked toward the front door hoping Leo was alone. It would be easier to talk to him about Dottie. Nell's outlook had changed since she cooled down after last night's disastrous phone conversation with Sam. She'd tossed in bed until one in the morning and then decided she was better off without that pompous ass. She had to admit, though, that his disapproval was a huge motivating factor in wanting to be a part of solving this murder. So, maybe he was good for something after all. She'd show him.

Leo opened the door a minute after Nell rang the doorbell. "Nell, come on in." They gave each other a warm embrace after she stepped inside.

"I didn't know if you'd have family here still," she said nodding toward the street, "but thought I'd pop over."

"Oh, no. The family's gone. Had to get back to work, you know. The car out front is someone visiting the house across the street. Sit down. Would you like a cup of coffee? I just made a fresh pot."

"That would be lovely, Leo. Thanks," Nell said.

"How about a cinnamon roll? You can't believe the food people have brought over here. The ladies from the church packed up the leftovers from yesterday and delivered them, too."

Nell's resolve to eliminate sugar had taken a nosedive after yesterday's sweet treats. "A cinnamon roll would be delightful." Leo ambled into the kitchen and Nell could hear coffee being poured.

"Cream and sugar?"

"A little cream or half-and-half would be great," Nell said as she followed his path into the kitchen. Leo handed her a mug and he put a large cinnamon roll each on two plates. "Sitting here at the table would be fine with me."

"Then we're closer to a refill, too." His smile was weak.

They sat down at the small oak table in the quant little kitchen. As Nell looked around, she noticed so many homey touches that Dottie had chosen. A large wooden fork and spoon were on one wall along with an old-time yellow clock with flowers by each number. Pictures of the grandkids and some of their artwork adorned the fridge. A red-and-white checkered tablecloth dressed the table that no longer needed leaves since Wayne and Tina had left home. Now Leo was alone and had to live in this house of memories every day. She understood what he was up against and wished she could make his burden lighter.

"Nell, I remember when Drew died and how sad we were for you, but I can see now a person never really understands until it happens to them. Dottie and I should have been better friends to you during that time."

Nell waved a hand in front of her face. "You were both very kind. As I recall, Dottie came over with food, too." Nell felt a lump in her throat form with the guilt of knowing she had an ulterior motive for visiting today.

"I don't know what to do without her. I wish I wasn't retired. Then I'd have somewhere to go and something to do with my time." Leo wiped at his eyes.

Nell's initial thought today was Leo was doing very well. His last statements revealed that his grief was the normal up and down after a spouse passed. Something she knew like the back of her hand. She was glad he was comfortable enough to let his emotions out in front of her.

She reached across the table and took his hand. "Grief is a difficult journey, Leo. I hope you'll call on me whenever you think I can help. Through my experience, I know it helps to talk to others who have been through it." She paused before taking a bite of her cinnamon roll.

"Thanks." Leo shook out his shoulders. "Pretty good roll, huh? Louisa Rolf was here this morning and brought them over. Made them herself, she said."

The roll almost caught in Nell's throat. She had to admit it was excellent, but darn it. Why did it have to be Louisa's? It was the perfect ratio between nuts, cinnamon, and gooey goodness. "Yes, simply delicious."

"Almost as good as your chocolate fudge with walnuts. Dottie said it was the best fudge she'd ever eaten."

"Had Dottie eaten my fudge recently?" Nell rubbed her left eyebrow trying to remember.

"We had a tray of desserts from the library bake sale. The plate was filled with different varieties of sugary treats. Dottie was making a huge production out of how good the fudge was and she knew it had to be yours. There were only a few pieces of each item so I told her she could have all the fudge and I'd have the molasses cookies, my favorite, and we'd split the rest. She agreed and ate the four pieces of fudge in one sitting, one right after the other." Leo exhaled. "How I loved that woman!"

"She was a character all right."

"Say, don't you do something else with food? A website or something? Maybe you could interview Louisa? You know, she'd love the attention." Leo couldn't hide his smile.

"You never know." *That would be the day.*

Leo seemed to have snapped out of his funk. This might be the time to approach him with some questions.

"Leo, I hate to bring this up, but do you know why Dottie died?"

"Her heart gave out. She was way overweight, didn't exercise, had high blood pressure, and sleep apnea. She was on a bunch of medications for it all." He raised his eyebrows and admitted, "We also usually fell into the sauce a bit on weekends."

"But did you have an autopsy done?"

"I was advised against it. I was told it costs quite a bit and the cause of death seemed cut and dried."

"Who advised you?"

"Hmm, let me think. I believe it was the assistant coroner. She was over here within a couple hours after I found my wife. And that's what I wanted her to say, too. I didn't want Dottie's body all cut up for no reason."

"So there was no autopsy."

Leo paused. "I hadn't intended on telling anyone this, but the coffin at the funeral was empty. I didn't want an autopsy, but after the kids came, they talked me into it. Wayne and Tina convinced me it was important for them to know if there was a particular reason she died. They mentioned knowing of any health issues would be good for them and the grandkids. You know, genetics."

"You did the right thing. Results from the autopsy will help your kids know their health history better."

"I guess, but I still don't like the idea of her body being cut up." Leo wiped at his eyes again. "It doesn't seem proper."

"I understand." Nell reached over and held his hand. "Believe me, Leo, I'm not enjoying this, but could you tell me exactly how you found Dottie the day of her death? At his grimace, Nell said, "I'm so sorry. Please?"

"I've told it enough times already, but sure, if you insist."

Nell nodded her encouragement. "Thank you."

"I was out of the house early that morning and over at the Bayshore Fitness Center to swim laps. I left Dottie in bed as usual. When I came home and walked in the door, I knew something wasn't right. Ordinarily, she would have been out of bed with the coffee brewing and making breakfast. The house was quiet. I walked to the bedroom and she was lying there, still as my coffee cup here. I went over to her and she didn't feel warm. She didn't feel cold either, but I knew she was gone." He pulled a handkerchief out of his pocket and blew his nose. "I called 9-1-1 and the rescue squad was here almost instantly. Officer Carson came within minutes and then Assistant Coroner Taylor. Soon, I was answering questions left and right."

"At that time you discussed her pills, eating habits, and level of activity?"

"Yes. Have you heard enough? Can I stop remembering now?" Leo ran his handkerchief over his eyes. "Why are you doing this to me, Nell? You went through almost the same thing when Drew died."

"I'm sorry, Leo, but I appreciate your patience so much. I only have a couple more questions," Nell soothed. She felt like a monster for making him go through it all. Wanting to cross her fingers for her most important question, Nell asked, "Was Dottie on warfarin, the blood thinner?"

"No. She wasn't on any kind of blood thinners. Why?"

All the air rushed out of Nell's balloon. She realized Leo deserved an explanation. "I don't know if you have heard much about Clayton Dunbar's death, but he was poisoned. I had a feeling Dottie might have been poisoned, too."

"*Poisoned?* You think Dottie was murdered?"

"I've been considering it. Would you let me take a look at Dottie's pills?"

"Do you think *I'm* a murderer? Dottie used to love those mystery shows, so I'd watch them, too. Don't they always say the killer is someone close to the victim?"

"Never in a million years would I think you had anything to do with her murder. I'm hoping Dottie wasn't killed, but if she was, we need to have the perpetrator caught." Then softly, she added, "Can I see the pills, Leo?"

From the look on Leo's face, Nell didn't know if she was going to be run out of his house on a rail or allowed to look over Dottie's meds.

"Follow me." Leo led her to the bathroom, scanned the long counter, and then opened up a large cabinet. He pulled out a basket full of pill bottles. "Have at it. I don't want to be in here." He turned and stalked out.

Nell picked up each bottle and read the label. No warfarin, just as Leo said. She opened each bottle and shook a few pills out to examine. Nothing looked suspicious. How could she be so wrong? She put the bottles back in the basket and returned it to the cabinet. As Nell maneuvered it back in place, she noticed the long hose of the CPAP machine. She knew quite a bit about the workings of this machine as her late Aunt Celia also had a CPAP. Nell used to visit her and help her around the house.

There should be a bottle of distilled water around, too. Sure enough. On the bottom shelf sat a gallon plastic jug that was almost empty. *Why was the machine in the cabinet? Had Dottie stopped using her CPAP? Could that have had something to do with her death*? Nell caught her breath. She remembered Dottie mentioning something about how wearing the machine wasn't very romantic. Maybe it was the last night Dottie hadn't used the CPAP because they had an intimate encounter. Leo might be feeling responsible. Dottie's death could be natural after all. She'd spare him any more questions.

Nell walked back to the kitchen where Leo was seated at the table. "I'm happy to inform you all of Dottie's pills looked to be in order. Thank you for allowing me to check."

Leo only nodded his head in response.

"Do you know that one of the churches in town offers a grief workshop for those who have lost a loved one? When Drew died, I didn't go to a group, but afterward wished I would have found one. If there isn't one in Bayshore, I'm sure you could find a group in Green Bay."

"Pastor Gene mentioned it. I might check it out."

"Good. But remember, you can call me if you need a listening ear." Nell gave Leo a quick hug and headed to her car. She was relieved her suspicions about Dottie's death hadn't panned out. However, putting Leo through his pain again didn't make her proud.

Before pulling away from the curb, Nell called Elena to see if she was available and willing to meet for lunch. Hearing lunch was a go, she drove over to The Two Sisters, a well-established restaurant and bar. It'd been a mainstay in Bayshore for more than thirty years. The dining spot had recently been purchased by an out-of-state party who kept the name the same. The new owners, Kate and Kallie, were sisters from California who saw no reason to change the sign. Nell had visited one of their restaurants before in Shawano, Pedro's Panini Palace. If they worked the same magic here, then Bayshore was in for a treat.

The restaurant was located next to the Oconto River with a dock and patio which made it a favorite in good weather. Even though it was December, the place was still a popular hangout. Nell parked her car and strode into the dining area. Elena wouldn't be there for thirty minutes, so Nell sat at a table, ordered coffee and a glass of water. She tried to get everything she discussed with Leo straight in her mind and organized, so she could share the information with Elena in a concise manner.

Nell's heart soared, thinking her fudge gave Dottie some joy before her passing. She was sure Clayton enjoyed his, too. He always had in the past. Hmmm, they both ate her fudge. Now *that* was a coincidence.

Chapter 15

"See, Nell," Elena said as she pulled another slice of the pizza they were sharing onto her plate, "there wasn't anything funny going on with Dottie. She died of natural causes."

"I know that now, but initially it looked suspicious. Poor Leo. What I put him through!" Nell took a deep breath, enjoying the aroma of the Jumbo Supreme Deluxe #4 pizza, picked up a sautéed mushroom and popped it in her mouth. *Every bit as good as before.*

"I liked Dottie. She was friendly whenever I saw her, even though we didn't know each other well. I'm glad she wasn't murdered."

"Me, too." Nell sipped her water and picked a chubby chunk of sausage from her slice. "I'm starting to think I may not need to doubt Scott Marshall's cause of death, either. But I know I'm right about Clayton. The way Hazel found his body tells me something is off. Someone must have deliberately given him more of some type of blood thinner."

"One murder will be easier to solve than three," Elena said. "I never liked the idea there could be a serial killer in Bayshore." Elena shook her upper body. "A shiver ran down my back just saying Bayshore and serial killer in the same sentence."

"I don't think our little burg is prepared for those 'big city' problems." Nell paused, taking another bite of pizza. "Chief Vance, I mean Chief Chuck, was so upset when I mentioned my various activities, especially the fact I went into Clayton's house unauthorized, I ended up leaving his office in a hurry. I wish I had asked him how he was going to investigate my theory."

"It's just as well you didn't. My guess is that he wouldn't have been in a sharing mood." Elena shook her head. "He may not want to investigate your 'theory' at all."

"You're probably right. Speaking of being in a sharing mood, tell me about your date with Herb." Nell gave her eyebrows the Groucho Marx double raise.

"Don't give me that look. It wasn't that kind of date." Elena smiled and fiddled with an earring. "We had a lovely evening. The food at The Wharf was exceptional, but the best part was the way he kept us both laughing. He brought up fun times I hadn't thought of in years."

"Are you thinking there could be something more to this relationship than laughs?"

"I don't want to speculate and jinx it. I'm enjoying the way things are right now. Have you heard anything from Sam?"

"Yes, and I'm so irritated with him I can't even bear to watch NCIS. My chubby Mark Harmon look-alike has turned out to be a skunk."

"Why? What happened?"

Nell shared with Elena about the phone call she had with Sam, and the two longtime friends finished their meal amid talk of men and murder.

"Mom, do you have time to talk?"

Nell adjusted her phone, paused the TV, and gave her full attention to her son. "Of course. There's no one I'd rather talk to, Jud."

"Thanks for calling and leaving me a message about Mr. Dunbar. I remember how much you used to like him. Sorry that's it's taken me so long to get back to you, but, you know..."

"Yes, I know." Nell laughed. "Young men have busy lives. Would it be better if I emailed?"

"Text, Mom. Emails stack up on me and when someone calls, I can't always talk. If you text, it's a better reminder to get back to you."

"Point taken. I'll text next time. You're right, though, about me always getting along with Clay. When I called you, I didn't even know the whole story."

"Whole story? What's up?"

Nell knew she said too much. Jud wasn't keen on her investigating murders either, but she had to continue. "Clayton was murdered."

"Are you serious? That's horrible! Who would do that?"

"That's just it. Someone killed my good friend and we don't know who did it."

"I don't like the sound of this, Mom. What do you mean 'we don't know who did it'?"

Nell could imagine the look on his face. He was never good at hiding his feelings. "The chief of police asked me to help out. I have his blessing to investigate to my heart's content."

"Wait. You're telling me, out of the blue, the police chief in Bayshore asked you to help?"

"In a manner of speaking. You have nothing to worry about, Jud."

"Nothing to worry about? You've had a close involvement in two murder cases within the last year. Why would I worry? What's Sam have to say about this? After talking to him a few times on the phone, I take him to be a steady guy."

"I'm not deaf yet, so please lower your voice. I'm no longer seeing Sam."

"I'm sorry, Mom. I thought you liked him. Everything was working out for the two of you. You seemed so happy." Jud paused and then challenged, "What happened?"

"We had a difference of opinion."

"Might the difference of opinion have something to do with your insistence

61

about participating in a murder case? A case I'm sure the police can handle without the aid of my retired mother."

"I took early retirement. Don't put me out to pasture yet."

"Well?"

"Well, what?"

Nell could hear his exhaled breath. "You're admitting you disagreed about the murder investigation, causing you to stop seeing him?"

"Yes."

"If you won't listen to Sam, I wish you'd listen to me. I'm worried about you and I'm sure he is, too. Let the police handle it."

"This time the killing was personal. Clayton Dunbar was a friend of mine. I knew him before you were even born."

"Mother, it's okay to be upset about your friend's murder. What I don't understand is why you feel the need to help the police. Don't you trust them to get the job done?"

"It's not exactly that. I came up with information in two other cases the police didn't have and the chief had to admit I helped them solve it. I know I can help this time, too."

"I can see I'm not getting anywhere with you. I have to go. I love you, Mom. It's why I worry."

"Thanks, Jud. I love you, too."

"And, Mom. Be careful."

Nell put her phone down and repositioned the dogs around her on the couch. She had a lot to think over as she released the pause on the TV. However, none of her thoughts had anything to do with stopping the investigation.

Nell tinkered with the wording of her next blog review. After spending more time than she cared to admit, she was proud of the end product.

Nell's Noshes Up North

Two Sisters
Bayshore, Wisconsin

The homey atmosphere of the Two Sisters restaurant lends the right feel to a place known for its pizza. However, many other dishes are created and eaten with relish at this longtime Bayshore favorite. I'll post a review of one of their delicious entrees soon. Today, it's all about the pizza.

The last time I dined at Two Sisters, I shared the Jumbo Supreme Deluxe #4 with a good friend. It was not the first time, nor will it be the last, that I lose myself in the aroma, the taste, and even the feel of this decadent pie. The title should give you, dear reader, the gist of the size and ingredients. Jumbo – the pizza was so huge my dining companion and I shared it and still each had a huge portion to take home. If supreme and deluxe each bring to mind a plethora of tempting components topping the pizza, your thoughts would be correct.

The Supreme Deluxe numbers (we ordered #4) refer to kinds of crust, sauce, cheese, and meat. When you order one of these specialties, you can have unlimited veggies on top. We ordered a partially whole wheat crust with garlic baked inside, a blue cheese béchamel sauce, with a mixture of fresh mozzarella and diced smoked Gouda. Sausage, pepperoni, and bacon crumbles dominated the next layer. Our choice of vegetables was caramelized onions, black olives, diced fresh tomatoes, and sautéed mushrooms.

When I saw the waitress turn the corner carrying the gigantic pizza tray, my mouth watered. The aroma hit my nostrils before the tray hit the table. It was comforting, like an old friend who is coming for a welcome visit. When those flavors hit my tongue, I was in ecstasy. Even though I've eaten #4 several times, the taste exploded in my mouth. Everything was perfect: the garlic in the crust, the lush blue cheese of the sauce, the smoky flavor of the Gouda, and the caramelization of the onions. In less capable hands, this pizza could have been ruined by too many aggressive flavors, but it wasn't overpowered at all by the garlic or the blue cheese. My every bite was truly a delight, and my friend agreed with me on this point.

Now to the bottom line. This pie is expensive. Considering we divided the cost and I took my portion home and had three additional meals already made, I think it was a bargain.

New owners are at the helm of the Two Sisters, and it's our opinion they are steering this eating establishment in the right direction. It looks like smooth sailing is on the horizon.

A true nosh or truly nauseous —You Decide!

Nell pushed publish and sent her blog entry into cyberspace. She was pleased she had put her wandering thoughts to good use. It was a relief to get her mind off murder for a few minutes. Now, though, she was back on the case. Her next step would have to be going to Chief Chuck's office to find out about his game plan in this murder inquiry. Nell hoped he still welcomed her input and didn't make an ugly scene. *Why couldn't he be more pleasant to her? She was helping, for crying out loud.*

She did a little channel surfing and came upon an episode of *NCIS*. Her thumb pressed down hard on the previous channel button. She loved the show but nope, she was not going to think about any portly Mark Harmon wannabe tonight.

Chapter 16

Big, beautiful snowflakes filled the early morning air as Nell yanked open the door to the police station. She had taken the dogs on a short walk earlier which had invigorated her and pepped up her mood. She decided not to make an appointment, but show up at the station unannounced. She loosened her ice-blue scarf and took off her gloves as she entered the lobby.

"Mrs. Bailey?" the smiling woman at the desk questioned. "Do you have an appointment?"

Nell looked at her nameplate again. Judy Schurz. Yes, she looked familiar. She has to be a former student. "No, Judy, but I was hoping I could get in to see the chief. It's important business."

"I'll see what I can do." Judy rose from her chair and as she walked past Nell, whispered, "I'll try, but he's cranky today."

Judy hardly had time to get to his office when Chief Chuck came thundering out to the lobby, his brown beady eyes the size of peas. *"What?"*

Nell looked around. Was he talking to someone else? Nope. Those eyes were drilled in on her. "I thought maybe you'd have a minute to talk to me about the case," Nell said. "I have some questions for you, Chief Chuck."

His eyes widened, but then he stepped aside and escorted Nell into his office. As soon as she was in the room, he closed the door. "Stop calling me Chief Chuck," he blustered.

"You said I could."

"I changed my mind. It sounds stupid, so stop."

"Fine. Now what has been done about my theory of excess blood thinners being the cause of Clayton's death? How are you going to figure out if this is what happened?"

"Your *theory*? As I told you before, Nell, I'm not going to share information with you. I'm allowing you to nose around and share info with *me*."

"Oh, so it's a one way street."

He nodded. "That it is."

"It seems to me you'd be more appreciative of an honest citizen who is going out of her way to help. From my last visit here, it was fairly obvious you hadn't seriously considered someone slipping Clayton more warfarin until I mentioned the possibility. I'm only looking for an update so I can be even more helpful."

Chief Vance pursed his lips. "Go ahead and sit down."

Nell's rear hit the soft cushion before he could change his mind.

"The death of Clayton Dunbar is officially a murder investigation." The seat squeaked as he sat down in his leather office chair. "Your tip about the medication was a good one, and I do appreciate it. However, you are always on the verge of pushing too far. You're going to get yourself in trouble, Nell. I don't only mean with the police department, but possibly with the perpetrator, too. He may come after you."

"Why would he come after me? You'll be happy to know I've kinda changed my mind about there being three murders. It's probably a case of 'one and done' and the killer isn't going to do anything else to cause suspicion."

"Thank God you have the thought of multiple killings off your mind." The chief shook his head. "I haven't anything to tell you. This is a slow process. I don't think we're going to find Clayton Dunbar's killer right away. If it eases your mind, we're waiting for the autopsy results and the lab is backed up. So even though I appreciate your input, I don't like to get too excited until the autopsy is completed."

She immediately thought of mentioning Dottie's autopsy, but knew Leo wasn't ready to share that particular fact. Also being the police chief, Vance may already know. "I'd wondered if an autopsy was being performed," Nell said. "We could get ahead of the game by doing a lot of the investigating into blood thinners before we even receive the results to see if the research confirms it."

"It could also be a big waste of time and manpower if the autopsy shows he died of arsenic or some other kind of poisoning. The taxpayers of Bayshore deserve better." He shuffled some papers. "I'm going to need you to run along now. I have work to do."

"I need something to go on. I don't know what to do next."

"You'll have to figure that out yourself," he said. "Isn't that part of your super sleuth mission?"

Nell noticed the corners of his mouth curl into a barely disguised grin. She got out of her chair and headed toward the door. "Thanks for your time. You can count on me to return." She turned and said, "See you later, Chuck," and hightailed it out of the station.

I'm going to need you to run along now. What a demeaning and dismissive statement! Although her desire to retaliate by calling him just plain Chuck and making a getaway was not the height of maturity, either.

Nell wasn't lying when she told the chief she didn't know what to do next. A cup of coffee at the Mocha Chip to think it over would help her determine her next direction. Maybe she'd even have a sweet treat to activate her brain. No. No sweet treat. She needed to find her willpower again.

She parked her car in front of the shop and saw a small woman with an adorable short bob of auburn hair coming out of the pharmacy. It could only be one person.

"Leigh!" Nell shouted as she moved toward her.

"Nell, what are you doing here? It's so good to see you."

The longtime friends shared a quick hug. "I'm going into the Mocha Chip for coffee. Do you have any time to spare?"

"Not really, but I can always squeeze in a few minutes for you." They walked into the shop, went to the counter to give the worker, Tonya, the order, and found a table. They removed their heavy coats and scarves and settled in for a long winter's chat.

"Ohhhh, I love that turquois ring. Did you make it?" Nell gushed as she examined Leigh's many rings and other jewelry she wore today. "Can I try it on?"

"Here." She handed the ring to Nell, who slipped it on and waved her fingers in admiration. "And, yes, I made it. I ordered some stones from New Mexico. I'm introducing a new line."

"You were made to design and create jewelry." Nell handed the ring to Leigh with regret. "You're such a natural at it. Metallic Dreams must be booming. How is Ed? Is his metal work taking off, too?"

Tonya came over with their order. "Double espresso for you," setting the cup in front of Leigh, "and a chocolate caramel mocha and turtle brownie for you." She set the second order in front of Nell.

"Thanks," they said almost in unison.

"The business has risen past our wildest dreams. Ed's fine, and busier than he wants to be. He's limiting the number of customer orders he'll create. He does excellent work and it all takes time. We've found that people who don't mind waiting don't mind paying a higher price for better quality. So things are going well." Leigh sipped her coffee. "What about you? Keeping yourself out of trouble? You're coming over to our house for Christmas, aren't you?"

Nell thought of Jud in Alaska, and how far away her brother, Gary, and sister, Renae, and their families were. They didn't get together every year for Christmas. No one liked to drive in undependable winter weather. She thought of her parents, who had been gone for well over thirty years. How she missed them! "I'm not getting together with my family this year, so if you want me, you've got me."

"Wonderful! You know we always want you. You're a part of our family," Leigh said as she touched Nell's hand. "Why don't you bring Sam? He'd bring his special brand of humor to the occasion."

"I can assure you that isn't going to happen. Right now, Sam Ryan and I aren't on speaking terms." Nell took a bite of the brownie. She had wanted to skip the brownie, but her willpower had caved in.

"What happened? Why haven't you told me this before?"

"It just happened a few days ago. He treated me like a child." When Leigh's eyebrows shot up, Nell continued. "Sam said he was 'putting his foot down' and I was not to investigate Clayton's death."

"Whoa, girl! It's obvious he had no idea who he was dealing with, the poor fool."

"Fool is right. He called me a few days later to patch things up, but didn't apologize." Nell licked some chocolate off her finger. "He still didn't want me to investigate. Who does he think he is?"

A tiny smile on Leigh's face appeared as she said, "A man who has his own business and is used to what he says being the ways things are done."

"You are so right," Nell said as she offered her fist to Leigh for a bump. "He was treating me like an employee, not as a partner."

"Don't give up on him too soon," Leigh advised. "All he needs is an attitude adjustment. He may come around."

"I don't know about that ever happening, but I do know something else. I've done some investigating and found out what I feared is true." Nell lowered her voice. "Clayton was murdered."

"Murdered?" Leigh moved her head closer to Nell's over the table. "Are you sure of that, or are you speculating he was killed?"

"I'm sure of it. Chief Vance told me that he was poisoned, but he thought it was accidental. I was suspicious, so I did a little investigating and gave the chief my theory." Nell scanned the coffee shop and whispered, "Vance is investigating it as a murder."

"Who do you think did it? Do you have any theories about the murderer?"

"Not really. Initially I thought Dottie Dumpling and Scott Marshall may have been killed, too. It seemed too coincidental when I realized they each had been at Clayton's open house."

Leigh's eyes widened as she asked, "You think there's an active serial killer here in Bayshore?"

"I don't think that anymore. I went to talk to Leo about Dottie's death but it seemed so natural." Nell shook her head. "I hated putting him through all my questions."

"What did Pam Marshall say when you questioned her?"

"I haven't questioned her. Clayton's death is the only murder." Nell paused and took a sip of coffee. "Maybe I shouldn't have dropped the idea so soon."

"Do you know Pam? I didn't see you at Scott's funeral."

"I don't know her at all, but it sounds like you do."

"I know her through the store. She's a regular customer of mine. Pam buys lots of jewelry, especially bracelets and necklaces. She and Scott were in several times last summer and autumn ordering garden figures from Ed, too."

"Do you know any personal info on them?" Nell asked, and then took another big bite of brownie.

"Probably not much more than what you would have read in his obituary. Scott had some heart issues, but that's not too different than a lot of other men his age. According to Pam, he worked out, watched his weight, and went to the doctor regularly. She was shocked when he died at their kitchen table." Leigh rubbed her forehead. "My heart goes out to her."

"You've given me food for thought. Perhaps Dottie Dumpling died of natural causes and Scott Marshall and Clayton Dunbar were murdered."

"I didn't mean to get you all wound up about Scott's death being a murder, but if there's any chance it is, I think we ought to know."

"You're right, and I'm not going to be able to put this idea to rest until I've talked to Pam Marshall."

Chapter 17

George and Newman were at the kitchen door wagging their tails when Nell walked into the room. She bent down to pet them and then gave them each a piece of a mini-wheat biscuit as a treat. The boys liked the crunch of the cereal. There was irony in the fact she was doing a much better job making sure her boys weren't overweight than herself.

Going to the fitness center was a huge improvement on her meager physical activity in the past. And she wasn't having the food binges she had before and didn't eat as much dessert, either. Well, except for a few relapses lately. Nell reminded herself it takes baby steps.

She had already divided the leftovers from yesterday's pizza lunch into three containers. The sugar in the mocha and brownie were urging her to eat more sugar. She knew she didn't want any more sweets, so decided to have an early pizza lunch. Unlike some, Nell loved cold pizza. She pulled out a nice plate and a cloth napkin. She sat at the table in the dining room and slowly ate her lunch, not gobbling it down as she had in the past. As always, she had two little friends watching her every move. They didn't jump up and beg, but sat politely, waiting for the bite of crust which would come to them at the end.

The big question on Nell's mind was how she could talk to Pam Marshall about her husband's death. The grieving widow may not want to talk to her at all or it could be a dead end. Should she come out immediately with the truth behind her questions? Would doing so make Mrs. Marshall more helpful or would she want to throw Nell out on her rear?

Nell felt the vibrating in her pocket and realized she hadn't taken the mute off her phone from being at the police station. Ahhh, Leigh.

"Hello."

"Hi, Nell. I'm knee-deep in work on a pair of earrings right now, but it came to me it might be difficult for you to approach Pam to speak with her about her husband's death. I thought maybe I could call her and see if she is willing to discuss it with you. What do you think?"

"I think you're a lifesaver," Nell laughed. "I was trying to come up with a strategy right before you called. I'd appreciate your help."

"Glad to be at your service. I'll call her right away and if she's home, I'll text you with an answer. I'll also text you if she's not home so I don't leave you hanging."

"Thanks, Leigh. I'll wait to hear from you."

Over the next few minutes, Nell willed her text signal to go off. She had turned the sound back on when Leigh called. Now her phone was like the proverbial watched pot that never boiled, or when her former middle school students thought the hands of the clock never moved during the last fifteen minutes of the day. She picked up the newspaper, but couldn't get into it. Finally the anticipated text signal rang.

It's a go. She was hesitant, so be gentle with her. Good luck. 555-2722

Nell breathed a sigh of relief and silently thanked God for good friends. She texted back a thumbs up and happy face emoji. She pondered whether to give Mrs. Marshall a few hours to think about the two of them speaking or if she should call her right away. She opted to contact her immediately, so the mourning woman didn't get nervous or change her mind.

"Hello."

"Hello, Mrs. Marshall?"

"Yes."

"This is Nell Bailey. My friend, Leigh, let me know you are willing to speak with me. Is this a good time?"

"I guess."

"Would you be willing to meet me in person to discuss your husband's death?" Nell asked. "I think that may make it a little easier than trying to do this over the phone."

Nell held her breath as she listened to the silence on the other end of the line. Finally a soft agreement.

"If I have to do this, I think talking in person will be better."

"Mrs. Marshall, you don't have to do this. If you're uncomfortable, I won't bother you again." Nell knew she was doing the right thing by offering a way out, but crossed her fingers, hoping she wouldn't take it.

"No. We can meet. Leigh trusts you and thinks this is a good idea."

"Thanks. Do you want to meet somewhere or should I come to your house?"

"Please come here. I don't want to go anywhere. My address is 3481 Ontario Avenue."

"Okay. I can be there in an hour, or is that too soon?"

"That's fine."

Nell hit the End button on her phone and called to her dogs. "George! Newmie! Wanna go for a walk?"

The boys jumped off the couch, shook themselves off, and started dancing around the room. Looking down at them, she remembered Drew often saying, "Simple pleasures are the best." She put a sweater on each of them, bundled herself up, and off they went for a long walk.

The snow on the road crunched as they turned off Adams Street and continued to walk the Presidents' Streets, Nell's mind full of possible questions to ask

Mrs. Marshall. She didn't want to cause her any undue stress, although the thought of her husband being murdered probably had already put her over the edge. She needed to be mindful of Mrs. Marshall's emotions and find the answers to her questions at the same time.

George, Newmie, and Nell were all a bit tired by the time they returned to the house. Nell applied some fresh makeup and ran a comb through her hair. She glanced over at the boys who were already curled up on the couch settling in for a long nap. Then she was off to Ontario Avenue.

Nell pulled into the driveway of the Marshall home with a mixture of dread and anticipation. She walked up the sidewalk of the lovely two-story home and rang the bell. Within a minute, the door was opened wide by a pale and slight woman. Her limp blond hair washed all color out of her face.

"Come in, Mrs. Bailey."

"Oh, please call me Nell."

"Then you call me Pam." She ushered Nell into the living room. "Make yourself comfortable. I can take your coat."

"Thank you." As Pam left the room with her coat, Nell took in the beautiful room with the large tree sparkling with Christmas decorations. Her heart went out to the woman. From now on, this most joyous time of the year will always bring memories of losing her husband.

"Is there anything I can get you, Nell? Coffee, tea, a soda?" Pam asked, wringing her hands.

"No thank you. Please relax. I'll try to make this as short and painless as I possibly can." Nell had no idea how she could do that, but she'd try.

Pam eased into a chair and questioned, "What is it you'd like to know? My husband died of natural causes, most likely from a heart attack."

Nell realized there was no more time for pleasantries. They were getting right into it. "I'm hoping that's what happened, too. I'm not sure if you're aware of this, but Clayton Dunbar's death is being ruled a murder..."

An audible gasp came from Pam's lips.

"I know it's shocking news. You were at his open house, but how well did you know Clayton?"

"Not very well, but Scott did. They used to meet up for coffee at different restaurants in town."

A possible clue. "Do you have any idea what their connection was, how they knew each other?"

"Not really." Pam paused and pressed her lips together. "I remember he always took his briefcase with him."

"Do you know if anyone else met with them?" Nell's voice took on a higher pitch. "Could they have been working on something together?"

"I'm not aware of any projects. Do you think this is important?"

Nell shrugged. "I'm not sure."

"How did Mr. Dunbar die?"

"He was poisoned. I think it was an overdose of warfarin, the blood thinner but I'm not positive. This takes me to my next question. Did your husband take any blood thinners?"

Pam shook her head.

"Was there anything out of the ordinary on the morning of your husband's death?"

"I don't think so."

"I realize I'm asking a lot, but could you go over the events on the morning of the death?" Nell knew this wouldn't be easy, but hoped Pam would pull through.

"We got out of bed that day as usual and Scott came downstairs right away to start the coffee. I took my time getting dressed and then came down. Scott went back upstairs to put his work clothes on as he had been doing some tinkering out in the garage."

Pam rose to her feet suddenly. "Excuse me, I need a glass of water. Are you sure there's nothing I can get you?"

"I'm fine. Take your time." Nell thought she might have a path to go on with the coffee meetings with Clayton, but wanted to stay and ask Pam as much as she could.

Coming back into the living room, Pam exhaled, "I feel better now. I can do this. While Scott was changing, I started the turkey bacon and eggs. He came into the kitchen and sat down at the table. I plated up his breakfast and set it in front of him." Her light blue eyes were dwarfed by the gigantic bags hanging beneath them. She whispered, "Scott then kinda slumped over and now my world has changed forever."

She started to cry and Nell rushed to her side to comfort her. "This is so hard, but I'll be all right." She held on to Nell as if she'd never let her go.

"I'm so sorry, Pam. I lost my husband five years ago. I know how much it hurts. Maybe I shouldn't have come."

"No, it's okay. Every day is like this. I start crying out of the blue." She released Nell and hugged herself. "Please go on with your questions."

Nell was surprised she was encouraged to continue, but after giving Pam a few minutes, took advantage of it. "Are you saying he hadn't eaten any of his meal?"

"None of the eggs and bacon, but when he came down to start the coffee he had already eaten something."

Nell's heart soared. Another clue. "What did he have?"

"Scott had such a sweet tooth. I later noticed he had been nibbling items from a dessert plate."

"What kind of desserts were on the plate? Did you make them yourself?"

"I'm more of a salty snack person and Scott shouldn't have too many sweets, so I don't bake much anymore. This was a tray of brownies, cookies, and bars from the library bake sale. He especially liked the candy. He had been saving them for last. I noticed all of the pieces of fudge were gone."

Chapter 17.5

The weathered newspaper clipping was pulled out of the envelope with love. Saturday, July 20, 1985, was written on the front of the envelope in familiar handwriting—my own.

> *The body of Charlotte Roper, 33, was discovered Friday morning in her Rockville, Maryland, townhouse. There had been no reports of any disturbances from the neighbors. From the nature of the wounds, foul play is suspected.*

Foul play is suspected? You think? The number of cuts and viciousness of the kill screamed murder. There was no way they could have been self-inflicted or an accidental slip of a knife. I ended up with so much blood on my clothes I had to drive fifty miles away to find a place to burn everything, including my shoes. No evidence left at all. No one would ever suspect me. No one ever has and I plan to keep my record perfect.

What a pity the paper didn't write out all the gory details! Was their readership too squeamish? Another disappointment was the dearth of valuables. I was led to believe Charlotte was worth more. I was forced to hunt down an additional victim in a little over a year. This kill was practically a waste of time. But I still enjoyed it.

Chapter 18

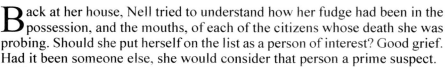

Back at her house, Nell tried to understand how her fudge had been in the possession, and the mouths, of each of the citizens whose death she was probing. Should she put herself on the list as a person of interest? Good grief. Had it been someone else, she would consider that person a prime suspect.

She'd ended her questioning of Pam rather abruptly after hearing about the fudge. Nell had felt like either fainting or vomiting, and knew she had to get out to her car. She drove a couple blocks away from the house, in case Pam was watching out the window, and then stopped to catch her breath. She finally made her way home. The boys were fast asleep and didn't greet her at the door. Each of them lifted his head from the couch to look at her and sleepily put it back down. Nell appreciated being able to sit down by herself and consider her options.

The idea of going back to the police station and admitting all to the chief didn't thrill her. He'd probably give her the fisheye and tell her to do no more nosing around. Maybe he'd even say she was a possible suspect. Telling all to Chuck Vance was definitely out.

Treating it like a coincidence was a thought. However, Nell realized all three of the deceased victims eating her fudge was too similar, even for her.

How many people knew about the fudge connection? Had anyone else heard Clayton telling her how he planned to eat it at the end of the night? Who were the others who were around them? The Library Bake Sale appeared to be the link.

A friend brought the fudge to Clayton. Who was that friend? A sudden thought made Nell sit up straight. Were the trays of goodies Dottie and Scott had eaten from also brought to them by friends? If they were and the friend was the same, that person could be the murderer.

Leo picked up the phone on the second ring and Nell wasted no time asking her question. "Leo, did Dottie go to the library and purchase the tray of sweets, or did someone bring it over to you?"

"I don't know. What difference does it make?"

"I'm not sure that it does, but it might. Can you remember?"

"What can I say? One day it was here. Someone could have brought it over, but I didn't see anyone. Of course, I didn't see Dottie bring it in the house, either."

"Okay, thanks. I'll be over to visit you soon."

Nell hesitated calling Pam so soon after leaving her house in a rush. Instead she'd see if Hazel knew who had brought the fudge to Clay.

"Oh, it's you, Nell. Have you found the murderer yet?"

"Not yet. I'm still searching for clues. Would you happen to know who brought the dessert tray from the library to Mr. Dunbar?"

Hazel paused. "I don't know. I wasn't here when it arrived and was trying to remember if he mentioned the name. I don't think so."

"Thanks, Hazel."

"Let me know when you figure it out, dear."

"I will."

Another dead end. Looks like she'd have to call Pam. At least she'd know if she purchased the tray or it was given to her.

"Hello, Pam. Nell Bailey."

"Yes."

"I'm sorry to bother you again so soon, but could you tell me if you bought the dessert tray with the fudge or did someone bring it to you as a gift?"

"Actually, neither. Scott came home with it. As I said, he had the sweet tooth in the family."

"Do you think someone could have given it to him?"

"No. Scott went to the library and bought sweets every time they had the sale." Pam sighed. "Too many years of those desserts, especially that fudge, could have killed him."

Nell feared the last part of Pam's sentence could be all too true.

The Library Friends put on the bake sale and Nell decided contacting someone in that group would be her next move. The person she delivered her three batches of fudge to was Norma Crenshaw. She dug her phone out of her pocket.

"Hello, Norma? This is Nell Bailey. How are you today?"

"Fine, Nell. What can I do for you?"

"I'm hoping you can help me with something. I'm thinking about the wonderful dessert trays the Library Friends create for each bake sale. Is there a pattern for how they are designed?"

"We chose five types of sweets and put four items from each type on the platter. We appreciate that you gave us so much fudge. We put four pieces on a lot of different plates. People always comment on how much they enjoy it. We like to put it on as many trays as possible. I think you could package and sell that fudge. You'd have a winner."

"Thanks. Does anyone else donate fudge?"

"No, yours was the only fudge we served this year. We get a lot of repeat business because of your fudge."

"Wow. Thank you. I appreciate the information and your kind words," Nell replied.

"Any time. You know the Library Friends are always looking for new members, Nell. Many hands make light work."

"I'll keep that in mind." Nell rang off and did some calculating. She had cut each batch of fudge into sixteen pieces before bringing it to the library. Those pieces would go on four different platters. Take that times three for the number of batches and her fudge would have been present on twelve dessert trays. There had been three deaths from three separate plates. What about the remaining nine trays? If Clayton, Dottie, and Scott had fudge from the same batch, there would be one more platter that may have been contaminated. Is there one more person who died, but who others took as a natural death?

Another question burned in Nell's mind. How would poison have gotten into her fudge? Could one of the Library Friends have laced her fudge with a lethal substance? She knew many of the caring people who donated their time and worked tirelessly to keep the library running. She couldn't imagine any of them would do such a thing.

Much as she loathed the idea, Nell knew she had to make another trip to Chief Vance's office and share with him her latest discovery. She glanced at the clock on the mantle. Too late to go today. Thank goodness she had a reprieve from a confrontation two times in one day.

Instead she opened her blog to see if she had any new replies to her posts.

Monica 410

I was so happy to read your review of The Alibi. That supper club is one of my favorite places to go for a tasty meal. It's exciting for me to know you agree with me on wonderful food and excellent spots to dine. I know when you recommend a place, it will be good. Thanks, Nell.

Red Stiletto

Your recommendation of The Whole Enchilada a few months ago was well received by my friends. It's become my favorite spot for fajitas. We are in the planning stages of a trip to Bayshore for a day of shopping in a few weeks. What's a great pizza place there?

After thanking Monica 410 and directing Red Stiletto to yesterday's blog posting about Two Sisters, Nell pondered how she'd spend the rest of the evening. She wanted to keep her mind off what was sure to be an ugly scene tomorrow at the police station.

George and Newmie were awake and stretching. She walked to the sliding glass doors and called to them. "Outside? Wanna go outside?"

They responded in the affirmative and were up and out within a minute. Nell watched them from the cozy confines of her warm living room. She doled out treats when they returned and thought about supper. There was some beef stew in the freezer that she could defrost in the microwave. It was a good cold weather meal containing lots of vegetables along with the beef. Good plan.

The aroma of the stew made her mouth water even though it was microwaved. It brought up nostalgic memories of her mom making it on a cold, winter night. Then she thought of how Drew raved when she made the same recipe. A good remembrance, but with it that feeling of loss for her mom, dad and husband. She finished her bowl, saving two pieces of meat to give Newman and George. The boys swallowed the morsels without even chewing. They had a good life. Sometimes she wished she could be so carefree.

As the three settled down on the couch, Nell couldn't stop the dread of tomorrow's meeting from overtaking her mind. She flipped on the TV and surfed through several channels. *Wasn't there anything other than cop shows on anymore?* She finally found a light science-based comedy to give her a few laughs.

The hours passed as Nell mindlessly flipped the pages of a magazine while watching TV. Then she uttered the magic words, "Who wants 'last pee of the night'?"

The boys shook themselves awake, jumped off the couch, and headed to the door. As Nell waited for them to come in the house, she wondered if she'd even be able to sleep. If the thoughts of tomorrow's meeting weren't bad enough, she was worried each victims' love of fudge had somehow killed them. But not just any fudge—her fudge.

Chapter 19

A reprieve. As Nell prepared for church, she realized that Chuck most likely wouldn't be at the office today. She had another twenty-four hours to prepare her case before she had to face him. She hoped she could come up with the right words to let him know about the fudge, but also avoid becoming a suspect.

As Nell pulled in to the parking lot of the First Christian Church she was thinking about Dottie's funeral there. Was it only Thursday? She had been so busy looking for clues, it seemed a lot longer ago than Thursday. She saw a man entering the building out of the corner of her eye as she shut the car door. Could it be Leo? Her heart went out to him as she recalled the difficulty of that first time attending church alone.

She hung up her coat and hurried to the doorway of the church. Nell scanned the pews. She spotted Leo, who had chosen an area far away from anyone else. He might not want to talk to anyone, but she wanted to give him the chance.

She rushed over to him. "Would you mind if I sit next to you?" Nell noticed his grimace, but didn't let it scare her off.

"You can sit down, but I don't feel like talking."

"That's fine. I don't want you to sit alone." Nell gave him a weak smile.

"I'm going to do a lot of things alone from now on. I'm trying to get ready for it." Leo pulled a handkerchief out of his pocket and wiped his eyes.

The awkwardness of the situation made Nell uncomfortable, but she remained silent next to him as he had requested.

After the pastor's motivating service, many parishioners spoke to Leo, so Nell chose to use the moment to walk away. He was safe with other people who knew his loss.

The sun was shining when Nell got home from church. Some of the snow had melted, but according to the forecast it would probably refreeze before the day was over. She put on her boots and rounded the boys up for a walk. All three of them enjoyed the outing, even though it was somewhat sloppy. The fresh air and movement lifted her spirits. George and Newmie were happy to check their "pee-mail" which had gone without their attention for several hours.

She made a salad for lunch, which included dried Door County cherries, pecans, and gorgonzola cheese. Fairly healthy and oh, so yummy. She set her bowl in the dishwasher as the telephone rang. She pulled it out of her pocket and was pleased to see it was her former student, Zane Colsen.

The doorbell rang in less than thirty minutes. Nell looked out the window and saw an older blue Jeep Liberty in the driveway. It was hard for her to come to terms with Zane having a driver's license. *Wasn't it just last year he was in her classroom?*

"Zane! Thank you for coming over." Nell brought him in the house and gave him a warm hug. He towered over her now, so she had to look up at him. "When did you get your license and, more importantly, how are you enjoying driving a car rather than riding your bike?"

"Mrs. B., how can you even ask such a question? I love driving." Zane bent over to pet the boys. Nell gave him credit for making friends with her dogs. A few months ago he had been afraid of them after a bad experience with a dog when he was younger. "I've been a licensed driver for eight days, but I was gone to the conference for four of them."

"Congratulations. Are the good people of Bayshore safe on the streets now?" Nell smiled and gave Zane a wink.

"Sure thing, Mrs. B. Either Mom or Dad took me out every night driving from the time I had my temps until I took the test. They're letting me drive our old Jeep almost every time I ask." Zane put a finger to his lips and whispered, "I think they're going to give it to me."

"Good for you." Nell walked him over to the garage door. She pointed out the burned out light bulbs on the ceiling and handed him a box of new ones. "You'll need to use the ladder which is right over there."

Zane had the bulbs changed and the ladder put away in less than ten minutes. "Do you have anything else for me to do?"

They walked back in the house. "No, but I did ask you over here for another reason. I heard you used to do errands for Mr. Dunbar and..."

He raised his eyebrows. "You want my help in your investigation?"

"Zane, I..."

"I had my fingers crossed that was the reason you wanted to talk to me. I knew you'd work on this case, since he was a teacher, too." He leaned forward as he rubbed his hands together. "When are we going to start? I don't need to be home for a couple hours."

Nell bit her lip. "I'm sorry you got your hopes up, but I only want to ask you a few questions."

His shoulders slumped, and Zane mumbled a faint, "Oh."

"Your answers could be very important, though. How often did you go to Mr. Dunbar's house?"

"Monday, Thursday, and Saturday were my regular days, but sometimes he called me to come over at other times, too. If it snowed on a different day of the week, he'd have me shovel the sidewalk. He paid by the week and gave me extra if I worked for him on the other days. Sometimes I'd pop over just to see if he needed anything."

"Did you knock and wait for Hazel to let you in?"

"Only the first time. Mr. Dunbar told me she was too busy to go running to the door every time I rang the doorbell. He said to knock and then come in on my own."

"You didn't need a key?"

"Heck, no. He never locked his doors."

"Did you tell anyone he kept his doors unlocked?" Nell held her breath.

"Just Mom and Dad. Mom marched right over to try to get him to keep them locked. She was concerned for his safety. They both really liked Mr. Dunbar. He was their teacher back in the old days."

Nell smiled and nodded her head. "Yes, he taught quite a few students over the years. Do you know of anyone else who came and went from the house as freely as you did?"

Zane hit the side of his head with his finger several times. "Gee, nobody I can think of right now."

"That's okay. What kind of errands did you run for him?"

"I'd bring in firewood, put up Christmas lights and decorations outside, rake leaves, that sort of thing."

"Did you ever do any work inside the house?"

"Oh, sure," Zane answered. "I'd go up in the attic and bring stuff down and later take it back up. I'd get on the ladder to clean the chandelier and other kinds of high work. Hazel wasn't much for using a ladder. I divided up his pills and cleaned the TV and computer screens. I..."

"Wait a second. You distributed his pills?" Nell leaned toward him.

"I put them in those daily container things. Yeah."

"I know Clay, er, Mr. Dunbar took a lot of medication. How did you know how much to give him out of each bottle? Wasn't it confusing?"

"It sure would have been if there wasn't a paper saying which were his day and night pills, and how many of each. There were some I had to cut in half, too. He had one of those pill slicer things and it worked pretty darn slick."

"Did Mr. Dunbar write the medication directions out for you?"

"No, there was a sheet from the doctor's office. It listed all his pills and quantities on it and I followed the directions." Zane added, "For the supplements, he told me to read what it said on the bottle. If it was one pill a day, I gave it to him in the morning. If it was two a day, I put one in the morning dispenser and the other in the one at night."

Zane pushed his hair out of his eyes and looked over at Nell. "Mrs. B., are you okay?"

Nell realized she was perspiring as she wiped away the moisture from her forehead. "I'm fine. Just processing what you told me. Where is the sheet with his meds kept?"

"In Mr. Dunbar's bathroom in the drawer under the one that has the dispensers. Did I give you a clue? What was it? If I gave it to you, I should at least know what I said," he wheedled.

"I'm not sure what you gave me, Zane, but I want to thank you for coming over so quickly. Let me get my purse."

"Just add it to next time."

"That sounds good. Would you mind if I called you again if I have more questions?"

"*Mind?* Are you kidding?" On his way out he turned with his phone in his hand and said, "I'm already waiting for the call."

Nell wanted to be sure Clayton's pills had nothing to do with his death. She hadn't looked in his other prescription bottles when she was at his house. A quick call to Hazel would remedy that fact. They could go back over to his house. Unfortunately, there was no answer when she tried calling. She left her name and number on the machine and asked Hazel to return her call.

Nervous energy so filled Nell she couldn't sit down or relax. She settled on a course of action. This wasn't the way she wanted to spend a Sunday afternoon, but knew it had to be done. After finding an address in the phone book, she hit the road.

She pulled up in front of a charming, little bungalow in an older part of town. *This was not what I expected.* Nell summoned up her courage, approached the wooden door, and rang the bell.

The owner, almost as tall as the doorway, appeared with a surly, "What the hell do you want?"

Nell swallowed hard. "Chief, I have something I have to tell you and it can't wait."

He stepped out on the stoop and closed the door behind him. "It's going to have to wait. I can't believe you'd come to my home."

"It's important, and you said I needed to tell you information I picked up in my investigation." Nell shivered and rubbed her arms.

"You're not coming in my house. Have you ever heard of a phone?"

"I wanted to talk with you in person."

Vance dropped his head, paused, and then said, "Against my better judgement, out with it."

"Standing in the cold sharing my facts was not how I pictured our meeting."

He didn't budge. "Talking to you on my doorstep isn't how I pictured my Sunday," Vance growled. "Spit it out, or go home and call me."

"I might have poisoned the victims."

"You've got to be kidding me. What are you talking about?"

"Clayton Dunbar, Dottie Dumpling, and Scott Marshall all had recently eaten my fudge from the Library Bake sale before their deaths."

The chief gave Nell a hard look. "Call Judy tomorrow and make an appointment to see me early in the afternoon. I'll tell her to expect your call. Don't tell anyone about this and don't you dare do any more nosing around. We have some serious talking to do tomorrow."

"Thanks for listening, Chief." Nell walked back to her car with the sound of the front door slamming in her ears. She had no intention of sharing with him that she planned to go back over to Clayton's house and hadn't dreamed of asking for his permission. As soon as Hazel called, that's where she'd be. What Chuck Vance doesn't know won't hurt him.

The pins and needles Nell was sitting on kept poking her with no sign of relief. Looking at the phone did not make it ring. She made another call to Hazel in case she was home now and hadn't checked her messages. Again the answering machine clicked on and Nell left a message, making it more urgent this time. She went to the kitchen to put together her supper.

"Good. I have some of my shrimp dish left and I can reheat it," Nell said aloud. She looked down at George and Newmie who had followed her to the kitchen. "This way I won't be in the middle of a big recipe when Hazel returns my call." They silently agreed and watched her as she moved around the room.

All too soon supper was finished and the trio was back in the living room at loose ends. If Hazel called now, they'd need to set something up for tomorrow. It was dark outside and she didn't want anyone to see the lights on in Clay's house.

Time to post a restaurant review in her blog. Nell cleaned her glasses and then gathered the notes she had taken on several different dining locations. She chose one particular establishment she had enjoyed and read what she'd written to remind herself of the highlights. Then, she began to write.

Nell's Noshes Up North

The Crusty Heel
Howard, Wisconsin

The sign outside the new restaurant in the old branch bank building boasted the words "The Crusty Heel." Thankfully, the picture wasn't of an encrusted foot, but a tempting bread basket. The building had been closed for several months while the interior was transformed from a formal corporate work space to an inviting place intended for relaxation. The renovators worked their magic so nary a thought of mortgages or car loans would ever come to mind while customers ate their fare.

My dining companion and I appreciated the change in the atmosphere and felt at home in the comfortable setting as soon as we entered. We were shown to a table with a thick khaki-colored tablecloth and rich chestnut-tinted napkins. We were handed menus and a wine list we browsed at our leisure. We chose to forego a drink before eating and had wine with our meal. It didn't take us long to make a choice as we had already viewed the menu online. A basket of crusty rolls was delivered after our orders were taken. A trio of butters accompanied the bread—plain, garlic, and honey. All of the pieces of bread were heels, some crusty and others soft enough that the comforting butters made them melt in our mouths. Neither of us could stop at one heel. This proved the line in the menu under the name of the restaurant to be true. It read "Restrict carbs tomorrow if you must, but enjoy the heels today."

Our salads came, and I took one more piece of bread to eat with my fresh dark greens, grape tomatoes, cucumbers, orange peppers, ripe olives, and shreds of parmesan. The peppercorn ranch dressing hit all the right notes. The crunchy homemade croutons answered the question of what was done with the pieces of bread which weren't made into heels.

My order of pan sautéed pistachio-crusted halibut with cherry beurre blanc arrived with gorgonzola mashed potatoes on the side. The sauvignon blanc appeared with perfect timing. I cut a piece of the crusted fish, dragged it through the sauce and up to my mouth. It had crunch and depth, and I closed my eyes in ecstasy. Then, the bite of gorgonzola mash comforted my mouth in warm joy. I was served a healthy portion and devoured every bite.

My friend received two bone-in pork chops grilled with prosciutto and aged provolone. It was topped with sautéed wild mushrooms and a balsamic glaze. A loaded baked potato was her choice of starch and a glass of Pinot Noir was her poison.

Nell stopped a moment as she reread the last line. *Oh, good grief!* Then she resumed writing.

She raved about her meal, too. The pork was juicy, yet earthy and the mix of flavors blended perfectly in her mouth.

We're both anxious to make the short drive back to Howard located on the north side of Green Bay. If the sandwiches are anywhere close to as delicious as this dinner, we'll be more than satisfied. At any rate, we know the crunch of the bread will make the trip to the Crusty Heel worthwhile.

A true nosh or truly nauseous? —You Decide!

Nell reviewed it several times and then hit publish. She'd had over an hour of relief from thinking of the murder, well, almost. Once she wrote of Elena's choice of "poison" her mind was focused on Clayton's mysterious death. Why hadn't Hazel called her?

Chapter 20

The shrill ring of her phone alerted Nell awake. Had she overslept? She picked it up from the bedside table and answered without checking Caller ID.

"I'm so happy to hear your voice, Nell. Is everything all right?"

"Hazel, is that you?"

"Yes. After receiving those messages, I thought you were in real danger."

"No danger. I needed you to get back to me as soon as possible."

"I came home late last night. My daughter had taken me on a day trip to the Upper Peninsula to visit my cousin. We stayed later than we planned and then had car trouble. I was so tired when I got home I went straight to bed without checking the machine. I'm so sorry."

"Don't worry about me. It was so cold out last night, I worried about you. Were you able to stay warm?" Nell asked.

"I was cold for a while and my daughter's cell phone couldn't get any reception to call for help. Then a nice young man and his wife stopped and, by golly, he changed the tire for us. Bless his heart." Hazel's voice brightened. "There are still good people in this world."

Nell thought about another man and wife who had changed a tire to help a young teacher out of a tough spot. Almost forty years had passed since Leo and Dottie came to her rescue. "Yes, there are."

"Tell me, what is it that had your underwear all in a bunch last night."

Nell would have preferred to have gone over to Hazel's and explain in person, but it might be easier this way. "I'm hoping you'll let me back in to Clayton's house."

"I don't know."

"Please, Hazel. I think there's a big clue there waiting to be discovered."

"When you put it like that, I guess I have to say yes."

"It won't take long. Can you be ready for me to pick you up in an hour?"

Nell had to wait for several school buses to make the turn toward the middle school. She tapped her fingers on the steering wheel as they moved slower than molasses in January in front of her. She was still waiting for the buses when her cell phone rang.

"Don't worry, Hazel, I'll be over to your house soon."

"I'm so sorry, dear. My daughter is here to take me to Green Bay for my nine o'clock appointment. With all the excitement, I forgot all about it. We'll have to go to the house another day."

"Oh." Nell wanted to ask if she could get the key and let herself in, but knew Hazel would not like the idea. "Okay, I'll call you later. Good luck with your appointment."

Talk about bad luck. Nell turned her car around and headed to the Mocha Chip. Before she left the car, she called the police station. Judy had been apprised of the meeting and it was already on the schedule. Judy said the chief wanted to see Nell at one o'clock. Nell agreed to be there at that time.

She walked to the counter and ordered plain coffee. No scrumptious sweet treat for her today. She didn't want to be in a food fog when she talked to Chuck. Chief Vance. Whatever his name, he was going to be furious with her and she had to be sharp in order to present her points. She took a chair at a small table and was served her coffee as soon as she was seated. Would calling Hazel after seeing the chief be too soon? Nell really wanted to get in that house.

Nell's back was to the door, but that didn't stop her from knowing who walked in the coffee shop. The foghorn known as Louisa Rolf had entered the building. Nell heard her loud, vibrating voice at the counter ordering coffee and a piece of banana bread. Then, out of the corner of her eye, she saw her sit down with a couple other customers.

Nell didn't look in Louisa's direction so no acknowledgement was required, but she couldn't help listen in as Louisa started chattering to her friends in her usual harsh tone. Nell tried to concentrate on sipping her coffee and planning her strategy with the chief. It was hopeless because Louisa's incessant honking couldn't be ignored. Just as she planned to leave and had a few sips left, one item caught her attention.

"Yolanda called me last night and said she's planning on coming up here tomorrow. She said she wanted to start cleaning out the house. I think it's about time. She hasn't been up here since her father died," Louisa sniffed. "What she *should* do is schedule his funeral."

Nell didn't bother listening to the rest of the conversation. Yolanda up here tomorrow? She might throw away the pills. Her evidence would be lost. She had to get back in that house today.

Nell's hand shook as she pushed Elena's name on her phone. She needed to talk this over with someone, and who better than the Lacey to her Cagney? After the appropriate pleasantries, Nell related to Elena about her appointment with Vance and the reason she wanted to go back to Clayton's house.

"I have so much to tell you I don't know if I can remember it all," Nell bemoaned. "Do you want to meet for lunch? Maybe you could give me some fresh insights."

"I'm so sorry. Herb is picking me up and we're going out for lunch before doing some Christmas shopping together."

"Christmas shopping?" Nell asked. "Is this relationship turning serious? It has been too long since the last time we talked."

"Not serious, just fun. I hate to let you down, but I have to finish getting ready."

"That's okay. I should go home and take the boys for a walk. I'll get my ducks in a row for my future interrogation."

"It won't be that bad." Elena laughed.

"You never know. Have fun on your date."

"Thanks, but Nell, don't do or say anything stupid."

After fifteen minutes of waiting in his office, Nell was irritated. Where was the chief? He had requested this specific time and was nowhere to be seen. Was he doing this on purpose? *What a jerk!*

Chief Vance strolled in to his office and took his seat behind the desk. Without a greeting or apology for keeping her waiting, he leaned back in his chair with arms folded. "Tell me about your candy."

Nell explained about the Annual Library Bake Sale and how the dessert platters were comprised. She related how each person had some of her fudge shortly before death. She mentioned the unnamed friend who brought one of the trays to Clayton. Vance sat with steepled fingers and without commenting as Nell told him everything she thought was pertinent.

"Thank you, Mrs. Bailey," Chief Vance's voice was low and even.

"What do you think? Could my fudge have killed these people?" In contrast, Nell's voice was shrill and rushed. "How could it have happened?"

"I don't know. The answer may be revealed when we get the results of Clayton's autopsy." Vance put his hand up when Nell started to speak. "As I mentioned before, the lab is backed up."

Nell took a deep breath and blew it out. She knew she had let emotion get the better of her. "Chief, my only concern is for justice. Please know I had nothing to do with anyone getting murdered. If my fudge turns out to have had something to do with it, I have no idea how it could have been contaminated."

"I don't think you had anything to do with the case, and that's just how I want to keep it."

Nell rubbed her eyebrow. "I'm not sure I know what you mean."

"Your candy has made you a part of the investigation. I'm not saying you're a suspect, but this is reason enough for you to stop looking into it any further." He picked up a file, put on his reading glasses, and looked at her over them. "No more poking around."

"Understood, Chief." She *understood* what he said, but didn't promise to *abide* by his edict.

Back in her car, Nell figured her fudge gave the chief the perfect reason to shut her out of the investigation. No wonder he was so calm. As soon as she talked to him on his stoop yesterday, he had figured out a way to stop her.

To add insult to injury, Elena was not going to be around to help her. Nell had to face the fact with Herb in the picture, Elena's time to sleuth would be diminished.

She drove past Clayton's house. Nell parked her car on the side street to avoid any curiosity from people driving by on Main Street. She scouted out the neighboring houses and walked to the back door. She rattled the knob, knowing full well, it wasn't going to pop open. Nell checked the one window that was within reach and realized she'd have to break it to gain entry. *Should she go that far?* Yolanda was coming tomorrow and she needed to get in and check those pills. However Elena's final words on the phone were ringing in her ears. *Don't do or say anything stupid.*

On a whim, Nell drove to Hazel's house. She parked in front and called her with high hopes.

Hazel opened the front door and started down the sidewalk as Nell opened the car door.

"I am so appreciative of you consenting to let me into Clayton's house. As I mentioned, it shouldn't take me long." Nell waited for Hazel to snap the seatbelt. "I trust your appointment went well."

"There was major trouble with my hearing aids. I was missing out on parts of conversations and filling in what I thought was said. My daughter let me know how often the words I filled in were wrong. The doctor straightened it out. I hope you find what you need this time," Hazel said. "I thought you'd have already figured out the killer by now."

"Real murders aren't solved as quickly as they are on TV. I wish it was the case, though, as I want to see Clayton's killer found and punished as much as you do."

They parked on the side street and walked to the back door. Hazel fumbled with the keys, but finally was able to open the door. "I'm not used to monkeying with a key. I had one because I had a small room here and stayed overnight at times. I never needed to use the key, though. I'm going to sit down while you do whatever needs to be done. It's been a long day." She dragged a finger along the end table near the couch. "I probably should come over and dust soon."

Nell hurried to Clayton's bathroom to check on his medications. She pulled out the basket of pills from his cabinet, then the dispensers from the drawer. Zane said the amounts allotted were on a sheet from the doctor in the drawer beneath the dispensers. She opened the second drawer and it was right where he said it would be.

"I wish you'd hurry up and find who murdered Mr. Dunbar." For such a slight older woman, Hazel sure could make herself heard.

"I'm working on it," Nell called back.

She opened the dispenser to the night after his death and checked it against the meds on the sheet and the pills in the bottles. They checked out. The 3 mg of warfarin was exactly the same in the dispenser and bottle. She then examined the day dispenser. All of the prescribed meds were accounted for and correct. *How could she be so wrong? Was all of this for nothing?*

Not one to give up, she took a look at the over the counter supplements. The amounts weren't on the sheet. Zane said if two pills were indicated on the back of the bottle, he put one in for both the morning and night. Nell looked for the bottles which suggested two a day. She again checked the dispenser. Everything was in order. She opened the other night containers for the rest of the week. No discrepancies.

Her last chance was the morning supplements. There was a large bottle with multivitamins. She shook some out in her hand and checked it against the morning dispenser. One in each container for the rest of the week. Before she put them back in the bottle, a number caught her eye. These were large white pills with the number 10 on one side.

Heart pounding faster and almost in her throat, Nell looked at the night dispenser. The café au lait colored tablet for 3 mg of warfarin had a 3 on one side in the same way. She looked up the colors of the blood thinner on her phone. The size of the pill increased, but it was the same shape. The number 10 on a white pill meant 10 mg of warfarin. Clayton was taking 10 mg of the med in the morning and another 3 mg at night when he should have only been taking 3 mg each night.

This was intentional. Someone had come into this house with a bottle of multivitamins, but it was filled with warfarin. She held the proof. The hard part was ahead of her. How was she going to tell the chief she had been in Clayton's house again?

Nell went back in the living room to share her findings with Hazel.

"How could this have happened?" Hazel asked. "I don't understand."

"I'm trying to figure it out, too. Didn't you tell me that Clayton mentioned to you that he had a lot of bruises lately?"

"Yes, he covered them up with his long sleeves and long pants."

"Too much of a blood thinner like warfarin can cause excess bruising." Nell paused, and rubbed her left eyebrow.

"Get to the point, dear. I'm not getting any younger."

"Having the additional 10 mg of warfarin each day took its toll. We don't know how many tablets were taken out of the vitamin bottle, but it looks to me like Clayton was poisoned gradually." Nell pulled out her phone and dialed.

"Bayshore Police Department, Judy speaking."

"Judy, this is Nell Bailey. Could I please speak with the chief?"

"I'm sorry. He's not available right now."

"The information I have could break the case. It's that important."

"Well, I..."

"He's there, isn't he?" Nell fumed. "Did he tell you not to let me see or talk to him?"

"I'm really not at liberty to say."

"Tell him I'm inside Clayton Dunbar's house and I've uncovered evidence." Nell heard Judy talking to someone and then a loud curse.

"Stay right where you are," he said. "I'll be there in a matter of minutes." A receiver slammed down in her ear.

The doctor must have worked wonders with Hazel's hearing aids because she heard the siren first. "I hope no one is seriously hurt."

Nell paused to listen. "No, Hazel, that sounds like a police siren and not the rescue squad."

"It sounds like it might be coming right outside the door. Somebody around here must be in big trouble."

There was an ear-piercing bang against the front door. "That would be me. I'm the one in big trouble."

Hazel opened the door and saw the chief and two deputies. Nell had the distinct impression they were here to arrest her.

For as calm as Chief Vance was when he spoke to her earlier, his appearance was the opposite now. His brown hair was uncombed, his face was the color of a Door County cherry, and Nell could see fire in his eyes.

Maybe she should have come here without getting Hazel involved.

Chapter 21

When she was able to return home finally, Nell called her sister, Renae, who lived in Minnesota. She'd been keeping her updated on the situation. "When the chief and two deputies arrived to the house, one of them drove Hazel home. I think the other one stayed to keep Chief Vance from killing me. He was so wild and he had such a maniacal look on his face, I was relieved not to be left alone with him."

"Why don't you stay out of it, Sis? I worry that you're going to get in over your head with all these upset officers and the murderer you're hunting. You could even get yourself killed."

"Don't worry, I'm fine. I kept my cool and listened to him without comment," Nell said. "I know I didn't cooperate with him the way he wanted, but it was for the greater good, wasn't it?"

"What you say may be true, but it's not making me rest any easier at night."

"I suppose I can go back to not telling you anything until it's all over like I used to do," Nell offered.

"No," Renae shot back. "I want to know, good or bad."

"Okay, then I'll finish telling you what happened. When the chief stopped ranting and took a breath, I led him into the bathroom and shared my findings. He calmed down and began to examine Clayton's medications. Chief Vance isn't happy with me for disobeying his orders, but he did end up thanking me. I consider that to be a huge development."

"Good. I feel a little better about the situation now." Renae exhaled a giant sigh. "However, I don't imagine this is the end of it for you."

"You know me well, Renae. I'm already plotting my next move."

What is my next move? Nell had spent several hours with the chief going over and over every piece of information she had gleaned during the course of her investigation. His face regained its natural hue and his temperament cooled way down as he recognized the breadth of the help Nell offered. There wasn't a way for her to act in an official capacity, but Vance finally came to terms with allowing her to be an unofficial part of the inquiry. This was an upgrade from being allowed to "nose around."

She had picked up a sub sandwich from the shop on the highway and positioned herself in front of the TV. This was an old, bad habit Nell had worked on breaking. Tonight was a temporary setback. She ate her supper, being sure to save a few morsels for the boys to devour at the end.

A cooking show droned on, but the Christmas baking competition failed to hold her interest. She flipped over to a movie channel and caught a repeat of *The Deliberate Stranger*, the old movie about Ted Bundy. The actor portraying the serial killer was Mark Harmon. *Wouldn't you know?* She had seen some pictures of Sam as a younger, thinner man and still thought the resemblance to Harmon was significant. Even as upset as she was with Sam right now, she would never consider him to be a killer. Then she shook her head as she remembered a murderer was exactly what she thought he was when she first met him.

She pulled George and Newmie closer to her as she burrowed into the couch half watching the movie and half thinking about what might have been.

"Benita?" Nell picked up the phone on the second ring and heard a sigh on the other end.

"It's so good to hear your voice. I hope this isn't too early to call?"

"I've been up for a while. Is everything okay?"

"Yes and no." There was a pause as Benita groped for words and then let them fly. "Dad misses you so much. He's like a grumpy, old bear that has been shaken out of hibernation. No one can do anything right. He snaps off everyone's head."

"I'm sorry for that, Benita, but I don't see why you're telling me."

"I'm telling you because you're the reason Dad's so grumpy. I'm not saying it's your fault. It isn't. But with you, he was the happiest I'd ever seen him. Now he's miserable."

Nell shrugged. She'd given Sam a second chance. "I don't know what to tell you. I—"

"Don't shut me down, Nell. Is there any chance we could meet for lunch today? I could come to Bayshore."

"I would love to see you, but how about I drive up to Marinette? I need to go to the veterinarian's office for dog food anyway. Would 12:30 work for you? I'll let you pick the place."

"How about Smiley's Diner?"

"That's a wonderful idea. I haven't been there in ages. See you at 12:30."

The knot in Nell's stomach started out tiny as she showered and changed into her charcoal gray pants and black sweater. It grew larger as she drove her car into the Smiley's parking lot and saw the giant set of teeth grinning down at her dwarfing the sign on the roof. By the time she pulled open the door, the troublesome knot was almost in her throat. She couldn't understand the reason for this attack of nerves.

Nell scanned the small dining area of booths and immediately recognized

Benita's long, silky, black hair. Benita turned and waved her over. She stood up and greeted Nell with a big hug.

"I've missed you so much, Nell."

"I've missed you, too, dear. It's only been a few weeks, but time has a way of marching on, doesn't it?" She slid into the booth and noticed it wasn't the tight squeeze it had been in the past.

"Yes. What happened between you and Dad?" Benita said, her wide, dark eyes drilling into Nell.

"Oh, well. We haven't even ordered yet. Let's relax and catch up first." That's when Nell knew this is what had caused her earlier uneasiness. Benita was there to put her on the hot seat.

They browsed the menus and made their selections. The table chatter was so strained Nell gave it up. "I'm sorry, Benita. I don't feel comfortable telling you details of a situation that should be none of your concern. Your father and I have the right to some privacy."

"Oh, I'm not fishing for details of your love life." Benita's face turned flamingo pink. "I'm certain from what I've been able to pull from Dad, he made some boneheaded statement and won't back down. I want to speak with you today to see if you would ever consider getting back together with him if he apologized. Is that a possibility?"

"You have the situation in a nutshell."

The waitress brought out the food at that moment. She set a plate in front of Nell that could have fed several people. She had ordered the liver, bacon, and onions platter and they meant *platter*. The gigantic plate was full of meat and onions. The American fries were served on the side along with the coleslaw. Benita was presented with a heaping chicken taco salad in a crispy shell. Both diners dug in with delight.

As their hunger abated and the pace of their eating slowed down, they picked up their conversation where it left off.

"Without going into detail, your assessment of Sam's position is accurate."

"So you agree Dad is a stubborn old goat?" A smile peeked out from the corners of Benita's mouth.

"I didn't say it quite like that, but in essence, yeah." Nell gave her a half-grin.

"Is there a chance, Nell? That's what I need to know. Is there a chance for the two of you to get back together?"

"It all depends on Sam. Can he own up to his mistake? Or even more important, does he realize what he said to me was unacceptable?"

"I'm not sure. I hope he does, and that he'll admit it."

"He did phone me one time and wanted to go back to the way things were, but didn't offer an apology. I called him on it and haven't heard from him since." Nell looked at Benita who was shaking her head.

"I know exactly when that was. It was unbearable being around him afterward."

"Unfortunately the things you're telling me make Sam sound more childish all the time. Adults don't behave this way."

"He's a good man, Nell. You know he is. A few weeks ago I thought I would one day call you Mom."

Nell shook her head. "He is a good man, but don't get ahead of yourself. Even at that time we were a long way from tying the knot."

"Will you listen to him if he tries again? Please tell me you haven't given up on him."

"If your father can get his act together, I'll listen to him. I'm not promising any more than a willing ear."

"That's all I'm asking." She grinned from ear to ear. "Give him a chance to make things right."

Benita and Nell paid their bill and headed for the door, doggie bags in hand. Going past the counter they were stopped by Zoe, a friend of Benita's, who Nell had met on several occasions.

"What do you think of Benita's new boyfriend?"

"What do you mean? She didn't tell me anything about a new man in her life." Nell looked at Benita with raised eyebrows.

"We were kinda busy with another topic. I'm going out with an old friend. You've met Jaron."

"Of course," Nell said. "He's so funny. The three of you and some of your other friends are all so close you remind me of the old TV show, *Friends*."

"Exactly. That's what I told her," Zoe laughed. "I think it would be hard to date Jaron. I love him like a brother."

"I think it's wonderful!" Nell said. "The best policy is to be friends first. Don't forget some of those 'friends' became a couple by the end of the series."

Nell left the two giggling pals and walked into the sunshine of the beautiful December day. She lingered in the car, lost in thought before driving over to the vet's office. Love must be in the air. Elena and Benita each have a new significant other. She looked in the rear view mirror before backing out, thinking of her own situation.

Alone again. Naturally.

Once in Bayshore, the old Mercury Sable practically drove itself out of her way down Main Street and past Clayton Dunbar's house. She saw a moving truck parked on the side street with Clayton's chocolate-brown BMW, and a police car behind it. Yolanda must be using her dad's car. A glance at the house and Nell realized the problem. There was police tape around the building. If Clayton's daughter was trying to clean it out and move items, she'd come to a standstill.

Nell slowly drove around the block deciding whether or not to stop. On her second lap around the house, she noticed Chief Vance and Clayton's daughter standing outside the back door. Yolanda appeared to be yelling.

Nell drove past and on to the Mocha Chip. Her presence wasn't needed at the house and most likely wouldn't be appreciated. Yolanda especially wouldn't be happy if she knew Nell was the one who gave the police the clue that caused them to close the house.

Nell ordered her plain coffee in a to-go cup and found a table facing a window. She watched the world outside, hoping to see the chief or Yolanda go by. Nothing much was happening on the street and Nell considered going to the counter for a sweet roll. She turned her head to look at the delicacies behind the glass, and when Nell turned back to her coffee there was Yolanda right outside the window in front of her. The door to Mocha Chip opened and in she came. She looked a little worse for wear with wisps of blond hair escaping her chignon and a trail of mascara streaking her face. Holding her head high, Yolanda stormed to the counter and ordered a caramel cappuccino.

When Yolanda turned away from the counter to find a seat, the first person she laid her eyes on was Nell. She charged over and plopped her purse on the table. "Thanks a lot, Nell Bailey. The chief of police told me you were the person who put the hold up on my moving plans today. The truck is on its way back to Green Bay. Who knows how long I'll have to wait before I can get the house cleaned out."

"Hello, Yolanda." Nell did her best to remain respectful. "I'm sorry this is causing you extra trouble, but if your father was murdered, the clues need to remain intact."

Yolanda pulled out a chair and sat down. "I know. You have no idea how hard it was for me to get the motivation to come up here and get going on the house. Now to be delayed like this brings my spirits way back down."

"I understand." Nell patted Yolanda's hand and gave her a tissue. "I'm here if you want to talk."

"It's been so hard to accept someone murdered Dad. I don't want to believe it." Yolanda wiped at her eyes and then curled her lips. "The Bayshore police are like a bunch of Keystone Kops who aren't able to solve the case. I bet the chief couldn't even figure out who owns a parked car."

"That's not true. I know you're upset, but our police department has a good record of solving crimes. They'll figure it out." Nell finished her coffee. "Are you staying in Bayshore long?"

"It's up in the air. While I'm here, I'm going to make arrangements for Dad's funeral," she replied. "And another thing, where are the autopsy results? His body has finally been released, but no results yet. Talk about incompetency."

"In all fairness, I've heard the lab is backed up. That's not the police department's fault." Nell looked out the window and noticed Louisa walking in their direction. "I see you have a friend coming, and it's time for me to take off anyway."

Yolanda glanced out and rolled her eyes. "Oh, great. Rumor mill Rolf is headed my way."

Nell only had to nod at Louisa as she left and Louisa arrived. She couldn't help but laugh thinking of Yolanda. *Some people never change.*

On her way home, Nell took a chance and drove past The Dining Room, Elena's home décor shop. She was in luck. Elena's new blue Subaru Forester was parked on the side of the building. She was working fewer hours because her grandchildren were all in school and her daughter, Julie, wanted to work more often. Elena was happy to fulfill the role of owner and decision maker, and retreat from the position of "every single day" salesperson. Her true talent was in ordering popular goods and decorating the showroom.

The bell over the wood door rang as Nell walked in to the store. She could see Elena at the end of the room, repositioning a centerpiece on a lovely oak table. They walked toward each other and hugged.

"When you were Christmas shopping with Herb yesterday, did the two of you go to any jewelry stores, by chance?" Nell teased.

"How you talk! I told you we're enjoying each other's company. That's all." Elena smiled and pushed her bangs aside. "Come back to the office where we can sit down and visit until I have a customer."

Once seated in the back, Elena recounted the fun she had the day before. Then, Nell updated Elena on the happenings in the murder case since the last time they spoke.

"Chief Vance has finally started to appreciate you. That's a good thing," Elena said.

"If he hadn't after everything I've brought to his attention, he would cut off his nose to spite his face." Nell chuckled. "I've come to the conclusion Chuck's a really good guy."

"You're back to Chuck, are you?" Elena asked.

A smile was Nell's only answer. "When Yolanda was complaining about him to me earlier, it crossed my mind maybe she had killed her dad and wanted to get rid of the evidence. She was so adamant against the police it seemed excessive."

Elena looked thoughtful a moment. "We have to consider everyone at this point. It would take a cruel person to poison someone with warfarin. Do you know of any reason Yolanda would have an issue with her father?"

"No, but with relatives it's usually money." Nell paused. "I wish I'd have thought to ask her if she was going to inherit all of her dad's estate."

"That would have been awkward."

The door opened and a middle-aged couple entered the store.

"I'll get out of your way, but think about everything we've discussed. We can talk later."

Nell drove past Clayton's house one more time on her way home. It looked closed up tight. Driving past the pharmacy, she noticed Zane Colsen getting out of his parked car. He waved at her with a big smile. For the briefest of moments she considered him. "Could he have fooled around with the pills because he wanted to get in on a murder investigation?"

No. Not Zane. She shook her head as if shaking the mere thought out of existence.

Chapter 22

The sunshine of yesterday had disappeared and gray gloom had taken its place. After a short, but careful spin with George and Newmie through the neighborhood, Nell sat down with a cup of coffee and planned her day. She was as anxious as Yolanda to learn the results of Clayton's autopsy. She was positive the excess amounts of warfarin would reveal itself, but would there be another lethal substance added to the mix?

Nell still thought her fudge might have had a role to play. Could a murderer have overdosed Clayton with warfarin and then poisoned the fudge for Dottie and Scott? Nell thought Dottie's autopsy might shed more light on the situation than Clayton's.

Nell wanted those results. One more sip of coffee for courage and she'd give Chuck a call. She knew Judy would put her through to him now.

"Yes, Nell. What's on your mind?" The chief's tone was much more pleasant than in past conversations she'd had with him.

"I'm wondering about the autopsy results. Do you have any idea how much longer it'll take?"

"Ordinarily I'd say I have no way of knowing, but they came in last night," Vance said. "I've contacted Yolanda."

"That's good." Nell paused, waiting for the information. "Aren't you going to tell me?"

"You already know. Telling you is only a formality. Warfarin. He was overdosed with warfarin."

"Was there anything else suspect in his system? Could something have been in the fudge, too?"

"No. You're off the hook. The warfarin was the only fatal substance in his body. You can breathe a sigh of relief."

Nell shook her head. "What about the other two murders? My fudge could have been the cause of death."

"There aren't two other murders. Dottie Dumpling and Scott Marshall eating your candy was coincidental. I spoke to a woman who worked at the bake sale and she assured me your fudge is well known throughout town." Vance chuckled. "I like sweets. Maybe next time I'll have to buy a platter."

Nell let that comment pass. "Chief, I think Dottie and Scott were murdered, too."

"Drop it, Nell. We have our hands full finding Clayton's killer." The chief spoke to someone in the background. "If that's all, I have work to do."

Nell rang off, but she had another idea. If the results came in for one autopsy, could they have come in for another?

The phone rang several times before it was picked up. Nell heard the pain in Leo's voice when he answered and wished she didn't need to ask him any additional questions. She tried to console and then cheer him up. All in vain. Leo had chosen to dwell in misery for the time being. Seeing no way to soften the blow, Nell asked her question.

"I hesitate to ask you this, but have the autopsy results been delivered yet?"

"Nell, I'm getting mighty darned tired of your questions. If the only reason you're calling is to grill me, you can stop it. I've had enough."

"I'm so sorry. I..."

"How about this. When the report comes in, I'll call you. Will that work?"

"Leo, I didn't mean to..." Before she could finish, Leo was off the line.

Nell's heart ached for him knowing how deeply she had hurt her old friend. She promised herself she would make it up to him. For now, it would be wise to let some time pass by before she approached him again, even if she had no questions about Dottie.

There was the possibility Dottie's death was natural, and Scott's, too. Chuck was sure of it and he was the chief of police. Nell had a feeling, though, and her feelings had been on the money before.

Since she wasn't going to talk with Leo for a while, Nell decided to call Pam. Perhaps she had thought of something else. What Nell was particularly interested in was if Pam had any more information about those coffee meetings Clayton had with her husband.

"Thanks for agreeing to see me again."

"Come on in." Pam held the door open for Nell. "I can't imagine what else you need to ask me."

Nell was guided to a chair and sat down. "I'm devastated over Clayton Dunbar's death and am trying to make sense of it."

"He was an old man, around ninety," Pam said. "You can't be surprised."

"I'm surprised it was murder. I could have accepted a natural death."

"But why are you here?" Pam wrung her hands together, pain evident on her face. "How do you expect me to help you?"

"I don't mean to upset you. I've been wondering about those coffee meetings Clayton and your husband shared. Have you thought any more about them?"

"No."

If I'm not careful I'll have Pam irritated with me, too.

"Do you know how long they'd been meeting or even what restaurant they frequented?"

"I'd say they've met once or twice a month during this last year. As far as the place, I think they spread their business around and went to anywhere in town that serves breakfast."

"Okay, thanks. How about other people? Do you think anyone else attended?"

"There could have been others, but Clayton was the only one Scott mentioned."

Nell sat forward in her chair. "Any idea on the purpose of the meetings?"

"No, Nell. They were friends. I think they liked to get together and talk. Scott was so fond of Clayton that he told me when he picked up the dessert tray from the Library Bake Sale for himself, he also bought one for Clayton and dropped it off at his house."

"There goes that theory." Nell ran her hand through her graying hair.

"Theory? What are you talking about?"

"I thought Clayton Dunbar, Dottie Dumpling, and Scott all having eaten the fudge from the Library Bake Sale was more than a coincidence. Maybe the fudge was poisoned. At least the candy that Scott and Dottie ate."

"Poisoned? Scott wasn't murdered."

"Are you sure?"

The color drained from Pam's already pale face. "I thought you were asking questions in order to get a handle on Mr. Dunbar's murder."

"I was. I am, but I think there's more to it." Nell explained her thoughts and the clues she'd learned. Pam was more receptive to her ideas than Leo had been. She shared information without prompting, and when Nell left, the two of them were on friendly terms. She knew she could return if she needed to follow up on anything. Pam even hinted she would be willing to help in the investigation.

Finding out Scott Marshall was the person who brought the tray to Clayton cleared up one question, but presented a new one. Was it now more or less of a coincidence each of the victims had eaten her fudge shortly before they died? Was someone trying to set her up as the murderer?

George and Newmie jumped up on the couch to snuggle next to Nell. She petted them as they settled in, and soon both of them were fast asleep. The music playing softly in the background, rather than the blaring of the TV, aided Nell in relaxing her mind. She planned to rest for thirty minutes and then start examining her clues. Instead, she soon was sawing logs right along with her boys.

She woke up in the middle of the night and made her way to her bed, the boys following. She felt new aches and pains as she moved and knew the last few days of activity had exhausted her.

Nell woke up early with plans to decorate her Christmas tree. She kept an artificial tree in the garage all put together so it was easy for her to drag it in each year and throw some ornaments on it. Most years she took more time and care while adorning her tree, but lately she'd been so involved thinking about the murders in town, the days had gotten away from her. By this time last year she would have already had her tree up for a week.

She put the coffee pot on, hitched leases to collars, and took the boys for a short walk. The crisp air coaxed the two dogs to finish their business in a hurry and the three returned to their cozy home. Nell lugged in the tree, the bins of ornaments, and other decorations.

Her thoughts went back to the real trees Drew used to insist they buy each year. The strong pine aroma was heavenly, but at times Drew had turned the air blue trying to straighten the tree. *The things one remembers*. After the tree was straightened out, Drew disappeared into his office until all the decorating was completed. Then he came out and made a huge fuss over how beautiful everything looked. How she missed her husband!

Nell did much more than throw some ornaments on the tree. She adorned the mantle and other areas of the house, too. The wooden nativity scene was displayed in the usual spot on the buffet surrounded by different size candles. It had been a present from Drew for their first Christmas together, so it brought another warm memory. The porch in front also gained some attention. When she was finally satisfied her home was festooned with enough appropriate Christmas decorations, it was almost evening. She had taken some time out at lunch to make tuna salad and eat a sandwich. Other than lunch time, her decorating had taken the whole day.

Nell was delighted with the results. Drew would have been impressed. Now she was tired and plopped on the couch for a few minutes with her little buddies by her sides. The tuna salad tasted so good supper would be another sandwich and a lettuce salad.

She moved up from the couch and lit the fir tree scented candle she had positioned on the coffee table. The aroma ensured her living room offered the wonderful ambiance of a real fir. With a flick of her wrist, a flame appeared in the gas fireplace. She sunk into a chair and closed her eyes for a few minutes. Nell had managed to keep her mind off murder for most of the day. She wondered if Elena had any more thoughts about the case. She pulled her phone from her pocket.

"Nell."

"Hi. Are you busy?"

"As a matter of fact, yes. I'm almost out the door to go to Daisie's Christmas program at the elementary school."

"Oh, how about lunch or supper tomorrow? I'd love to go somewhere for fish."

"I'm so sorry. Tomorrow Herb and I are going to the Resch Center to see the Trans-Siberian Orchestra concert."

"How wonderful! We'll talk some other day then. Have a great time! Give Julie and the kids my love."

"Thanks. We'll get together soon."

Nell put her phone back in her pocket and picked up the TV clicker. She scanned her saved movies from the DVR and chose a light romantic comedy with Cary Grant. An oldie, but goodie. Romance. She was happy for Elena, who deserved to have a man in her life. What troubled Nell was her need for Elena's detective abilities. Bouncing ideas off her friend helped her put everything in perspective. What was she going to do now? She had an idea simmering under the surface, just waiting to break through.

What about Pam Marshall? She had volunteered the last time Nell was at her house. However, she might be too closely involved since her husband was one of the victims. Or, did that make her an even better partner? She would be able to offer a deeper insight to Scott's habits and routines. There was the possibility she may suddenly remember something important without realizing its significance. She should review any pros and cons of working with Pam. She'd sleep on it before making the call.

Chapter 23

"Hello, Pam? This is Nell Bailey."

"Oh, hi."

"I hope I didn't get you out of bed."

"No. I hardly sleep anymore."

Nell had second thoughts about asking for her help. Pam sounded down, almost depressed. She'd still ask her to go to lunch, though. "I was wondering if you'd be interested in going for lunch today."

"Today? Well, I don't know." There was a short silence. "I suppose I could. I've hardly been out of the house since Scott died. Oh, wait. Are you planning on somewhere in town?"

"I thought so. Would you rather go out of town?" Nell rubbed her left eyebrow.

"No, I think that's probably a good idea. It's time for me to make an appearance in Bayshore."

"I'll pick you up. Is 11:30 okay?"

"Yes."

Nell hoped she hadn't made a mistake asking her to lunch. Pam sounded dismal and weak today. But there was no going back now.

Nell pulled in Pam's driveway and saw her exit her house by the kitchen door. She opened the passenger side door and greeted her.

"How's Miners' Fish House sound to you?" Nell asked.

"That's fine." Pam offered a tentative smile and snapped her seatbelt.

By the time the duo walked into the restaurant, Nell had Pam laughing like they were old friends. They walked back to the dining area and found a table. Lynn, the waitress, welcomed them with menus and went to fetch them each a glass of beer.

Pam turned serious and whispered, "I hope no one thinks it's unseemly I'm out, laughing, and drinking a beer."

"Good grief, woman! You do realize we're in the twenty-first century, don't you?" Nell shook her head. "Women don't have to wear black and mourn for a year any more. That was never healthy. We need to get back to normal as soon as we can. It's high time you're out."

"Thanks. That makes me feel better."

Lynn came back with their beers and they each ordered the deep fried perch special. Nell took a sip and urged Pam to feel free to share anything she'd like. It could be about Scott or anything else. Nell was still considering asking Pam if she'd help her with investigating Clayton's murder and maybe her husband's, too. But, she was interested in finding out more about Pam before extending the invitation.

"Scott grew up in Bayshore and wanted to move back here after he retired. He had been an attorney for thirty-eight years. His two grown sons both live out of state."

"*His* two sons. Aren't they yours, too?" The other information had been in his obituary, but it didn't state he had a wife before Pam.

"No. We'd only been married four years." Pam wiped her eyes. "Scott had finally found happiness after years of pain. Now he's gone and can't enjoy it."

"I'm so sorry." Nell patted her hand. "You don't need to say anything more."

"Oh, I want to say more." Pam pulled her chin up. "There has never been a more evil, vindictive shrew than his ex-wife. She made his life miserable."

"Did you know Scott's ex-wife well?"

"You better believe I did," Pam replied. "I was his personal secretary, or I should say administrative assistant."

Nell automatically drew back.

"From the look on your face, I can tell what you're thinking. It wasn't like that. I'd only worked for him a year." Pam waved her hands in front of her face and chest. "You can see I'm no young gold-digger. There wasn't any hanky-panky going on between us. Claudia, his first wife, was an over privileged, spoiled socialite, who ruined everything she touched, including the lives of Scott and their sons."

"How horrible!" Nell gasped. "How did you and Scott ever end up married?"

"Claudia wanted a divorce. From what Scott told me, he had tried to leave the marriage for years, but she wouldn't let him go. Then she found greener pastures in the form of a new partner in the firm. Jefferson Klein was the son of the founder and almost twenty years younger than Claudia."

Nell tilted her head.

"I hate to admit this, but she was gorgeous. She must own stock in Botox. Claudia and the young buck looked the same age."

"Did they get married?"

"That's the thing. She was sporting a ring on her finger she could hardly lift. It forced Scott's hand into retirement. He didn't want to work with the new partner, who would be married to his ex-wife. But as it turned out they never tied the knot."

"What happened?"

Into the dining room hustled Lynn, balancing a tray with their piping hot fish dinners. She set them down and the new friends began to eat.

"This is like a soap opera, Pam. I can't wait to finish eating to hear the rest.

You have to tell me while we chew." Nell dipped a piece of perch in the tartar sauce, took a bite, and savored the crunchy fish.

"I quit working for the firm a couple months later because I had become Jeff's assistant. I didn't feel the loyalty I had for Scott. Before I left, I noticed the frequency of Claudia's midday visits to Jeff's office." Pam shook her head. "The walls were paper-thin."

"Are you talking about afternoon delights?" Nell giggled.

"From what I could hear, they both were exceedingly delighted. Anyway, Scott and I had become such close friends during that year, we started meeting for coffee and then for dinner. It turned into love. The decision to marry was an easy one. We moved here where he wanted to relocate, and I thought we were going to live happily ever after. It wasn't to be." Pam turned her face away and rubbed the tears from her eyes.

"I know. It's so sad, but you gave him happiness for as long as you could."

Pam straightened up and dragged one of her fries through ketchup. "Yes, I did."

"You haven't told me yet. Why didn't Claudia and Jeff get married?"

"We thought they probably had, but about six weeks ago Scott's son, Joel, called him. Neither son usually discussed their mother, but this time was different. Joel grumbled about how his mother had contacted him and hinted around for money. He mentioned Claudia also called his brother, Mason, with the same request. Joel said she hadn't married."

"Oh."

"We never did learn the reason. My guess would be Jeff caught on to her wicked ways. He escaped before it was too late. Poor Scott put in all those years and when they divorced, Claudia received a huge settlement. She came from money, so I don't understand why she would need any from her sons."

"Too bad Scott hadn't asked for a pre-nup or made a better deal somehow. I mean, since he was a lawyer."

"That's what I thought, but he was so relieved Claudia wanted out, he willingly complied with her wishes." Pam leaned over the table and whispered, "After talking to his son, Scott was afraid she might come here next."

"Did Scott think Claudia would try to extort money from him if she came to Bayshore?"

"Yes, and he told me he wouldn't give her any." Pam shook her head. "I'm not so sure. She had a way of being annoying to the point he might have paid her off. Again."

"Would you have any idea if Claudia had ever had any run ins with the police?"

"I never heard of any, but I'd have no idea if she did during the last four years. I only know she's underhanded and has an uncontrollable temper. It's a bad combination."

As they lingered at the table, Nell decided to go for it. "You mentioned earlier you'd be willing to help out in any way you could. Are you serious about getting involved?"

"Getting involved?" Pam asked. "If you think Scott was murdered, it means I'm already involved. What do you want me to do?"

"For the most part, lend a listening ear. Then give me your opinion of my ideas." Nell took her last bite of fish. "I might want to talk on the phone or meet on short notice."

"Short notice? Like today?" Pam smiled, then lowered her head. "I want to help, but not every day is a good one for me. Sometimes I don't even want to get out of bed."

"I understand, and don't want you to do anything if you aren't up to it."

"On the other hand," Pam continued, "I thought today was going to be a non-functioning one until you called. I straightened myself out and here I am. Maybe I'm stronger than I think."

"That's the spirit. How about when I call you, you decide if you want to assist me depending on your state of mind? I'll be fine either way, and you don't need to feel bad if you're not up to it," Nell suggested.

"That would work for me."

Nell dropped Pam off at her house, and before she even pulled in her own garage, she considered Scott's ex-wife, Claudia, a suspect. Could she have shown up in Bayshore as Scott anticipated? Had she shown up, did her evil deed, and disappeared?

Nell saw the name on her ringing phone and couldn't stop her heart from skipping a beat. Would this call turn out any better than the last one?

"Hello." Nell tried her best to keep her voice even and low.

"Hi, honey," Sam murmured in the deep sexy tone that made her melt. "I miss you."

"From the noise in the background, it sounds like you have a crowd tonight. At least you're keeping busy."

"Friday night fish fry in Wisconsin. You know how it goes." Sam paused and then added, "You used to come up here and join me for a meal."

Nell let that statement hang without comment.

"I should have called you before. I'm sorry."

Nell couldn't stop herself from asking the obvious question. "Are you sorry for not calling me sooner or for something else?"

"I'd like to talk with you in person. This phone stuff isn't for me. I want to see you."

"What do you have in mind?" Nell asked.

"Can we get together tomorrow night? I know it's late notice, but I needed to make arrangements for someone to tend bar for me. My usual guy was unavailable and it took me a while to find someone else. I thought we could go out to a nice spot for a relaxing supper, away from the bar. We'll be able to talk."

"Your invitation sounds intriguing. I'd like to see you."

"Great. I'll pick you up. How about six?"

"Why don't we meet somewhere?" Nell suggested.

"Oh. Okay. Where would you like to go?"

"Let's meet at Riversfront in Peshtigo. Alright with you?"

"Sure, that's fine. I'm looking forward to seeing you." Sam's voice lowered. "I have some amends to make, sweetheart."

"See you at six, then."

Nell hit the button and set the phone down. *Amends to make.* A positive step forward. She picked up Newmie and danced around the room while George yipped at her feet.

Chapter 24

The water was running in the shower and Nell was about to step in when she heard the ringing of her phone. She turned the water off, wrapped a towel around herself, and went to her bedroom to answer it. The caller ID said it was Leo. She still had a little over two hours before she needed to meet Sam, so she had time if he was looking for some comforting words.

"Hello, Leo."

"Can you come over?" Leo rasped. "The police are here and they have the autopsy results. My Dottie was killed. Someone poisoned her."

"I'll be right there." Nell threw on her clothes and headed for her car.

An officer met her at Leo's door and blocked her way. "Sorry. This is an active investigation and you can't come in here."

"Let her in. She's here to see me," Leo called from the kitchen.

The officer turned. "Chief?"

Nell heard Chuck Vance's voice. "Yeah, she can enter."

She rushed to Leo's side and gave him a big hug. "What can I do to help?"

"I don't know. I've never had a wife killed before." He started to sob. "Who would do such a thing?"

Although she wanted to laugh at his phrasing of the words, she remained serious. "We'll figure it out," Nell assured. "Have you called Wayne and Tina?"

He nodded, "I have some other calls to make. Will you help me?"

"Of course. Have you called a lawyer yet?"

"I don't need a lawyer." Leo glared at Nell. "I haven't done anything wrong."

"I know, but you should have one present anyway. Don't say anything else to the police."

Nell made the calls and took care of some other business while they waited for Terrence Monroe, one of the prominent attorneys in town.

She wanted to get a chance to speak with the chief and have some of her questions answered, but Vance was giving her the stink eye. He walked over to her.

"Why did you insist on Leo calling Monroe?"

"He needs to have representation. He's so upset, who knows what he'd say?"

"I'm not looking at her husband for the murder. It's going to take a long time for the lawyer to get here. All this time wasted." He turned and walked away.

Within an hour, Terrence Monroe knocked on the door. He sat down with Leo to answer questions from the police. Nell was relieved the chief didn't make her leave.

"Do you have antifreeze in your garage, Leo?" Chief Vance asked.

"Yeah. I used it to do some basic auto maintenance on our car. Why?"

"Could you tell us where in your garage it's located? Ethylene glycol was found in your wife's system. It can be lethal and is found in antifreeze."

"Oh, my God!" Leo stood and headed to the garage door. They all followed him to a high shelf to the right of the car. "Here it is. We no longer have a dog, but when we used to, we always kept this container above his reach. It's still the place I keep it."

Nell knew the substance was sweet and if not kept out of the reach of pets, they could get into it and be poisoned.

An officer pulled down the antifreeze from the shelf. "This container is ancient."

"Yeah," Leo agreed. "I haven't used it in a long time."

"A bitter substance is added now so pets aren't attracted to it, but this old stuff probably is still sweet." The officer handed the container to the chief.

"Ethylene glycol itself is colorless so it could be added to another liquid without changing the color," Vance said. "It could easily be taken with water."

"Wouldn't Dottie have noticed either the sweet or bitter taste?" Nell couldn't keep quiet.

"I'm only allowing you here for moral support as a friend of Leo's," warned the chief. "Keep your thoughts to yourself."

"I can't imagine how Dottie could have gotten into the stuff." Leo shook his head.

"That's what we're trying to figure out." Vance looked around the kitchen. "You don't have a water purification system, do you?"

"You mean one of those contraptions where a man brings in water every week?"

"Either that, or something hooked on to your faucet?"

"No, we get our drinking water from the freezer door. It's so handy."

"You don't ever buy purified or distilled water bottles for any reason?"

"I can't think of any." Leo's eyes were wet, and he pulled out a handkerchief to wipe them.

"Is there another place where you keep water? Some place where only Dottie would drink it?"

Nell had a thought and left the room. She returned from the master bedroom with Dottie's CPAP machine and the nearly empty gallon container of distilled water.

"That's right. I forgot all about her machine," Leo said. "But she didn't drink that water. It comes up the hose and she inhaled it through the mask."

"Don't say one more word," Terrence Monroe cautioned.

"Come on, Terry." Vance walked over and took the machine and water from Nell. "Chances are this is only distilled water." He took the cap off and smelled.

"Remember the substance is odorless," Nell reminded. "You're going to have to take it to the lab, unless you want to taste it."

The chief glared at Nell and asked for a glass. "I want to exclude this distilled water right now, so we can move on to other liquids in the house."

"If you're going to do that, Chuck, put a little on your tongue. Don't take a big swallow." Monroe moved closer to the chief.

Vance poured a little in a paper cup, dipped his finger in, and put it in his mouth. "Could be my imagination, but I think it tastes sweet." He then grabbed a clean glass and took a big drink of water.

"No. I don't believe it." Leo stood up. "Dottie wouldn't drink green antifreeze."

"What I tasted wasn't colored. Not all antifreeze is green anymore," Chuck said. "It could have been watered down so it wasn't as noticeable."

"I don't like the direction this conversation is going," Leo complained.

"Leo, be quiet," Monroe warned and turned to Vance. "What now?"

"This machine and water are going to the lab. The old container of antifreeze is coming with me. I want Leo down at the station for further questioning and we'll take it from there."

Terrence Monroe was giving Leo a ride to the station so Nell was taking her own vehicle. As she opened the car door, she noticed Chief Vance was by her side. "That will be all for now."

"What do you mean?" Nell closed the door. "I need to be there for Leo."

"Leo has his lawyer to guide him. You've done enough for tonight." He walked to his car and left Nell standing alone, contemplating her next move.

She sat in her car and started the engine. The radio came on and she looked at the clock. It seemed to glare at her—7:57. With a sinking feeling, she remembered she should be in Peshtigo having "make-up food" with Sam. She dug in her purse for her phone. Three voicemail messages were waiting.

6:23 "Hi, Nell. I'm at Riversfront. I take it you're running late. I hope you arrive soon. I can't wait to see you."

6:48 "Please call or text me and let me know you're all right. I hope you haven't had car trouble. I called ahead and reserved the romantic table in the corner. If we don't claim it soon, they'll give it to someone else. I miss you."

7:17 "Did you change your mind about meeting me? I would have appreciated being told you didn't want to see me rather than being stood up."

He was hurt and angry. Why hadn't she heard her phone ring? She realized she had set her purse and coat in the spare bedroom, so she was away from the phone most of the night. She listened to the first two messages which carried concern. The last one was of a colder variety. Nell returned his call, but there was no answer.

She apologized, and said she was headed to Riversfront now and hoped he'd either still be there or would return.

Nell pulled in the parking lot of the restaurant, searching the cars for Sam's Crown Vic. She didn't see it, but it was a big area. She entered Riversfront and scanned the bar patrons for Sam. Spotting a single stool across the bar, she moved over to it and heaved her tired body up.

"What's your pleasure?" The smiling bartender stood before her. His youth and energy made her realize the extent of her exhaustion.

"A whiskey old fashioned, sweet with olives, please. And I have a question."

"I'll try to give you an answer as I mix your drink." His perfect white teeth and dark hair contrasted in the most appealing way. Nell knew if she was in her twenties, this guy would be of great interest to her.

"I'm looking for a man who was here earlier. I was supposed to meet him, but was delayed."

"Do you mean Sam?"

"Yes. How long ago did he leave?"

"About an hour ago." He set the drink in front of her. "Excuse me a minute."

Nell saw him say something to the female bartender, who turned to look at her with a smile. The smile faded, which made Nell remember her appearance. She hadn't taken a shower or put on any makeup. She'd thrown on old clothes and it had been hours since her hair had seen a comb. She looked at the people around her, who were dressed in holiday finery. She was in the midst of some company's Christmas party. She took a sip of her drink while wishing she could be swallowed up by the floor.

The handsome bartender walked toward her with a beautiful bouquet of flowers. "He brought these for you and left them here. Sam seems like a great guy."

"He is," she murmured as she leaned over to smell the blooms. "Was he upset when he left?"

"Sorry, but I'm staying neutral."

She pulled out her phone and sent Sam a text message apologizing again and saying she would be at the restaurant for another hour. She hoped he would return.

Every time the door opened, Nell held her breath, only to be disappointed. This was an evening where Sam was going to apologize to her, but now she was the one who needed to make amends. What a horrible turn of events!

Then she thought of Leo and his predicament. Nell knew he hadn't killed Dottie, but who else would have had access to her machine and the gallon of water? Did someone come in their house and poison the water the same way someone went into Clayton's house and put warfarin in his vitamin bottle? Had someone also gone into Scott and Pam's house and poisoned Scott?

Theories of the murders alternated with thoughts of her relationship with Sam. She'd put her phone on the bar so it was waiting to alert her of a call or text. It remained silent. After watching the door and making her drink last for an hour and fifteen minutes, Nell walked out, leaving the bouquet on the bar. She'd touched the soft delicate petals. *Maybe these flowers can work their magic for some other couple tonight.*

Chapter 24.5

I picked up another envelope. This was labeled Tuesday, January 21, 1991.

> *The body found stabbed Sunday in a suite at the elegant Coral Flamingo Resort in Sarasota, Florida, was identified as forty-two-year-old Raymond Bennett, III of New York City. He had been attending a conference with some employees to upgrade the technology in his third generation real estate empire. The resort was notified when Bennett was a no show for Monday morning's presentation.*

Ah. I remember this kill. The mark had been to an exclusive jewelry store and bought up the place for his new wife. Those gems were easy to fence. Time well spent stalking old Ray.

The article continued about family members, service organizations, all the good deeds this well-respected member of the community accomplished. Blah, blah, blah. What was this, an obituary? No time for that now. I'd much rather think back to the look of utter shock on his face when I turned the knife in his gut.

The warmth of this memory makes me nostalgic. I dig around in my file cabinet until I find the file labeled New York Real Estate. I open it and pull out the fake white rabbit's foot that's attached to a key ring chain. Really, Ray? How much luck did this rabbit's foot give you? I look at the spot of Ray's blood on the foot. If I was a worrier, I'd have burned that foot long ago. The way DNA tests have been used these past years, having it in my possession could be a disaster. But I'm not a worrier. What reason would anyone have to test this foot? More important though, I'm never going to be caught.

Chapter 25

The stress of the day hit Nell full on as she pulled the car out of the parking lot and headed for home. Even though she had brought up the possibility, Nell took Dottie's murder especially hard. She had not prepared herself adequately for her friend to have died this way. Now it was all too real, and Leo was at the police station being questioned. She started to itch from the unkempt feeling of not having time to shower and throwing on old clothes.

Nell tried to keep herself from thinking about Sam, but it didn't work. Had she blown her last chance for the two of them to get together? Surely he would understand after she explained she hadn't stood him up on purpose, but had been enthralled in the case. She had lost track of time. Or would mentioning helping Leo and the police give him an excuse to repeat his claim she was too involved? No. She had been helping a friend. Her hand automatically wiped the wetness away from her eyes, as she parked her car in the garage and hurried in the house.

She greeted the boys, let them outside, and checked her answering machine. Nell hoped Sam had left a message on her landline phone.

Nothing.

She looked over at the patio doors to see George and Newmie staring at her. She let them in, gave them treats, and then headed to the shower. She needed to wash away this disappointing night.

Nell realized when she awoke she hadn't eaten any supper the night before. There really was a first time for everything. She let the dogs out, put on a pot of coffee, and dropped two frozen waffles into the toaster. Adding syrup and blueberries would make a simple, but good breakfast. After she fed Newmie and George, the three of them went out for a walk. The early morning was cold, but bright. Nell hoped the fresh air would help her organize all the thoughts churning in her mind about the previous day.

Walking around the neighborhood helped her calm her swirling emotions. She felt strong now and able to face any obstacle in her way. By the time the three winter warriors returned home, Nell knew what to do. She hit Sam's cell number from her contact list and listened to the sound of repeated ringing.

"Sam. I've tried to call you several times, but have only been able to leave a message. I would like to talk to you. If you've decided to sever our relationship for good, you need to let me know."

She dressed for church and looked for Leo upon her arrival. Was he still at the station?

After a motivating sermon from Pastor Gene, she drove home and looked at her machine for the telltale blinking light. No messages. Oooookay.

Nell took the rest of the day for herself. She didn't think about the murders or about writing anything on her blog. She called her sister, Renae, and brother, Gary, to catch up. She also phoned a couple friends from out of state, Kris and Stacy, and enjoyed laughing at their antics. She texted Jud and said she was free all day, if he wanted to chat. She was delighted when he did. As she listened to his voice, she realized the older he got, the more he sounded like his father. Nell assured her son that she wasn't in any danger and that the police had a good handle on things. She ended the day watching old movies and trying to keep her mind off Sam.

Nell woke with renewed vigor to continue with her plan. She worried that Leo's questioning Saturday night upset him and called to offer to visit. There was no answer, so she left a message stating her concern.

She moved on to the next item on her agenda and made her next call.

"Bayshore Police Department, Judy speaking. How can I help you?"

"Good morning, Judy. This is Nell Bailey. Could I speak with the chief, please?"

"Hi, Mrs. Bailey. I'll see if he's available."

Nell didn't have to wait long.

"Yes, Nell?" Chuck Vance's voice was all business.

"Thanks for speaking with me, Chuck. I haven't been able to contact Leo. Please tell me he's not being held in jail. Also, what did you find out about the distilled water?"

"Hold on a minute." There was a pause and then a deep sigh. "I'll no doubt regret this, but could you come down to the station?"

Nell jumped out of her chair. "You know I'll help in any way I can."

"I didn't say 'help'. I don't want to talk over the phone."

"I'll be down right away." Nell ended the conversation before the chief could change his mind.

She changed into her gray jeans and a soft lilac sweater. She did a quick makeup job and ran a comb through her hair. She smiled at her slimmer reflection in the mirror while thinking how she could acquire as much info as possible about the case. After a smooch on the head to George and Newmie, she was out the door.

Judy beamed as she guided Nell down the hall of the police station. "Chief, Mrs. Bailey's here."

"Thanks," said the chief. He hadn't looked up from his work. "Have a seat."

Nell sat down and waited as the chief shuffled some papers. He finally stopped and stared across the desk at Nell. "You were right. Both Dunbar and Dumpling were murdered. It's difficult for me to admit a civilian had it figured out before I did. Good job, Nell. You kept after the truth when I completely blew you off. I wanted to tell you face to face how sorry I am for not listening to you." His words were solemn, but he had a small smile on his face.

"Thanks, Chief. I appreciate those words." Nell couldn't stop herself from making the comparison between Sam and Chuck. Even though Chuck was unhappy he was wrong, he had apologized, and in person. Sam's ability to do the same was questionable at best.

"I've swallowed my pride and am willing, make that anxious, to hear any of your other thoughts about this case." Chuck leaned back in his chair, waiting.

"You've caught me a bit off guard. I'm usually trying to sneak in a question here and there." The idea of being taken seriously made Nell's heart soar. Where to start?

"I'll fill you in on what we've got right now. Leo went home after we took his statement. The distilled water and CPAP machine have been sent to the lab. I requested a priority rush on it as we've had two murders. I'm sure we'll get the results soon as it won't take nearly as long as an autopsy. A couple officers and I compared a few drops of Leo's colored antifreeze with some of the distilled water we held back at the station last night. It tasted exactly the same to all of us, but the water was clear."

"So you're saying Leo isn't a suspect?"

"I'm saying the antifreeze in his garage wasn't the poison. Something else was the source of the ethylene glycol that Dottie swallowed."

"Poor Dottie. Why didn't she taste the sweetness?"

"For one thing, I suspect she inhaled the odorless substance rather than drank it, and for another, Leo said Dottie had consumed a few drinks before she went to bed. She put her mask on and fell asleep. I wonder if she passed out and wasn't able to notice anything."

"If it had been a natural death, I thought maybe Dottie hadn't used her mask that night and the stoppage of breathing was what killed her." Nell shook her head. "I would say this was a freak accident, except it was done on purpose."

"What I want to know now is what other thoughts do you have swirling around in that pulsating brain of yours?" Chuck asked, tapping his own head. "Your instincts seem to be better than mine."

"Music to my ears," Nell said, and smiled. "We need to look into Scott Marshall's supposed heart attack."

"Now that could just be a coincidence. People in town do die of natural causes, you know. I..."

Nell silenced him with a look.

"You're right. I was falling right back into form."

"Old habits die hard."

"You have the floor, Nell. Tell me why you think Marshall's death wasn't by natural causes."

Nell adjusted her pink glasses and took a breath. She proceeded to fill the chief in on the financial problems of Scott's ex-wife and her possible visit to town to tap him for money. She also mentioned the meetings Scott had with Clayton.

Chuck took notes on the information she gave him. "I'll run Scott's ex-wife through the system and see what we can find. Is there anything else? Are you sure you don't want to throw in Scott also ate your fudge?" He released a deep chuckle and Nell soon joined him.

"However, that's not as funny as you think. I was concerned someone had taken note of those who bought my fudge and were getting rid of them one by one. Tracking that list down would keep us busy. A lot of platters of goodies with my candy were sold."

"And it all would have led back to you. I'd hate to think of having to keep you in my jail." He gave Nell a wink. "I can't think of anything else right now. Thanks for your help. Can I call you again?"

"You bet." Nell stood up and headed for the door.

"Everyone raves so much about your fudge that I want to try it one of these days." Chuck's grin put a somewhat different spin on their meeting.

"I think that can be arranged." Nell left the building with her own smile lighting the way.

Nell searched her memory for everything she knew about Chuck Vance on the way home from the police station. She pegged him as being around her age. He had been Chief of Police for at least ten years and was previously one of the officers. She remembered his wife died after a long illness around the time he became chief. That was quite a few years before her husband, Drew, died. She couldn't remember if Chuck had children or anything else about him. She didn't know much, except he possessed the maturity to admit when he was wrong without being goaded into it. Sam could take a few lessons from him.

Sam. The ball was in his court. Maybe he'd call her, maybe he wouldn't. She reveled in the knowledge she would be fine either way.

The boys greeted her in the usual manner when she stepped in the door. She glanced at her landline. No messages. She pulled her cell out of her pocket and placed a call.

"Hello."

"Hi, Pam. This is Nell. How are you doing today?"

"You know how it is. I wake up in the morning thinking everything is good and then remember Scott is gone. When does that feeling end?"

"The timeline isn't the same for everyone because grief is different for each person. I know what you're going through. I wish I could help you. You sorta have to find peace in your own way. For me, it took several years."

"That isn't what I wanted to hear, Nell. I want to feel better *now*. I go to bed each night wishing it was all a dream and I'll wake up in the morning with Scott beside me."

"I understand, Pam, I was the same way. Things will get better. I promise."

"I hope so," Pam said. "Is there a reason you called? I jumped in with my issues right away and didn't let you speak."

"I called to see if you wanted to go out for lunch. If this is one of the days you're not up to it, I'll understand."

"You know what? I think going out might be just what I need. It will give me something to do instead of mope."

"Great. How about I pick you up at 11:30?"

"I'll be ready."

What a difference a week made! Pam walked out of her house looking much healthier than Nell had ever seen her before. She'd taken time with her hair and makeup, and it made a huge difference. She opened the car door and slid on to the seat.

"You look beautiful, Pam."

"Thanks, but I wouldn't go that far. After our talk this morning, I decided it was time to go back to my usual beauty routine. I'm going to start my exercise DVD again, too."

"Good for you. Keeping active will help you stay focused."

"Where are we going for lunch?"

"If it's all right with you, I'd like to go to The Shenandoah. It's a neighborhood bar and grill, except it isn't in my neighborhood," Nell explained. "Great pizza, chicken, and sandwiches, but I like to go on a Friday night for fish, too. And the owner, Cal, makes a mean mixed drink."

"Fine by me. It'll be nice to go somewhere unfamiliar."

As Nell turned into the parking lot, Pam said, "I've driven past this place when I've gotten my hair done at QT's Beauty Bar."

"Yeah, that's a few steps down the street. I hope you'll like The Shenandoah as much as I do. Be sure to notice the back bar. It's beautiful."

They entered the building to a big greeting from Cal, and made their way to the dining area. They found a table, ordered sodas, and perused the menu. Pam went with a small vegetarian pizza. Nell heard the loud rumbling of her stomach and answered its call. She ordered half a chicken and sides, so she could eat her fill and take the rest home.

"I looked at the back bar as we walked past. You're right. You don't see anything like it in newly built establishments." Pam's warm smile highlighted her pretty face.

"I love the character of older buildings. I always feel so at home here." Nell paused, then decided to share her information. "I know you've agreed to help me investigate Clayton Dunbar's death. Well, I have some news."

Pam nodded her head as Nell continued. "Dottie Dumpling's autopsy results are in and it turns out she was murdered, too."

"Two murders in this little town? Outrageous!" Pam turned to Nell with wide eyes. "What does this mean in relation to Scott's case? Do you think he could have been killed?"

"I don't know. He could easily have died naturally, but I think we need to look into it. Don't you?"

"Definitely. I can't imagine anyone wanting to kill Scott, but if someone did, I want to know the truth," Pam said. "On second thought, I do know someone who is mean enough to want him out of the way. Claudia, his ex-wife. She's capable of even the most heinous act. What do you want me to do?"

"Turns out Dottie was also poisoned, but by a different substance than Clayton. The police suspect ethylene glycol, or possibly antifreeze, was put into her CPAP machine. Inhaling it killed her."

Pam drew in her breath. "You're kidding."

Nell shook her head. "I wish I was."

"That's diabolical."

"Can you think of any way that someone could've come in to your house and put poison on something only Scott would use? He doesn't have a CPAP machine, does he?"

"No. I'll have to think about other possibilities. I wonder if there's any way Claudia could get in while the two of us were gone."

"Maybe." Nell paused, but then forged ahead. "By any chance, was there an autopsy performed on his remains?"

"No. I thought it was his heart and didn't see the need." Pam looked over at Nell. "What? What do you want to say?"

At Nell's hesitation, the light came on in Pam's eyes. Her face paled as she whispered, "No. Please tell me you don't want to exhume his body."

The server brought the food at that moment. It smelled and looked fantastic, but only one of them could eat.

Chapter 26

Pam practically jumped out of Nell's car before it stopped in front of her house. She grabbed the pizza box containing the entire pie Nell had coaxed her to bring home. "I know you're trying to solve a couple of murders, but I'm going to need some time to consider digging up Scott's body. If he was murdered, I know Claudia is the culprit. As much as I'd like to see her fry, it's difficult to take such a drastic step. Maybe she'll be found out before I have to make a decision. That could happen, couldn't it?"

"Possibly. I'm sorry I upset you, and perhaps unnecessarily. I haven't mentioned this idea to the chief, so I don't know if he'd even think to ask you to have it done. Again, I'm so sorry."

"I'll think about how someone could sneak in the house and poison Scott." Pam shook her head. "I'm not making any promises about an exhumation. I'd like to erase that thought from my mind."

"I'm sorry I mentioned it. I'll call you soon."

Nell watched her walk in the house looking like a different person than the one who had exited it less than two hours before. The washed-out look was back on her face and she moved as if in physical pain. Knowing Nell had caused it filled her with guilt. Sometimes she couldn't let things alone. She should have asked Chuck if he thought exhuming the body was a good idea. How would she feel if someone wanted to exhume Drew? Nell shivered and pulled away from the curb.

Nell opened the sliding glass door to let the boys out and then put her leftovers in the fridge. Even though Shenandoah's chicken was deliciously crispy and hot as always, she had lost some of her appetite, too, when she realized how much she upset Pam. Perhaps she should concentrate on who killed Clayton and Dottie, and drop the idea of Scott Marshall as a third victim.

Before she set the thought completely aside, there was one lead she hadn't looked into yet. Nell found her old phonebook with the yellow pages. She began calling restaurants in town to see if Clayton and Scott had their morning coffee together at any of them. Nell finally hit pay dirt when she called Maude's, a small diner on the outskirts of town. She arranged to go out there and speak with Maude in person.

The restaurant had found its niche in making a good breakfast and lunch, so it was no longer open for an evening meal. They closed at three and Nell made it just in time.

Nell noticed Maude watching her from behind the counter as she came in the diner. The portly woman came forward and introduced herself.

"I'm Maude. Come over here and we'll sit at this table. I need to take a load off my feet."

"Thank you for agreeing to speak with me." Nell sat down at the table. Even though she had been here for many meals, she had never spoken to the owner, who made all the desserts and was the head cook. Today she saw Maude close up for the first time. From the lines on her face and the gray hair under the net, Nell realized the woman was older than she had thought.

"Sure, although I don't think I have any more to tell you than what I said on the phone."

"You mentioned Clayton and Scott came down here regularly. How often would they come in? Once a month or so?"

"I'd say it was more like once a week."

"And how long had they been coming here?"

"Let's see." Maude rubbed her chin. "About six or seven months, maybe longer."

"Could you ever hear what they were talking about?"

"I don't wait on tables. My talent lies in making the food. You know, funny thing, they always sat at the same table." She pointed to a large table in the corner.

"That's a big table for the two of them. I suppose they could've spread out paperwork on the empty area."

"Yeah. They brought their briefcases with them. And a laptop computer, but the woman was always the one using that."

"*The woman?* There was a woman with them?"

"I may work in the kitchen, but I can see out in the dining room. It's the way this place was designed."

"Sure, I understand. Do you know who she was?"

"I do not. I could never get a good look at her. They always sat in the same places and her back was to me. Let me get Phyllis. That table is in her section, so she would have waited on them. I'll let the two of you talk."

"Thanks, Maude. I appreciate your help."

A couple minutes later a woman with coal-black hair in a beehive and bright red lipstick, wearing jeans, a light sweater, and an apron, took a seat across from Nell. "How can I help you?"

"Maude told me the table in the corner over there is in your section. Could you tell me if you know who the woman was who used to come here with Clayton Dunbar and Scott Marshall?" Nell held her breath.

"Dottie Dumpling."

Nell exhaled. "Are you sure it was Dottie?"

"Positive. I've lived down the street from Leo and Dottie for years. Just from Leo now, I guess. The poor guy."

"Do you have any idea what they'd talk about when they came?"

"Not a clue. It's busy here in the mornings, so I'd set a pot of coffee on their table and they could help themselves."

"Was there ever anyone other than the three of them meeting here?"

"Not that I can recall."

"Thanks, Phyllis. You've been a big help."

What in the world was going on here?

Clayton Dunbar—murdered, Dottie Dumpling—murdered, Scott Marshall—dead. The three people who had been meeting for coffee for six months or more were deceased. And all within a matter of a couple weeks of each other. Coincidence? Nell didn't think so.

She parked her car outside the police station and hoped to have the opportunity to speak with Chuck. Judy's eyes twinkled as she asked, "Here to see the chief, Mrs. Bailey?"

"Yes, I hope he's not too busy."

Judy glanced down at the phone on her desk. "Looks like he's talking to someone, but I'll let him know you're here." She wrote something on a piece of paper and walked toward his office.

"Please have a seat. I'm sure he won't be long," Judy assured as she came back to her desk. "How's Jud doing?"

"Ah, Judy. Now it comes to me. You're Judy Anton." Nell shook her head and laughed. "I've been trying to place you. I thought maybe you were in a class of mine, but I didn't think so. You were a good friend of Jud's in high school."

"That's right. My family moved to Bayshore when I was in eighth grade, so you were never my teacher. I've been to your house many times, though."

"Of course." Nell grinned. "You were part of the 'movie night' group when you kids rented movies and ordered pizza. I haven't thought of that in years."

"I hadn't either until you came to the station."

"Well, Jud is fine. He's living in Alaska now."

"I'd heard that. I guess he doesn't get home much."

"No, not at all. I miss him," Nell sighed. "What about you? Married? Kids?"

"Yes to both questions. Jim and I have a two-year-old daughter, Kenley."

"Oh, how wonderful. You know, I always thought you and my son would get together. Judy and Jud."

"Believe me, I did, too. I drew more than one heart around those names," Judy chuckled.

"You wanted to see me?" Chuck towered in the doorway.

Nell told Judy she'd let Jud know they talked, gave her a wink, and walked with the chief into his office.

"Damn it, Nell." Chuck rubbed his hand down over his face. "I know I asked for your input, but that's all I wanted. Your *input*. Why would you approach Marshall's wife about exhumation before you talked about it with me? We aren't even close to making that decision. I want to concentrate on finding the murderer of Dunbar and Dumpling."

"So do I, Chuck. I'm sorry I spoke out of line, but I've become friends with Pam Marshall. I know she'd want to find out if her husband was killed."

"It's one thing to want to know, and another thing entirely to consent to have his body dug up from the grave. Don't you recognize the difference? Chances are now, she'll be uncooperative if I need to speak to her about other issues."

"No," Nell said. "I told you Pam said she'd think about how someone could get into her house. She wants to help."

"As you explained it, I think she wanted to get out of your car and away from you. She probably would have told you anything."

Nell huffed. That hurt. "If it's any consolation, it was hard for me to come over and tell you what I did."

"Why would that be any 'consolation'? It should have been hard for you. You messed up."

"I do have another part to tell you."

"Heaven help me." He threw his hands up in the air. "What else did you do?"

"I learned Clayton and Scott met once a week for coffee at Maude's. I went down there to talk to Maude and found out they've been meeting for several months. Also someone else met with them. Guess the identity of the woman."

"Woman? Was it Dottie Dumpling? Are you kidding me?"

"Yes, yes, and no. I thought you'd appreciate that nugget."

"That's a real lead. Right when I think I'll put an end to your shenanigans, you come up with something I can actually use."

"I hope it makes up for my other blunder."

"I'm pleased with this information, but I want you to think twice before you ask any more questions. Ideally, you'd give me a call prior to going out and interviewing someone, but I suppose I'm asking for the impossible."

"I do a lot of my sleuthing on the spur of the moment. Taking time out for a call might interrupt the flow of ideas."

"That's okay for the most part, but if there is anything sensitive, like an exhumation," Chuck looked over his glasses and gave her the stink eye, "you need to run it past me first." He stood up and Nell followed suit.

"Thanks. I'll be more careful," Nell assured.

"You better be."

She left the station considering the last expression on Chuck's face. Was there a hint of a smile there, or was it her own wishful thinking?

Nell took the boys for a long walk when she returned. It was good for all of them and helped her gather her thoughts about the murders. She strained to think of any reason Dottie, Clayton, and Scott would meet once a week for half a year. Especially with briefcases full of paperwork and a laptop computer in use. It couldn't be anything they wanted to keep secret because they were in public. Maybe they were on a committee for the city, although none of them were city council members. Did they all attend the same church and were working toward a mission? Nell knew they weren't, but perhaps they were representing three different churches for some sort of community church service. She could find out easily enough. Pam didn't know what the meetings were about and didn't realize Dottie attended. Was Leo aware of this coffee klatch? She'd try to call him again when she returned home.

Dottie and Scott both grew up in Bayshore and were the same age. According to their obituaries, they graduated the same year. Could they have been high school sweethearts and taken up an affair? Perhaps either Pam or Leo found out and killed them. No, that sounded ridiculous even to Nell. Why would Clayton Dunbar be included if the object of the meeting was steamy sex? And they wouldn't have met at Maude's little diner. No, this has to do with the paperwork they were going over and the information on Dottie's computer.

George and Newmie pulled on their leashes to get back in the house. Nell realized she should have put on their sweaters. It was cold outside.

She treated them and filled their bowls. The food would warm them up.

She glanced over at the answering machine, expecting to see nothing. The red light was blinking. Had Sam finally decided to respond?

"Nell, this is Leo. Chief Vance said it was all right for me to visit Tina, so I guess he doesn't think I'll try to leave the country. Anyway, I drove over there yesterday. She encouraged me to use the computer for email so she can send me pictures of the kids. I arrived home a few minutes ago, walked in the house, unpacked all the food Tina sent with me, and went over to the desk to check the computer for the pictures. It's gone. Someone entered my house and stole Dottie's computer!"

Chapter 27

L eo ushered Nell in the house and over to the oak desk in the large kitchen. She could tell that this was the computer's home by the light layer of dust outlining its spot. "It took me over twenty minutes to get over here. I'm surprised the police haven't arrived yet."

Leo turned his back and walked a few steps away from the desk.

"Leo? You did call them, didn't you?" Nell asked.

"Why do they have to be notified? I'd probably need to go down to the station to make a statement. I'll buy a new computer so Tina can send her pictures. Dottie complained that this model was obsolete anyway."

"Someone came into your home and stole your property. It's a crime and it needs to be reported. Maybe other items are missing. Have you taken a look around your house?"

Leo nodded. "Dottie's diamond earrings and wedding ring are in the jewelry box with lots of other gems." He choked up and whispered, "I should pack them up and give them to Tina."

Nell gave him a hug. "I know this is hard. You'll get through it." She backed off and said, "What about other electronics? Do you have a spot where you hide cash? Any expensive tools taken out of your garage? Leo, you need to call the police."

"I guess you're right." He inhaled a deep breath before he made the call.

Nell sat down at the table. She wanted to do an inspection, but knew she shouldn't contaminate the scene.

"They're on their way."

Within ten minutes, Leo opened the door to Chief Vance and Officer Wunderlin. The officer spied Nell and she thought she heard him mutter, "Speak of the devil."

While Wunderlin was taking Leo's statement, Nell pulled Chuck aside. "I was planning on asking Leo if he knew about Dottie's meetings with Clayton and Scott. Then I was going to ask him if he'd be willing to let me take his computer to the police department to find what our victims were working on together. But Leo called me before I had a chance to call him."

"When did you come up with this plan?" Chuck asked. "Less than two hours ago you were at the police station agreeing to contact me before you questioned someone about a sensitive matter."

"I thought of it while walking my dogs *after* I spoke to you," Nell replied. "Besides, I don't think it's a sensitive issue."

"Oh, well then by all means." He threw his hands in the air. "Which officer gave you the go ahead for bringing the computer down to the station? I know I didn't." Chuck's eyes had reverted back to the beady little pea stage.

"It was a good idea, though. Think of the information you could have gleaned."

The chief walked back to Leo and sat down with him at the table while the deputy started a search of the house. "Would you have a backup to save files on the computer, Leo? Something like a flashdrive?"

"I didn't use a flashdrive to save any work. I don't think Dottie did, either. Feel free to check her desk."

"How about the cloud?"

"I have a vague idea about the cloud, but our computer was old." Leo creased his brows. "Why do you want to know what was on our home computer?"

"Chief?" Nell interrupted. "Leo is a friend of mine."

"Fine. If you want to explain the situation, go ahead."

"Thanks." She sat down and took Leo's hand. "Do you know anything about Dottie meeting for coffee with Clayton Dunbar and Scott Marshall?"

Leo's gaze went back and forth between Nell and Chief Vance. "That's the reason you two are so solemn? Heck, yes, I knew."

Nell was on the edge of her seat and saw the expectation in the chief's eyes.

"Clayton and Scott were working on some project, and Dottie was hired to take notes. They met once a week and Clayton paid her well."

"How did your wife get that job?" Chuck asked.

"She was experienced as a bookkeeper. She worked at an accounting office before we had kids. Then she stayed home while they were young. Once Tina and Wayne were in high school, she took a job at a law office in Green Bay. She knew her stuff," Leo beamed. "She retired, but Clayton asked her about working for him a couple hours a week. Dottie said it was the easiest money she ever made."

"Do you have any information about Clayton and Scott's project?"

"No, but I figured it had to have something to do with money. Both of them have their fingers in a lot of pies in town."

Officer Wunderlin came back to the kitchen. "I couldn't find a forced entry, but a garage window is unlocked. Someone could have entered there. The items Mr. Dumpling mentioned all seem to be in their assigned spots."

Chief Vance stood and shook Leo's hand. "Please contact us if you think of anything else."

"I will. What do you think the chances are of me getting my computer back?"

"All I can tell you is we'll do our best. When we find the murderer, and we will, I'm sure we'll find your computer, too."

The two law officers left the house without looking at Nell. She glanced at Leo and found him staring at her wide-eyed. "What did he mean about the killer having my computer? I thought this was a robbery."

Nell explained what she had learned so far in her investigation and her theory.

"Please tell me you don't think Dottie working those extra two hours a week got her killed," Leo pleaded. "We didn't even need the money. She used it when she went on those shopping channels on TV."

Nell grabbed a tissue from the box and handed it to Leo. "I'm sorry, but that's exactly what I think. Those meetings caused all of their deaths."

"Why would someone kill them? They were all good people."

"I don't know why at this point. The police and I are trying to figure it out. Someone didn't want them to accomplish their goal. Then, the killer came in here and stole the computer so no one would know what they were trying to do."

"I can hardly believe it."

"You should believe it, and count yourself lucky you weren't here when the murderer came for the computer. Whoever is behind this means business. Three innocent victims' lives have already been taken. Is it a giant leap to think the killer would strike again in order to keep the reason a secret?"

Chapter 28

Snow had fallen overnight and covered the landscape with a sparkling film of crystal, making it more difficult for George, Newman, and Nell to trudge through the neighborhood on their daily walk. Nell couldn't concentrate on much more than taking care to remain upright. She shortened their usual outing and steered the boys back to the safety of their house.

After having their breakfast, George and Newmie plopped on the living room floor and fell asleep. Nell came in with her coffee and let herself sink deep into the recliner. She needed to talk to someone about the clues in the case. Nell thought it best not to call Pam. Chuck may have been right in thinking Pam wanted to get away from her. Instead, she hit Elena's number on her phone.

"Nell! I'm so glad to see your name on my caller ID."

"Good to hear your voice. Do you have a minute?"

"Sure. What's up? Anything new with the case?"

"A few things, but tell me first how everything's going with you and Herb."

"Great! We're having a lot of laughs. He's so comfortable to be around." Nell could picture the smile on Elena's face.

"I'm excited for you," Nell said and meant it. "It's nice to get a man's opinion on things sometimes."

"Yes, it is. Now tell me about the murder."

"It's murders. The results came in from Dottie's autopsy and she was poisoned, too."

"Oh, my gosh. You knew it, Nell. What's Chief Vance have to say about you being right?"

"I've discovered he's a standup guy. He wants my opinion on the case. Chuck actually said he's anxious for my views. He admitted he was wrong without me having to point out to him that he should apologize, as I had to do with Sam."

"You and Sam met and he apologized?"

"Not exactly. He was going to make amends, but I stood him up."

"I can tell I'm woefully behind on 'The Life and Times of Nell Bailey,'" Elena laughed.

"If you're drinking coffee, pour yourself another cup and I'll fill you in on every detail."

The two old friends settled in for a long chat. Over an hour later, Elena dispensed a couple pieces of advice. "I would be very careful if I were you.

You pointed out to Leo he was lucky not to have been in the house when it was robbed as the murderer wouldn't be too concerned with killing one more. Have you thought about how it concerns you? The secret must not get out you're trying to find the murderer. Consider the danger of trying to stop someone who doesn't care how many people are killed. I know that won't stop you, but please be extra careful. Also, you mentioned you'd like to go back to the police station and see what else the chief knows and hasn't told you. I don't know if you should. That might look like you're on a fishing expedition."

"You're right. I'd be fishing for information that he might have forgotten to tell me," Nell agreed. "I guess I should have something concrete to ask."

"I'm sure you could come up with a lot of questions. Be careful how you ask them, too. Even though you said he was very gracious about admitting his error, you might not want to push it. If Chief Vance is like most people in authority, he could be unwilling to have his decisions analyzed and discussed."

"Good point. You know, Watson, I really miss working with you. Your insight always kept me focused."

"Am I being fired, Sherlock?"

"No. You're busy with Herb, and we don't get together as much. I've even asked Pam Marshall to help with this case."

"Did she say she would?"

"Yes, but now she's upset with me about the exhumation."

"Oh, right."

"My request for her help may have been premature. I don't know if she's dependable. Besides, Pam would never compare to you."

"Thanks, Nell. You know if you're ever in a pickle, I'd back you up come hell or high water."

She rose from her chair and put the phone on its charger. The boys turned their heads to look at her, but made no move to follow. Nell rubbed her ear. After sitting so long and talking on the phone, it felt good to stretch. She made a loop around the house while thinking of questions to ask Chuck. She was walking a thin line. She wanted to have access to all the information that he did, so she could do her utmost to help. Yet by going to the station or calling him too often, she risked being looked at as a pest. Chuck wanted to know what she was going to do before she did it. She could try it his way. Nell retrieved her phone and made the call.

Judy transferred her call to the chief right away.

"Yes, Nell."

"Good morning, Chuck." She took a big breath and exhaled. "In keeping with our new plan, I'm calling to let you know who I'm going to talk to today."

"Okay. Good."

"I thought I'd go back to the beginning and interview the guests at Clayton's open house. I want to know if anyone saw someone going in or out of his private bathroom."

"Hold on there a minute. Someone from the department has interviewed each of them twice. None of them saw anything. A third time would be overkill."

"Okay. What about Brenda from Brenda's Good Taste Catering? Did you talk to her?"

"We did. Twice." The chief's voice rose. "We interviewed everyone who was in the house the night of the party. Twice."

"I just thought..."

"We are all accredited police officers, Nell. We know how to do our job. I've appreciated information you've given me in the past, but there's no reason to harass people who have cooperated and given us everything they knew. That's not the way to find the psycho who has murdered two, possibly three, citizens of Bayshore."

"I'm looking for a way to help."

"I know you are," Chief Vance's voice softened. "Maybe you should take a break for a while. Becoming too involved could put your safety at risk. I couldn't bear to have anything happen to you."

Before Nell could answer, she heard children's voices in the background. Chuck said, "Excuse me. The kindergarten class has arrived for a tour. I have to go."

Thank goodness she was saved by a group of five-year-olds. Nell had no idea how she would have responded to Chuck's last statement.

Nell stared at her iPhone. Was she imagining the tenderness of Chuck's voice as he spoke of her safety? When did that happen? Nell acknowledged her own thoughts of him had changed, but didn't realize it was mutual. Or was it? Maybe his concern for her was only of a police chief for a citizen of his city?

She kept those thoughts in the back of her mind as she plotted her path for the rest of the day. It was too soon to contact Pam Marshall, but she hadn't talked to Hazel for a while. Nell hoped she was doing well. She called and arranged to go over for a visit.

After a shower, Nell chose her good brown slacks. She drew in her breath as usual when she started to tug the pants up her legs. She was surprised at how easily they pulled up and buttoned at her waist. She walked to her full-length mirror. The difference in her appearance was evident. Why hadn't she realized it sooner? No matter, she was delighted and knew she'd continue going to the fitness center. She planned to look for her 'thin' clothes in the guest room closet soon.

Nell threw on a soft beige sweater and added a brown scarf to the mix. Gold hoop earrings and a couple gold rings completed her look. One glance out the window reminded her that she needed her short, black boots.

She was happy the visit was friendship only. She had no ulterior motive this time. Nell could see Hazel looking out the window as she drove her car in front of the house. The wooden door was open before Nell could reach it.

"I've been waiting for you to call me with news of capturing Mr. Dunbar's killer." Hazel stepped aside to allow Nell in the room. "Why haven't you contacted me?"

"Good morning to you, too, Hazel," Nell said removing her coat. "I haven't called because we don't know who the murderer is yet."

"Go ahead and take a seat." Hazel took the coat, draped it over a chair, and sank down in the soft chair. "Why is it taking so long?"

"It hasn't been quite three weeks yet."

"I know. Why's it taking so long?" she repeated.

After explaining to Hazel about the time frame for processing clues and the reality of lab backups, she wasn't any happier. "It looks like Yolanda will have to bury her father without knowing the identity of the killer. If the culprit was known and behind bars, the funeral would be less difficult for her."

"Most murders take a lot longer than three weeks to solve. Besides, we have some time yet before Clayton's funeral."

"Yeah." Hazel looked at the clock. "A whole two hours. You better get busy."

Nell's heart sunk. "What do you mean, two hours?"

"I guess you didn't get a call. I'm sorry I mentioned it."

"Are you telling me it's a private funeral and I wasn't invited?"

"I don't know," Hazel admitted. "Yolanda called me a couple days ago to make sure I knew and offered to provide a ride if I needed one."

"I'm sorry, but I'm going to have to cut our visit short. I need to make a call and find out if it's appropriate for me to attend the service."

"That's all right. My daughter will be here soon to take me to the church."

On the way back to her house, Nell remembered she hadn't read the paper yesterday or today to check for a funeral notice. She also hadn't been on Facebook in days. It would save making a call to Yolanda if she could find the information elsewhere.

She looked in yesterday's paper to no avail, but did find a short notice in the morning edition. It didn't say *private* so Nell prepared to head over to the church and pay her respects. Why was it so hush-hush? Only publishing the notice in today's paper would leave many people unaware until it was too late. She gave Judy a call to make sure the police department knew about the funeral.

The parking lot of St. Anthony's Church was almost full, with more cars vying for the remaining spots across the street. Nell wedged her Sable in a parking place and headed toward the entrance of the church. She wished she hadn't changed from her practical low boots to a fancier pair with heels. Her right foot was already throbbing.

Nell chose not to go up front. It was a closed casket, so no final viewing of Clayton was allowed. Many mourners were speaking with Yolanda by the remains, but Nell would offer her condolences later. Time was short, so she found a seat and surveyed the mourners. Everyone else must have heard about the service early enough. There was a capacity crowd with more people still coming in and taking the steps to the balcony.

The service was lovely as Father James reviewed Clay's love and tireless work for the Lord, his devotion to his family, and his efforts toward his hometown of Bayshore. Most heads nodded at the words, "a life well lived."

At the funeral luncheon, Nell found a single seat available next to Mayor Corbin. She claimed it and made small talk with the longtime city official. Trying not to appear too obvious, Nell attempted to turn the conversation from the national walleye fishing tournament coming to Bayshore in the summer, to Clayton Dunbar's contributions to Bayshore.

"Clay was always willing to do what he could for the city. No one could organize a benefit the way he did. Everything would run smoothly and a lot of money would be made," Mayor Corbin said. "I was on the city council for years before becoming mayor and Clayton Dunbar was an active participant in local government. Even though he never held public office, he put a lot of time and effort in to making our city better."

"He was such a good man," Nell agreed. "I suppose his work for the city ended these last few years as he got older."

"Not a chance. Clay was in great shape." The mayor rubbed his chin. "Actually, he'd been working on a project for the city for...maybe...eight months now."

Nell's heart skipped a beat. "Oh, Mayor. What was the project?"

"That's the thing, Nell. He didn't tell me. He said it was something exciting for Bayshore. He had a couple people working with him, too."

"Two others? Who were they? Do you know?"

"No. Clay was very tight-lipped about the whole thing."

Nell's shoulders drooped, but she tried again. "Did you ever see him with Scott Marshall or Dottie Dumpling? Or the three of them together?"

"I don't think so."

"Hmm. Weren't you curious about what he was working on, Mayor?"

"I was interested, but I didn't bug him about it. He hadn't asked for any city money to achieve his ends and he was so optimistic. I knew anything he came up with would have the best interests of the city at heart. If I had to guess, I'd say it had something to do with giving more money to one of our worthwhile programs. He truly cared about Bayshore."

Out of the corner of her eye, Nell caught Chuck coming to the next table with a heaping plate of food. From what she could see, one whole side of his plate housed desserts. *He does have a sweet tooth.* The chief looked to be in his Sunday best and not in his uniform. Nell waved him over to a recently vacated spot across from them.

"Come over and sit by us, Chuck. I was speaking with the mayor about Clayton. I think you should hear what he has to say." Nell looked at Corbin with a smile and gave him the floor.

She listened as the mayor shared his information about the project. When the chief pulled out a notebook and wrote down notes, Nell excused herself to say a few words to Clayton's daughter.

Yolanda Dunbar Nyland was a vision in black. Draped from head to toe in the dark shade, she looked like a relic from another century. Her ebony veil went over her face and past her neck, and her charcoal-colored dress touched the floor. Nell tried not to let her thoughts be too critical, as the poor soul's father had been killed. But she couldn't help thinking Yolanda's theatrical flair was alive and well.

"Yolanda, I'm so sorry about your father." Nell leaned in with a warm hug.

"Thank you. I thought I would have been better prepared for his death because of his age, but his murder threw me for a loop."

"It's understandable. I thought so much of your dad. I hope you know that. He helped me get my career on the right track as a young teacher."

"He thought the world of you, too. Sometimes by the way he talked, I thought he would have liked to trade me in and adopt you for his daughter."

"I know that isn't true." Nell laughed it off, but had the uncomfortable feeling it might be the way Yolanda saw Nell's relationship with her father. *Could the daughter have taken misplaced revenge against her father? Only if it was a standalone murder. Yolanda wasn't even in Bayshore at the time of the other two deaths. A partner, perhaps? If there was a jealousy/revenge scenario it could put Nell in the hot seat.*

There was a man behind Nell waiting to talk to Yolanda so she wished her the best and moved out of the way. Her thoughts about Yolanda were out of line. She noticed Chuck and the mayor were still chatting, and wondered what she had missed. She chose not to go back over to them and hoped Chuck would fill her in later.

Nell walked out of the church hall and toward her car. She hadn't gotten far when she heard a voice behind her.

"Nell, wait up." Chuck's long legs soon caught up with her. "Thanks for directing me to Mayor Corbin."

"Sure. Did he mention anything else while I was talking to Yolanda?" She held her breath and let it out.

"Not really. I jotted down his info and then we talked about Friday night's high school basketball game against Oconto Falls."

"Oh," Nell sighed. "I'm not expecting this, but have you been able to locate Leo's computer?"

"I guess I'm meeting your expectations then." Chuck exhibited a half smile. "We haven't found anything yet, so I'm glad I'm not disappointing you."

"I imagine it'll be difficult to locate."

"More than likely someone has it hidden away. We'll need to be darn sure where it's located before we can get a search warrant. And that, dear Nell, is easier said than done."

Did he just say "dear Nell"?

"What are you going to do?" She stopped and looked up at him.

"Old-fashioned, solid police work. It's what solves crimes." Chuck frowned and tilted his head. "I think a better question is, what are *you* going to do? I'm starting to recognize that look on your face."

"I have some ideas. You didn't happen to notice Pam Marshall here today, did you? She and Scott knew Clayton and celebrated with him at his open house."

"I didn't see her, but I arrived late."

"Her husband was helping him on his project for months. I wonder why she didn't attend."

"Some people have a harder time dealing with loss than others. Her own husband recently died. She may not have been up to it."

"Of course, you're right. Leo isn't here, either. I'm sure it was too much for him." She leaned on one foot to take the pressure off her sore one. "I think I'll go over to Leo's to see how he's doing. I also want to go over to Pam's in a day or two, when I think she's ready to meet with me. I'd like to see if we can locate Scott's briefcase. He could have all kinds of paperwork in there."

"This time I really am disappointing you. I've already been to see her myself and looked through his briefcase."

"What was in there?"

"Nothing that pertained to Bayshore or working with Clayton. It looked like documents relating to property they own and his will, among other papers."

"Wouldn't you know? I think I will take that ride over to Leo's now, though." Nell started to move away.

"Nell..." Chuck leaned toward her and reached for her hand.

"Oh, Chief. You're just the person I wanted to see." Neither Nell nor Chuck had noticed Louisa Rolf creeping up behind them. "I don't want to interrupt your little tete-a-tete, but I need to ask you about the new four-way stop on School Street."

Chuck looked at Nell with helpless eyes while she made a beeline to her car.

"Louisa strikes again," Nell laughed as she slid behind the wheel. "Poor Chuck. She'll have his ear for who knows how long." She pulled out of the church parking lot and headed to Leo's house.

Leo opened his arms in welcome. "Come on in and visit for a bit." He directed her to an easy chair in the living room.

"Thanks."

"You look like you may have attended Clayton Dunbar's funeral." At her nod, Leo continued. "I couldn't bring myself to go. He was a good man and all, but I didn't think I could handle another funeral. Not so soon." Leo brought a handkerchief out of his pocket and wiped his eyes.

"That's understandable."

"In particular, I didn't want to go to *his* funeral. You mentioned yesterday Dottie's death could be related to the work she was doing for him. I'm very bitter. If it wasn't for Clayton, Dottie might still be alive." Leo shook his head. "I can see you're all ready to argue against me, but I can't help how I feel."

"I won't try to change your thoughts and feelings. I don't want you to put roadblocks for healing in your path, though."

"I'll keep it in mind."

The two went on to discuss their children, the undefeated high school basketball team, and other news related to Bayshore. As Nell was getting ready to leave, Leo surprised her by bringing up the mysterious project. "You know, Nell, I've been racking my brain trying to remember if Dot every mentioned it. She might have, but I have to admit I'm not the world's best listener."

"Please don't beat yourself up over it. No one seems to know. I spoke with the mayor today at the funeral, but he only knew Clayton was working with two other people. He had no idea of the nature of the project. He figured it may have had something to do with offering money to one of the 'town's worthy causes'."

"Hmm, interesting. Why would it have taken months and months to arrange for a transfer of money?"

"Good point. I don't know, either."

"Anyway, thanks for stopping over. It's always good to see you."

"Take care."

Nell's tan Mercury Sable found its way over to Pam Marshall's house. Nell hadn't planned on speaking with Pam for a day or two yet, but why wait? She stood outside the house and rang the doorbell.

The door opened a crack and then wider. "I wasn't expecting you here."

"I know. I want to apologize for the subject matter of my last visit. Could I come in, please?"

Pam stepped aside and allowed Nell to enter. They moved toward the living room. "I'm listening."

"I'm so sorry I ever mentioned exhumation to you yesterday. I had no business talking about it and I realize how upsetting it was for you."

To Nell's dismay, Pam burst into tears. "I haven't been able to get the thought out of my mind. I want to help, but..." She lifted a handkerchief from the arm of her chair.

"No. Please banish the thought from your mind. Chief Vance let me know in short order an exhumation was not being considered. Talking to you about it was all my idea and not the police department's at all."

"You're telling me I don't need to make a decision?" Pam sniffled.

"I am. And I'll repeat how very sorry I am to have caused you so much pain."

"Please sit down, Nell. I can't tell you how relieved I am I don't have to decide either way." Pam sat and wiped her nose. "Scott can rest in peace."

"I understand, and I appreciate you welcoming me in your home." Nell looked over at the tree in the corner. It looked too dry. Watering the tree was probably one of the jobs Scott did and Pam hadn't even considered it. "Christmas is almost here. I know it will be difficult for you."

"It will be. I have no family, but I do have a place to go. Leigh Jackson has asked me to come to her house for the day."

"Fantastic." Nell smiled. "I'll be there, too. She makes every holiday so much fun. I'm glad you're going."

"Me, too. My life is changing so much from how I had planned it. Maybe the three of us will have a lasting friendship."

"I think it's a wonderful idea. A group of women can always be counted on to find fun and interesting ways to pass time. You'll fit right in with the rest of us." Nell stood in front of the tree. "Would you like me to water this? It looks a little dry."

"Is it? I hadn't noticed." Pam's eyes went up and down. "I'll take care of it, but thanks for bringing it to my attention."

Nell originally planned to ask Pam some questions about Scott and the project. She hoped some memory would be jogged loose. She didn't want to ruin the good feeling Pam was experiencing, so held back for another time. Plus, it looked like the two of them would get together more in the future.

Nell gave her a hug. "I'm so glad we have things straightened out between us. Again, I'm really sorry for making you go through that pain."

"It's over now. Don't give it another thought."

Two boisterous dogs climbed all over Nell as she sat on the floor and rolled a tennis ball back and forth. Finally, George took the ball in his mouth and went off with it. Newman chased after him and Nell saw it as her chance to escape. This evening she'd write a restaurant review on her blog to occupy her thoughts for a couple hours. She needed a break from all her theories about the murders. She sat at her desk in the office and looked at the last few emails her blog had received.

Santa's Helper

Nell, could you let me know of places in the area serving food on Christmas Eve? I've read ads in the paper, but they said either open on Christmas or closed Christmas Day. None of them mention Christmas Eve. My extended family seems to have acquired lots of preferences, so I thought it'd be easier to take them out for the meal. Help!

Crimson Tulip54

I've been reading your blog for months and want to let you know how much I enjoy your suggestions about food and dining spots. My sister lives in your town of Bayshore, and she told me there is some speculation about some deaths there. Is that true? Have you been looking into it? Has someone been poisoned or is it a rumor?

Nell closed her email. It didn't look like she'd get away from the murders. She'd postpone answering those questions until later. She dug up her restaurant notes and read through them. With her eyes closed, Nell brought back images of the Green Bay restaurant and flavors of the food. She tried again to chase away all thoughts of murder and allowed her mind to wrap itself around the memory of delicious food—a subject which was near and dear to her heart.

Nell's Noshes Up North

Jade
Green Bay, Wisconsin

The crackling of wood in the fireplace was a comforting sound in the dining room of Jade. My companion and I appreciated the beauty of the flames along with the heat as it spread through the room. The supper club had been a standby in Green Bay for years, but neither of us had visited it recently. New spots are always opening, and Jade was on the other side of town from Bayshore. We were anxious to see if it held up to our nostalgic memories.

The wooden tables were heavy and old, but that lent a sense of character to the atmosphere. We took our seats, ordered wine, and browsed the menus. I scanned the offerings in search of one particular dish I hoped to see. I was in luck. They still prepared Maple Whiskey Salmon. I didn't need to look any further. The choice was made. My friend chose a ribeye steak with sautéed onions and mushrooms.

Once the order was in, my glass of wine arrived and I took a few minutes to reacquaint myself with the decor. Not much had changed, but I liked how the room gave off the look of confidence and pride. The lovely white linen tablecloth and napkins delivered an elegant feel.

A dark green salad arrived for me, loaded with fresh plum tomatoes, cucumbers, sliced beets, and crunchy sunflower seeds. It was topped with garlic croutons, blue cheese, and their secret house dressing. I delighted in the salad while I kept my fingers crossed my salmon entrée had kept the same high standards.

We didn't have long to wait for our meal. My friend's steak sizzled as it was set down in front of her. The tantalizing aroma almost made me wish I, too, had ordered the beef. One look at the salmon set me right. I was in for a treat. A large, center-cut salmon fillet was before me with maple whiskey sauce dribbling down each side. I cut down and through the chopped walnut and Dijon crust to gaze on perfectly roasted fish. I could hardly wait until the bite reached my mouth. I closed my eyes to remove any other sensory interference. I only wanted to experience the salmon. It almost melted in my mouth.

My dining companion was thrilled with her steak. She said it was a perfect medium rare and she'd order it again. We both had baked potatoes and sour cream to round out our meal.

I've been asking myself why I allowed years to go by without stopping at Jade for a meal. I don't know the answer, but frequenting it often in the future will rectify that mistake.

True nosh or truly nauseous? —You decide!

Contrary to what she wrote in her review, Nell knew why it had been so long since she had been to Jade. It was one of Drew's favorite places to eat. A lot of old memories lingered around the iconic supper club. She hadn't been in a hurry to bring those thoughts to the surface. Now she was ready to return because she was moving on with her life. She may never straighten out her relationship with Sam or see the flirtation with Chuck go any further. But taking the idea of male companionship into consideration was progress and the end result didn't matter. She was under new management and directed herself toward getting the most out of life.

She read over her review again, but decided not to hit publish. Instead, Nell closed the lid of her laptop. She'd take another look at it later with a fresh eye.

Chapter 29

Nell parked her car on the street in front of Hazel's house and walked up to her front door. The inside door opened before Nell raised her hand to knock.

"Have any news to tell me?" Hazel stepped aside. "You can still come in, even if you don't have news."

"That's a relief. Otherwise, I'd be headed right back to the car." Nell went in and was directed to a seat. "I thought it would be nice to have a visit."

"Don't hand me that. I'm sure you want to ask me something."

"Can't I come over to see how you're doing the day after the funeral of a dear friend to both of us?" Nell sniffed.

"You could, but you didn't. What is it you want to know, Nell?"

"Good grief." Nell hesitated, but knew she was caught. "Okay, fine. There are a couple questions I would like to ask you." At Hazel's nod, she continued. "Do you have any idea what project Clayton was spearheading for the city? Dottie Dumpling and Scott Marshall were helping him."

"My, my, my. Three pillars of the community working together for a common cause. All dead in December. Do you think that's a coincidence?"

"No, and I must say I think you're being flippant about our friends' deaths. This isn't like you, Hazel."

"Maybe it isn't. I'm not myself anymore. I think about how someone came in Mr. Dunbar's own house to poison him. I was there all the time. They could have easily have poisoned me, too."

Nell reached over and patted her leg. "You're safe now."

"Am I? Are any of us safe?" she asked. "Someone could get into all the houses in Bayshore if they tried hard enough."

"Should I give your daughter a call? Do you want her to come for a visit?"

"No. Just because I'm old doesn't mean I need a babysitter. To answer your question, I don't know what Mr. Dunbar was working on for the city. He always had projects to keep himself busy."

"Were Dottie and Scott ever over at Clayton's home, or do you know if Clayton had meetings with them anywhere else?"

"They were over there a few times."

"Did they have paperwork or a computer?" Nell edged closer. "Do you remember the topic of discussion?"

"I served the coffee. I don't recall offhand. Give me some time to think back."

"Okay. I have another question."

"Figures," Hazel smirked.

"Do you know if there was ever anything going on between Yolanda and Vern Rolf?"

"Ever anything going on? How about for the last fifty years?"

"What are you talking about, Hazel?"

Hazel looked up at the ceiling, then stared at Nell. "It took you this long to figure it out. Their affair has been Bayshore's best-kept secret."

"You mean, they were a thing even before Yolanda's husband died?"

"Oh, yes. And I was in the perfect place to know everything that happened. You know the help always knew what was going on with the Crawley family on the "Downton Abbey" series."

"Hazel, I couldn't be more surprised. I was expecting you to tell me nothing was going on and you'd never heard of anything so ridiculous."

"I could have told lots of stories through the years. Most of them I've forgotten by now." Hazel ran a tissue over her eyes. "You know, I think the two of them could have been happy together. Poor Vern has put up with a lot through the years being married to Louisa. He and Yolanda are going to get together now, though."

"What do you mean?"

"When Yolanda was home for Thanksgiving, I overheard the two of them talking. Stuff like 'we've suffered long enough' and 'only a couple more steps to go until we're together forever'."

"Have you mentioned their relationship to anyone else?"

"No. I never would have said anything while Mr. Dunbar was alive. He would have been devastated to know how his daughter was carrying on with a married man."

"Could I get Yolanda's phone number? I'd like to have a chat with her."

Hazel copied the number from a tablet onto a piece of paper. "Now don't go hounding the poor woman. Her father's been murdered. She's overwrought."

"We'll see if that's true," Nell murmured. She stood up and took the paper with the phone number. "I have a lot of thinking to do about this situation. Please don't tell anyone else what you told me about their affair."

"I won't, but try to let me in on what's going on for a change. Is that too much for an old woman to ask?"

Nell parked her car in front of the police station and hurried inside. She hoped Chuck would be available to speak with her. She smiled as she saw him bending over Judy's desk in the lobby.

"Is there any chance I could sneak in and talk to you for a few minutes?"

Chief Vance looked up and returned her smile. "Sounds like a plan. Come on back." She took a seat in his office and he closed the door behind her.

"Thanks a lot for hightailing it away from me yesterday after the funeral.

I was left there for twenty minutes while Louisa criticized every traffic light in the city."

Nell noticed his twinkling eyes and knew he wasn't too upset. "Sorry about that, but I knew if I stayed, I'd be drawn into her conversation, too. Louisa is part of the reason I stopped by, or rather her husband."

"The long suffering Vern? What about him?"

She shared all the information she had heard from Hazel about the relationship between Yolanda and Louisa's husband. "Had you heard any of that before?"

"No. And I'm not happy to hear about it now. The younger officers sometimes go in for that kind of talk, but I don't enjoy it. I have to admit I'm disappointed you do."

"I'm not *enjoying* it. I'm wondering how their intention to unite could possibly fit in with the case."

"Are you referring to Clayton's murder? How would his daughter having an affair cause his death?"

"That cryptic message I just told you that Hazel overhead. 'We've suffered long enough' and 'just a couple steps until we're together forever' could be important. Yolanda and Vern are doing some serious planning."

"If Louisa was the one murdered, I might agree with you. But how does Clay's death influence the two lovers getting together?"

"Maybe Vern needed money to remove himself from Louisa's clutches. The story going around is Yolanda will be inheriting a bundle."

"Again with the rumors." Chuck shook his head. "Good police work doesn't depend on small town gossip."

"I agree, but sometimes you can put a thought in the back of your mind and it pops out later and saves the day," Nell offered. "Stranger things have happened."

"Okay, I guess I've learned not to discount anything through my years of police work." Chuck looked over at Nell. "Go ahead and find out anything you can on the Yolanda/Vern connection. You may be a little more discreet than one of my men would be."

"Thanks," Nell smiled. "I'll call her right now and see if I can stop over." She pulled the phone and the number out of her purse as she watched Chuck put on his coat and wave as he left his office.

"Hello."

"Oh, Yolanda, this is Nell Bailey. I'm so glad I caught you."

"This isn't a good time for me to talk. I'm on my way into the bank. I'll have to call you back later."

"Okay. Thanks."

Leaving the police station, Nell hoped Yolanda really would call her back.

She noticed Clayton's chocolate-brown BMW parked on the street in front of the bank. *At least she hadn't given Nell a song and dance.* She considered standing by the car and waiting for Yolanda to come out, but decided against it.

Instead Nell walked to Mocha Chip, purchased a caramel latte, and sat at a table by a window. She had the perfect view of the building and the vehicle.

She finished her latte and noticed Yolanda's car was still parked in front of the bank. *Evidently, she was doing more than cashing a check.* Nell went to the bakery counter and ordered a regular cup of coffee. As she turned to go back to her table, Leigh walked in the door.

"Nell. What have you been doing? We haven't talked in weeks." Leigh offered a big hug.

"More like days, but I've missed you, too." Nell laughed. "Come sit here with me."

"I'll order and be right there."

Soon the old friends were catching up and sharing stories.

"I hear you were able to connect with Pam Marshall. Isn't she nice?"

"Yes. I was pleased at how well we got along."

"I feel so bad for her. She's so alone," Leigh whispered.

"It looks to me like you're doing your part to get her involved. She told me you invited her over to your place for Christmas."

"The more, the merrier. She needs to be with people, and I can see a little mischief in her. You know, I think she could be one of us."

"One of us? Really? That's a pretty exclusive group," Nell joked. "Not many want to be included."

"I noticed her wicked sense of humor before her husband died. It may take her a while to get it back."

"We have a lot of time to help her in her journey. She'll make a good addition. I'll welcome her to the group with open arms." Nell took a sip of coffee. "What would you like me to bring on Christmas?"

"You don't need to bring anything."

"I want to."

"Then whatever you'd like."

An hour slipped by seemingly in minutes, and Leigh announced she had to return to her shop. They walked out of the Mocha Chip together and went their separate ways.

"See you on Christmas, Nell."

"Yeah, and now it's just a few days away."

A glance over to the bank revealed Yolanda had left. Nell checked her phone to make sure she hadn't missed a call, and then thought she'd drive over to Clayton's house to see if his daughter had returned. She saw no evidence of the BMW and decided to head home to try to get hold of her by phone.

She took a last minute swing past Hazel's and there was the brown car. Knowing an investigator cannot be timid, Nell parked her own vehicle and knocked on the door.

"Come in."

Nell pushed the door in a little at a time. She heard sobbing and steeled herself for an uncomfortable situation.

"Why are you here?" Yolanda sniffled. "I told you I'd call you back."

"I'm sorry, but I thought you might have forgotten, or maybe you didn't think it was important enough to call back."

"What is it? What is so damn important?" Yolanda glared at Nell.

Out of the corner of her eye, she caught Hazel shaking her head with wide eyes. Nell had already figured out this was not the time to ask questions about an extramarital affair. She had to think of something else fast.

Hazel to the rescue. "Sweetheart, why don't you tell Nell what you found out at the bank? You know she's helping the police investigate who killed your father."

"I've had a hard time believing Dad was murdered. I didn't want to accept it." She wiped at her eyes with a tissue. "But I do now."

"What happened?" Nell whispered.

"Safety deposit box," Yolanda sputtered. "It's empty."

Nell gasped.

"Please excuse me. I need to wash off my face." Yolanda headed to Hazel's bathroom.

Nell looked at Hazel with raised eyebrows.

"I'm not saying anything," Hazel responded. "You'll have to get all your information from the source."

"You're right. That's how it should be done." Nell touched her gold necklace. "It's only...I think we're getting closer to solving this whole case."

"Everyone in town will rest easier once the killer is known. I look at my pills each morning and wonder if there's poison in them."

"We're all uneasy, but I'm sure it will be over soon."

"How can you be sure, Nell?" Yolanda sneered as she came back in the room.

"Please relax, dear. Nell was only trying to soothe an old lady." Hazel went to Yolanda and took her arm. "Let's sit down here on the couch."

"I can leave, if you want me to go," Nell offered. "I want to help, but if you'd rather..."

"No, stay. I'll explain to you about the safety deposit box."

Nell tilted her head.

"I had been to Dad's lawyer's office for the reading of the will earlier this morning. Dirk Holden and I were walking over to the bank when you called me. The last time I had spoken to Dad about his will was, say...eight months ago."

"Eight months ago? About the time he started working on a project for the betterment of Bayshore?" Nell raised her eyes to the ceiling and then looked right at Yolanda. "I'm hesitant to mention this, but do you think your father cut you out of the will and moved the money somewhere else to go into his project?"

"Heavens, no. I already had my inheritance. Forty years ago, Mom and Dad gave my late husband, Erik, and me money to buy our resort near Sarasota, Florida. That place has been a little goldmine. We didn't have any children, so I'm not going to bequeath money or property to descendants. I told Dad to do whatever he wanted with his money. Besides, I had been to the reading of the will and knew about Dad's project for Bayshore."

"You were fine with the project?"

"Absolutely. It was just the kind of program in which Dad would be involved. He loved Bayshore and wanted it to prosper."

Yolanda had pulled herself together, so Nell continued with another question. "Would you mind telling me about it? No one has a clue."

"There was a reason for the secrecy." Yolanda looked at Nell, then Hazel. "This cannot get out to the citizens of Bayshore." At their agreement, Yolanda explained. "Dad's estate was worth well over three million dollars. He was giving a million each to the hospital and the Bayshore Area Humane Society. The other million plus was going to be divided equally among the churches and organizations in Bayshore. These groups needed to be civic or religious, but had to help people and had to have been operating for at least two years before his death. Dad was afraid of someone catching wind of his donation and creating fake organizations to get a portion of the money."

"How wonderful!" Hazel threw her hands in the air. "It couldn't go to worthier causes."

"Remember, Hazel, the money has disappeared," Nell said.

"No. The money for the project is still there." Yolanda combed her fingers through her hair.

"Well, what had been in the safety deposit box then?"

"Mother's jewelry." Yolanda's face drained of all color. "Dad had already told me I'd receive all the gems and I've been wearing a lot of the pieces. I'd only switch out the items every six months or so. Dad kept them at the bank. I didn't want to have him go down there every time I came home."

"When was the last time you checked on the jewelry before today?"

"Not since July. I had taken Mom's diamond out and several other pieces I planned to wear until Christmas. Then I'd exchange them for others. There were a lot of other gems in there, including Grandma's diamond ring and bracelet. Dad kept several pairs of gold cufflinks and his grandfather's gold pocket watch were stored in the box. An elegant pearl necklace which once belonged to a great aunt back east was a showpiece. The jewelry was worth a fortune. Now it's gone." Tears came back to her eyes.

"We can't narrow down the time of the theft." Nell rubbed her left eyebrow. "It could have been any time since July."

"I remember when your mother used to wear those huge diamond and ruby earrings. Are they gone, dear?" Hazel asked.

"Yes, they're gone." Now it was Yolanda's turn to put an arm around Hazel. "All of the pieces were insured, but the sentimental value is priceless."

"Did Clayton have any other deposit boxes in the bank?" Nell said.

Yolanda nodded her head. "Dad owned a great deal of property and had stock in many businesses. All the deeds and information were in separate deposit boxes. As far as cash goes, I know he liked to have a certain portion of his portfolio easily accessible. He always kept a box of cash. Those safety deposit boxes are still intact."

Nell sat forward in her seat. "I'm not sure I understand how someone could have taken the jewelry out of the bank box. Doesn't a person need a key and then have to sign to open it?"

"That's true. The bank log shows the last time Dad signed in to the box with the jewels was in late October."

"I'm sorry to ask this," Nell said, "but could Clayton have taken the gems and done something with them? Sell them perhaps?"

"No." Yolanda's glare said she would brook no further discussion on the matter.

"It doesn't look good now, but we'll figure it out. I understand why Clayton didn't want the whole town knowing about the donation, and you may still want to keep that aspect to yourself. Mayor Corbin may want to choose a time to present your father's donations to Bayshore as a surprise. However, it's of utmost importance that you tell Chief Vance everything you've told me," Nell advised.

"I know that." Yolanda looked at her watch. "I've already made an appointment to meet my attorney, Mr. Holden, at the police station in a few minutes." She smirked at Nell and mocked, "You didn't think I was going to tell *you* and not the police, did you? I want my father's murder and this theft to be solved, and that won't happen if I depend on some Jessica Fletcher wannabe."

Jessica Fletcher wannaba! She wasn't that old. Yolanda has gone straight back to form. Nell jumped from her seat and headed for the door. She said good bye to Hazel, and yelled back at Yolanda, "If you want to keep the donations a secret, make sure Louisa Rolf doesn't find out." She couldn't stop herself from adding a kicker. "But then again, I bet you're an old hand at keeping secrets from Louisa!"

Nell waited long enough to see Yolanda's mouth drop open. Then she slid in her car and pulled away.

Chapter 30

"Sam!" The patrons of Sam's Slam, Home of the Grand Slamburger, greeted the owner as he limped in to his establishment as he held tight to a cane. "Great to see you back among the living."

Benita held his arm for balance as she and her dad maneuvered to a low table, and sat down. "I wanted him to take it easy a couple more days, but he insisted he wanted to be here. I don't know why. He can't stand behind the bar yet."

"I need to get the feel of how things are going in my place," Sam groused. "I was going mad sitting at home."

"Heard you were out with a busted foot, but not how it happened." Jerry, a bald man with glasses, swiveled on his barstool.

"The doctor says my ankle is badly sprained, but I tell ya, if this is only a sprain, I'd hate for my ankle to be broken," Sam replied. "Last Saturday night I slipped on ice getting out of my car and got wedged between the tire and the curb. It took several hours for someone to find me."

"What a freak accident! It had to have been miserable," Jerry's wife, Wilma, added.

"It sure wasn't fun. I shivered so hard I never thought I'd lie still again. Then there was the pain." Sam shook his head. "I'm glad to be on the mend and here today."

"If somebody else had slipped, I might have accused him of drinking too much, but I know better with you, Sam. You mostly pour drinks for other people." Jerry raised his own glass.

"Yeah, I was sober as a judge." He pulled himself up and started toward his small office off the kitchen. The Bean was at his side.

She kept her voice low so the patrons couldn't hear. "Are you ready to call Nell yet? She doesn't know about your fall and has no idea why you haven't called her."

"Give it a rest. I'm not going to call her with you hanging over me."

"I don't know why you wouldn't let me call her last Sunday after we took you to the hospital." Benita helped Sam into his chair behind the computer, then propped his foot up on a liquor box. "She probably would've been here every day."

Sam scowled and looked at the door.

"Okay. I can take a hint." Benita left the office, but stuck her head back in and said, "Dad, please give her a call."

Sam picked up his cell and started to hit Nell's number. Instead, he listened again to her messages on his voicemail.

I would like to talk to you. If you've decided to sever our relationship for good, you need to let me know.

That last one was a doozy. Sam sighed and set the phone down. He dug around the piles of paper on top of his desk for paperwork to keep his mind off Nell.

By the time she walked in the door of her kitchen, Nell had chastised herself for the immature remarks she hurled at Yolanda. She admitted she enjoyed saying them, and seeing the shock on Yolanda's face. But after examination, she saw her comments as unkind and unnecessary. Yolanda was at a low point, and even though her words were also unkind and unnecessary, Nell should have taken the high road. She hoped Yolanda didn't take her snipping as any kind of threat. That was not how she meant it. *Well, how did she mean it? Good question.*

She let George and Newmie outside, but they didn't stray far from the patio. They were soon back in the house and raring to go. They wanted a walk, so she hooked their leashes up and the threesome left the house for a short spin around the neighborhood.

Nell couldn't let her mind travel too deep into thoughts about the case as the roads were slick and she had no desire to fall. She needed to keep her wits about her. After slipping and almost landing on the ground, she guided the boys to their comfortable house. As she doled out the treats, Nell wondered how she'd manage to find out what Yolanda was sharing with Chuck. She thought back to a few weeks ago when Chuck also made the Jessica Fletcher comparison. Then, she had a totally different reaction. The way each of them said the name wasn't similar in the least. Tone meant everything.

The phone rang and Nell was happy to see it was Chuck. They could put their heads together and figure this crime out.

"Hello, Chuck."

"I had an interesting visitor this afternoon."

Chuck's voice did not elicit a warm feeling. She smelled trouble.

"Oh?"

"Doggone it, Nell. Why do you insist on getting people riled up? Yolanda Dunbar Nyland is all bent out of shape because of words she had with you."

"I realize how inane this sounds, but she started it," Nell said.

"What?"

"Yolanda spoke to me in a derogatory manner and made unkind comments. I returned fire." She rubbed her left eyebrow with her left hand.

"I can't believe what I'm hearing. She didn't tell me anything about you holding a gun on her. Returned fire? Please tell me you don't own a gun."

"No, no. Not at all. We exchanged words, that's what I'm saying. I admit I wanted to take the words back after I hurled them. It was immature. My point is, I didn't go running to you about what she said."

"Are you calling Yolanda a tattletale? Really? As the Chief of Police of Bayshore I'm letting you know hearing gossip and personal bickering between people is not in my job description. I agree that you have a lot to offer as far as ideas, and I appreciate you as a behind-the-scenes person. Do you remember I said you could look into the Yolanda/Vern connection, but to be discreet? Where was the discretion?"

"I know I shouldn't have said it."

"As I've mentioned before, there is a problem when you are a...let's say, a first responder. You are a civilian, not an officer. When you get too close to an investigation, it could be a huge liability for the department."

"I know that, and I haven't asked to strap on a gun."

"Lord, help me!"

"Point taken, Chuck. I'll try to stay more in the background."

"Thank you."

"Any chance I could come down to the station now?" Nell asked.

"You're kidding."

"Just to talk. You said I offer good ideas. I need all the facts."

There was a long pause on his end. "How about the day after tomorrow? Can you wait until then?"

"Not tomorrow?"

"Not tomorrow."

"Okay, I can do that. What would be a good time for you?"

"Ten o'clock. Does ten work for you?"

"Sure. See you then." Nell put her phone back in her pocket and smiled. The chief was still willing to talk about the case.

The more Nell thought about it, the more her comments to Yolanda bothered her. She wouldn't be happy with herself until she apologized. If she had expected Sam to apologize to her, then she should apologize to Yolanda. Deciding there was no time like the present, she pulled a loaf of cranberry walnut bread out of the freezer to take as a peace offering. Nell wrapped it in a decorative red and green cloth napkin and was on her way to Clayton Dunbar's family home.

Yolanda looked genuinely taken aback when she opened the door and saw Nell standing before her. "May I help you?"

"Yes. I want to apologize for my comments earlier today. I'm sorry. I hope you can find it in your heart to forgive me," Nell said as she stood on the stoop.

"Come in." Yolanda stepped aside and closed the front door. "I wasn't expecting you."

"I'm sure not, but I have a peace offering." Nell handed her the loaf of bread. "Here's some cranberry walnut bread I made earlier and put in the freezer."

"Thank you. Do you have a habit of doing things for which you need to apologize?" Yolanda laughed as she took the bread.

"One never knows."

"Please sit down. Of course, I accept your apology and let me offer my own. I'm sorry for the way I talked to you. Mother and Dad raised me better."

"We're all under a lot of stress. Sometimes it gets the better of us," Nell said. "This is awkward, but I want to assure you I won't tell anyone about you and Vern Rolf."

"This certainly *is* awkward because I can assure you there is nothing to tell," Yolanda stressed. "I don't know who you're getting your gossip from, but you have been misinformed."

"Again, I'm sorry. You know how stories spread in small towns."

"I can understand it to a point. Vern and I were friends all our lives. In high school we dated, but we went our separate ways after graduation." Yolanda shook her head. "I suppose some people could make something of the fact we always get together when I come back from Florida. When Erik was alive, he knew about our friendship and it didn't bother him."

"Do you think Louisa is as receptive to the idea of the two of you getting together as your late husband was?"

"Who knows what that woman thinks? I've never been able to figure her out. She has the perfect husband, and she badgers and heckles him beyond belief."

"So, you aren't planning to run away together?" Nell questioned, a smile on her face to show she was kidding.

"What? No, never. Vern and I are not going to marry or have an affair or anything at all. I will repeat myself. You need to acquire better sources because your information is way off." Yolanda shook her head. "I'll tell you one thing, though. I've been after Vern for years to leave her. He deserves more out of life than to be forever married to a spiteful, gossipy shrew."

Yolanda was convincing, but Nell couldn't help think about the words Hazel had shared with her. 'We've suffered long enough' and 'just a couple steps until we're together forever.' Could Hazel have gotten it all wrong?

"Yolanda, do you think Vern will ever leave Louisa?"

"Never. He adores her. I can't figure it out." Both of Yolanda's hands went in the air. "After all these years, my talk of him leaving her has become a joke between us."

"Maybe Louisa is a different person with Vern than she is to the rest of the town."

"Maybe."

Nell changed the subject and shared pleasant memories about Clayton and then she took her leave. They parted on amiable terms with promises to go out for lunch sometime before Yolanda returned to Florida.

The old Sable started to shake as Nell drove past Hazel's house. She pulled over and parked in front when she noticed the older woman sitting in her chair in front of the window.

Hazel met her at the door. "What do you need now?" She gestured for Nell to enter.

"I'll only take a little of your time," Nell assured. "Do you think you could be mistaken about what you heard Yolanda and Vern talking about?"

"I'm an old woman. My memory isn't so good. I can be mistaken about a lot of stuff."

"When you heard Yolanda say 'we've suffered long enough'. Do you think it could have been 'you've suffered long enough'?

Hazel looked at Nell. "Possibly."

"Could 'just a couple steps until we're together forever' be something more like 'just a couple steps and you could be without her forever'?

"I suppose. I was having trouble with my hearing aids at the time. I had to get them adjusted."

"That's right. I remember your appointment was after Clayton's death."

"If I did get it wrong, I'm sure glad you were the only one I told. Yolanda would be upset if she thought stories were circulating about her in town."

"Thanks, Hazel. I've got to run."

Sam moved at a turtle's pace from his small office. Benita came running from the dining room when she saw him. "Why didn't you text? I want to help you."

"That's exactly what I don't want. I can't have someone hovering over me, getting in the way, trying to do stuff for me," Sam grumbled. "I need to walk, however slowly, by myself."

His daughter's face dropped. "You didn't call Nell, did you?"

"No. I'm not calling her until I can walk without this damn cane and a trussed-up foot. I feel like a Thanksgiving turkey."

"You aren't trussed up. It's a tall, walking boot so you can get around." She stood with her fists at her sides. "I'm not saying anything else about Nell...today."

"Good."

"But I think your stubbornness will look like rudeness to her."

"I thought you weren't going to say anything else." Sam caught the scathing look the Bean shot him. "The next time I see Nell, I don't want to look like an old man and have to explain about my fall. Having everyone here at the bar know about it is embarrassing enough."

The television was on for white noise while Nell put together her supper. She tore apart the lettuce for a salad with beets and avocado, and then cut up the onions for chicken salad to make a sandwich. George and Newmie were underfoot and were rewarded with a piece of cooked chicken breast she took from the fridge. She put both parts of her meal in to cool and sat down in the living room. Wouldn't you know? *NCIS* was having a marathon. She didn't remember the episode which was playing, so she kept watching. Her thoughts turned to Sam even before Mark Harmon was on the screen. Why hadn't he called her? She realized he was stubborn, but hadn't considered him to be ill-mannered as well. If it was over between them, she wanted their last words to be civil. Nell hated to admit it, but she was hurt. Maybe he wasn't the man she thought he was, and she should put him out of her mind.

She clicked the channel to a Christmas program, but seeing the cartoon Grinch made her think of Sam, too. The crabapple. Then, turning to HGTV, Nell landed on a show featuring beautiful tablescapes. As she strived to rid her head of all thoughts of murder and men, she considered having an impromptu get-together for some of her female friends. If she was going to do this, it would have to be tomorrow afternoon. That wouldn't give anyone much notice, but she'd make it clear she just came up with the idea and no one was a last minute invite. If people can't make it, no big deal.

She made up her guest list, including some who had never been to her house before. She'd make the calls and still have time tonight to run the vacuum and clean the bathrooms. She'd decide on the menu as she rested in bed before she fell asleep. She picked up the phone to call Elena first.

Chapter 31

"Happy Holidays, Merry Christmas, Happy Hanukah, and everything in between." Elena laughed as she entered and threw her arms around Nell. "I'm so happy I postponed going out with Herb until tomorrow. We haven't gotten together in ages."

"It's so wonderful to see you. And I'm happy you're early." Nell walked through the dining room toward the kitchen. "There are still some things I need to finish."

"I can help," Elena offered. "Your table looks lovely with your beautiful tablecloth and seasonal centerpiece."

"Thanks, both of which I bought at your shop."

"I know. I recognized them," Elena winked. "What can I do?"

The doorbell rang. "If you can get the door..."

"Sure. How many are coming?"

"Four more said they could fit it in their schedules." Nell took a pan out of the oven. Soon she heard Leigh's voice and walked out to the living room.

"I brought Pam with me."

"Great idea. I'm glad both of you could make it on such short notice." Nell gave them each a hug and took their coats.

"I put aside the earrings I was working on to finish later. Coming here was too tempting to pass up," Leigh said.

"Two more vehicles just drove up the driveway." Elena backed away from the window.

"That should be everyone then," Nell said. "I'll make introductions when they're inside."

When all were present and the coats safely on top of the guest room bed, Nell performed her hostess duties. The women gathered and looked at each other. Most knew or knew *of* Yolanda. Elena and Pam finally met. The one person who was acquainted with Nell and no one else was Judy Schurz, the receptionist at the police station.

"It's wonderful to meet all of you. I haven't been here since those parties with Jud. Now I've been asked by you. I feel all grown up. Thanks for inviting me, Mrs. Bailey," Judy smiled.

"You're gonna have to stop the Mrs. Bailey business. From now on I'm Nell." The others all agreed first names were the way to go.

Nell poured the merlot and the conversation was fast and furious as she brought out appetizers in fancy crystal dishes and platters of goodies to the table. They filled their plates and wandered back to the living room to socialize and sample the snacks and wine.

The hours quickly escaped amid belly laughs, small chuckles, and food. Lots of food. George and Newman loved all the attention from six different pairs of hands. Their favorite part of the day? The bits of appetizers that landed on the floor or bites of cracker Nell allowed them to be given. Leigh and Elena had been close friends with Nell for years and knew what food the boys were allowed. Yolanda, Pam, and Judy fit in better even than Nell had expected. They had stories to share and loved dogs. Who could ask for anything more in a friend? She was delighted she had thrown together this last minute party. It wasn't too much longer and a couple of the guests started making noises about leaving.

"Leigh, before you go, come in here with me and take a look in the guest bath. It's where I put the hanging wire flower you made." The two left the living room.

"Elena, do you know if there is a master bath in Nell's house? All the wine has caused me a bit of an emergency after drinking several cups of coffee earlier. All the liquid, you know."

"Oh, sure. Through the bedroom over there." Elena pointed her in the opposite direction.

A few moments later all the guests were back in the living room and getting serious about heading for home. The coats were returned, and Nell received lots of kudos for hosting the party.

Soon Nell was alone, happy with her successful gathering and with her ability to keep thoughts of Sam and the murderer off her mind. She picked up a piece of butterscotch candy from the floor. Must have dropped from someone's purse.

Nell poured herself another glass of wine to sip on as she started to transfer the food from her elegant dishes to plain storage containers. She had put out a darn good spread. Unfortunately now she had the stuffed, too-full feeling. And she had all these leftovers. This wasn't good, as she was trying hard to control her eating habits. Another splash of wine, and Nell had an idea. She'd make up five of her red and green plastic dinner plates with an array of items she served at her party and deliver one to each of her friends who had been at her house today. She wouldn't be ruining anyone's diet with her tempting treats as they were all of a healthy weight. Everyone said they loved the treats she'd made. Then she wouldn't have too much left, and there wouldn't be the possibility of a binge. She could put her cranberry spread in the middle of the plate and accent the edges with bars and other sweets. It would look festive and bright. She'd make the plates up now and leave them in the refrigerator while she talked with Chuck at the station tomorrow.

Then she'd come back to the house and pick them up for delivery afterward. Nell decided not to call her friends ahead of time; she wanted it to be a surprise.

Chapter 31.5

Man or woman, it doesn't matter to me. Women are exceptionally open to my charm. I think they like my face, the drawn out, sad look of someone who offers them no competition. I'm friendly and willing to please—until I have them in my clutches. As long as I can get them to open their door for me the first time, I know I have them. Today was a nice diversion.

Killing Nell has been a possibility and I've given it serious thought. At the very least, it would have been a joy to have poisoned her dogs. The dumb, little white one came over to me often to get a cracker and a pat on the head. The bigger dog, the schnauzer, wouldn't come anywhere near me and even woofed at me a couple times. Smart boy. But time is of the essence. Now I must get serious about packing up the jewels and heading out of town. You never know when I may be back. I've been known to disguise myself and fool people I've known for years. Nell Bailey, I may not be done with you yet.

Chapter 32

Nell was up early to give her boys a good walk around the neighborhood and then take care of some chores. Upon their return and after waiting for treats, George and Newman jumped on the loveseat, plopped down, and curled up. The scene they set looked so cute with a dog on each end, Nell grabbed her phone and took a picture. She was still chuckling as she used a stepstool to put the fancy dishes she'd used yesterday away in a high cupboard. After doing a few other odd jobs, it was time to get ready to go to the police station.

She relaxed under the stream of hot water in the shower and rubbed her new mango ginger shampoo into her hair. What a glorious scent! Nell took great care as she dressed in a pair of black pants and a soft pink sweater with small sparkles. The top had a shimmer without being gaudy. For a real bonus, nothing felt as tight as it did in the past, even after splurging a bit yesterday. She knew this time she was headed in the right direction.

With a kiss on the head to each of her boys, she opened the door to the garage. *On second thought, why don't I take Judy's platter with me? I can give it to her when I go to the police station.* She went back to the fridge and pulled out one of the plates.

Nell opened the door of the police station, balancing the platter of goodies in her other hand. She headed for the reception desk in the lobby but Judy was nowhere to be seen. The chief walked out of the hallway and over to the desk.

"Hi, Chuck," Nell greeted. "I have some treats for Judy. Do you know where she is?"

"She didn't come in today. Called and said something came up. It's the first time she's ever done that." Chuck came over to Nell and looked at the plate. "What do you have there?"

"Some sweets and savories, but this plate is for Judy."

"Darn," Chuck said, snapping his fingers. "Come on in to the office."

Nell left the plate on Judy's desk as she thought Chuck might try to finagle some of the treats out of her. Then she followed him down the hall.

"Have a seat." Chuck was already behind his desk. "What did you want to see me about today?"

"I'm wondering about progress in the case, and if you could share anything you and Yolanda talked about the other day."

"I already told you one thing we talked about—how irritated she was with you."

"I have some news for you on that front," Nell smiled. "I felt guilty about how I spoke to her and went over to her house and apologized. She told me she was wrong, too. I guess you can say we made up. She was even over at my house for a Christmas get-together yesterday."

Chuck leaned back in his chair and intertwined his fingers over his stomach. "As upset as Yolanda was when she came in, I wasn't expecting the two of you to make nice anytime soon."

"I've also come to the conclusion I was incorrect in thinking that she was having an affair with Vern Rolf."

"Whoa, what has brought on this newfound ability to admit mistakes?" Chuck gave Nell her first opportunity to see almost every one of his teeth in a wide grin.

"There isn't any newfound ability. I always own up to the truth." Nell smiled right back at him. "How about you and the department? Not everything turns out the way you expect, either."

"Point taken. And to prove I'm a good sport, I wish I had something to share with you. I really do." Chuck held his hands up. "However, there's no breaking news."

Nell exhaled. "I'm disappointed. I was hoping there would be a lead."

"Now don't you go off and try to stir something up," Chuck warned. "We've already had this discussion. A number of times."

"I know, I know." Nell got out of her chair and headed to the door. "The only plans I have for today are delivering trays of goodies to my friends."

The chief followed her out to Judy's desk. "Do you have any of your famous fudge on that plate?"

"Yes, and all kinds of other bars and treats, too." Nell noticed Chuck practically drooling. "I think I'll deliver them to her house. Thanks for your time, Chuck."

She picked up the plate, backed out the door, and caught the chief watching her with a half-open mouth.

Nell let the boys outside while she loaded the other four plates of treats in her car. She planned to go to Elena's first and hoped to catch her before she left with Herb. The boys were coming back in the house when the doorbell rang. George and Newman went into serious bark mode and bounded toward the perceived intruder. Nell pulled open the front door to find Yolanda standing there with a box.

"Come in, Yolanda."

"Thanks. I'll only stay a minute. I'm sure you're busy."

"Actually I was about to come over to your place, among others. Go ahead and sit down. I need to go out to the car for a minute. I'll be right back."

The boys were torn between keeping an eye on the visitor and following Nell, with Nell winning out. She came back in the house with a plate of goodies.

"I'm delivering a platter to each of the women who came to the party yesterday, but since you're here, I'll give it to you now."

"How thoughtful! Everything tasted delicious. Thank you." Yolanda handed the box she brought to Nell. "I enjoyed myself so much at your party yesterday I wanted to give you something in return."

"You didn't need to do anything. I had more fun than anyone." Nell lifted the top from the box and spread apart the tissue paper.

"This is the Irish linen tablecloth and twelve napkins Dad and Mom bought on their Ireland trip. Dad picked it out and it was always his favorite."

"Yolanda, this should belong to you." Nell touched the soft, delicate fabric. It was such a nice gift.

Yolanda smiled. "Dad would want you to have it. He'd be pleased with me that I thought to give it to you."

"I don't know what to say other than I'll always treasure this elegant keepsake."

Yolanda rose from her seat with her plate of treats, and Nell met her with a hug. "I think I understand why Dad liked you so much. Thanks for the goodies."

"Thank you, too." Nell walked her to the door and closed it after her. She set the box with her present on the table and went to the garage with a spring in her step. Her heart soared, thinking how a small kindness had affected Yolanda. She must remember how each person influences others around them. Nell had never really cared for Yolanda, but perhaps she should have made an effort to be friends. Yesterday, she had seen her in a new light. Now they seemed to be on track to a fulfilling friendship. She made a promise to herself to keep a positive attitude about everyone until she's proven wrong.

She backed down the driveway and turned in the direction of Elena's home.

She was in luck and had a good visit with Elena. Nell was pleased to spend some time chatting with each of her friends without care as the minutes slipped away. Getting with a bunch of friends is always nice, but so is having some private time one on one.

At Leigh's, Nell enjoyed their unique Christmas decorations and took extra time to give attention to Leigh's cats. She bent to pet Prada, while Coco weaved between her legs. Nell had to walk back to the bedroom to find the feline giant, Louis Vuitton, sprawled out on the bed.

"Oh, precious babies. I'll see you in a couple days when I'm here for Christmas."

"Louis is saying he can't wait to see you again." Leigh laughed.

"Yeah, I can tell by his excitement today."

"I'm always glad to see you, Nell."

"Thanks, Leigh. I have one more plate to deliver and then I'm heading home to be with my boys. I'm going to relax the rest of the day."

"Sounds good. See you Christmas Day."

Nell had knocked several times before she turned to walk back to her car, when the door opened and she heard a voice call out to her.

"Nell. Don't leave."

"Oh, good. I'm so glad you're home." She walked in the house. "I want to share some of these treats with you."

"Aren't you sweet? And it was so wonderful you had me over to your home yesterday. I had a better time than you could possibly know."

"I'm glad." Nell took a glance around the room which seemed to be in a huge disarray, totally different than when she had been here in the past. "I think I'll run along. You look busy. The boys will need to go outside anyhow."

"No. Stay a while. I'm finishing a few things up around here. Besides, I thought I saw a doggie door at your house."

"I have one, but they like it better when I open the door for them," Nell said. "They tend to only use it for emergencies."

"Sit down. I can't believe you let those stupid dogs run your life."

"I guess I can stay for a few minutes." Nell sat, but then squirmed in her chair. Something was off kilter.

A beautiful cut-glass bowl filled with butterscotch candies was offered to her. Nell took one and set the bowl back down on the coffee table.

"Don't mind if I do. No one ever gained weight from one piece of hard candy." She laughed as she fumbled with the wrapper and put the candy in her mouth. Her effort to lighten the moment was met with dead silence.

"What do you know about Clayton Dunbar's death? Any new clues?"

"I don't know much about it," Nell hedged. "Remember, I'm a civilian."

"Don't give me that. You and Chief Vance are thick as thieves. Tell me everything you know."

Nell could feel a thin layer of sweat form above her lip. "He's not all that willing to share. I go in to see him, but I never come away with much."

"What about that Dumpling woman? Do they know anything about her demise?"

"I wish I had some big news to tell you, but I thought you'd be more concerned about how your husband died."

"I don't need to ask you about that. I know exactly how Scott died. He had a bad heart, remember?" Pam pursed her lips and batted her eyes.

Nell's own heart sank, but there was no time to feel sorry for herself. She had to think. What was her best chance to escape? She'd have to play along. "Yes, I know and I'm sure the police realize that, too. There's been no talk of an autopsy." *Maybe she could keep her calm.*

"The only autopsy talk was from you, Nell Bailey. Not one other person thought he'd had anything but a natural death. Only you." Pam looked at Nell with wild eyes.

So much for keeping her calm. Nell shot out of her seat and charged to the door. "I have to leave."

"You're not going anywhere. Get back to that chair."

Nell tried to open the front door, but her nervous fingers couldn't complete the mission. She turned back to Pam and saw a gun in her hand. "Why are you doing this to me?"

"Because I can." Pam snickered and held up the pistol. "You're going to do whatever I tell you to do. Understand?"

Nell nodded.

"Good girl," Pam said. "You stopping in today is saving me a lot of work. I'll have you load up the boxes in my vehicle so I can make a clean getaway."

"You're leaving?"

"Don't play dumb with me. By now even you have to have figured out I killed Dunbar and Dumpling. I know you suspected Scott was murdered, but couldn't prove it without an autopsy. I would have put up a fuss about the procedure, but if it would have been performed, poison would have been found in the fudge he ate before dying. Your fudge!" Pam sneered.

"Pam, you had me fooled. I thought you were devastated over your husband's death."

"Oh, I was—when I needed to be. I'm a master of the theatre arts—long, suffering administrative assistant, heartbroken, helpless widow, woman on her own trying to find strength, and let's not forget yesterday's Oscar worthy performance—a cackling member of a women's group of friends."

"We accepted you."

"Of course, you did. It's exactly what I wanted you to do. I've had years of practice making others do my bidding."

Her lips twisted in the cruelest smile Nell had ever seen in her life. Then she looked in her ice-blue eyes, which appeared deranged as they moved from Nell, to the door, then to the window, and back again. *Why had she never noticed the coldness of those eyes before?*

Pam waved the gun at Nell. "Now we're going to walk into the bedroom. There are piles of clothes on the bed and suitcases on the floor. You're going to pack them for me. Then I have boxes in the garage ready to load into the car. If you put a move on it, this will all be over in less than an hour."

"I suppose my boys can wait another hour."

Pam stared at Nell. "Are you really that obtuse? *You're* not going back in an hour. Maybe I should have been more specific. It will all be over for *you* in less than an hour. And I hope your dogs die waiting for you."

Nell cringed at the hateful comment about her dogs, but she had figured Pam intended to kill her. By getting it out in the open, she knew she must do whatever she could to escape. She wasn't going to survive any other way.

"I can see those old gears in your head grinding. Don't start thinking you can get away. I heard about how you overpowered an assailant with your weight. That's not going to happen this time." Pam raised the pistol above her head. "This little baby is all the weight I need. If I have to drop you where you stand, so be it. I'm going to put your car in the garage when I leave whether I kill you now or later. That should give me enough extra time to get far away from this rat hole. If you want to breathe a little longer, start packing."

Nell began the strange work of packing another woman's clothes, knowing she would never pack her own bags again. She tried not to hurry. She needed time to come up with a plan.

"Why Clayton and Dottie? Will you tell me?"

"The burning curiosity of the amateur sleuth, is that it? You want to go to your grave knowing all my secrets?"

"Something like that."

"Where to begin." Pam rubbed her chin. "That's the question. Okay, I'll give you the short version. After marrying Scott Marshall, I thought I'd live the high life. Who knew he wanted to retire in his backward hometown as an ordinary Joe. I wanted more, needed more. An extravagant life in a big city awaits me now."

"You never loved him?"

"Loved him? Are you kidding? Love leaves you vulnerable. It's only for chumps." Pam watched Nell rolling pants and fitting them in for the maximum usage of space. "You're taking too long. I don't need any more of this junk anyway. I'll buy a whole new wardrobe. With the money I'll have soon, I'll be able to buy as many expensive outfits as I want. Scott turned out to be a real tightwad. I wasted too much time on him." She motioned to the suitcases. "Just bring the bags you've packed."

"Since you mentioned acquiring money, how did you manage to get your hands on those jewels?" Nell asked. She zipped up two pieces of luggage and moved them to the floor.

"Pick them up and let's go to the garage. We're wasting time."

She carried the suitcases to the red Toyota Highlander and saw several boxes lined up in a row waiting to be loaded. She also noticed a small covered vehicle. When Pam pointed the gun, Nell began to stack the boxes in the SUV.

"I was able to read through all the paperwork pertaining to the 'mysterious project' by going through Scott's briefcase. I think he was on to me, though, as he started hiding his case and even took it to the fitness center with him. I knew where he hid it at home, so when he was taking his morning shower, I was making copies. A copy of Dunbar's will was in the briefcase with all the jewels going to his daughter. After seeing all the money he was going to bequeath to this town, I was hoping to get my hands on lots of cold, hard cash. Time ran out before I could enact my plan to have his fortune 'donated' to me. I'll have to make do with untold riches in gold and silver trinkets." Pam's evil smile didn't look human.

"You had to kill Clayton, so the gems would be available and you wanted to get rid of Scott as he was on to you. Why Dottie? Was she suspicious, too?"

"That cow, Dottie, would never have caught on to me." Pam uttered a low chuckle. "I wanted to kill her. My skills had gotten a little rusty and I needed practice. Killing Dunbar gave me the old adrenaline rush. I lusted for the quick uplift of another notch on my belt. Nothing like it."

Nell resisted giving in to the feeling of doom that hovered over her head. "How did you get the valuables out of Clayton's bank security box? Isn't a signature needed to unlock it?"

"Once I had access to his paperwork, I knew the jewelry would make me a very wealthy woman. At least for a year or two." A low chuckle escaped Pam's lips. "I made my own secret plans with Dunbar. I visited him on several occasions after revealing that I make jewelry appraisals."

"You're a jeweler?"

"Of course not, you idiot. But he didn't know the difference. I would appraise each piece and have all the paperwork done for Yolanda in preparation for his death. He had given me all the jewelry and I took it home to view at my leisure. I made up several questions about the gems and went over to his house for an answer. That's when I dumped warfarin pills into the vitamin bottle. He called me on the morning of his open house and asked me to bring all the jewels over the next day and he would explain everything to his daughter. He wanted it to be a surprise and asked me not to tell her at the party."

"Your plan was about to be discovered." Nell tried to keep her talking.

"Not a chance. I've been in much tougher spots than filching some baubles," Pam bragged. "At the open house, I made sure his pill container was loaded with the strongest dose of warfarin and also dragged a tail of shrimp through a smashed up pill and coated it with cocktail sauce. Clayton was delighted when I served it to him on a toothpick. I couldn't take any chances. Later that night, I picked up a few small, but expensive antiques from the house. A gigantic handbag is my favorite accessory. You never know when it will come in handy." She laughed, but to Nell's ears it sounded more like a witch's cackle. "I never know who I'll have to kill."

A cold chill ran down Nell's spine. She half-expected to see a split tongue flick out of Pam's python mouth. Most of the boxes were already loaded. Her time was almost up. She knew Pam wouldn't have any pity. She had to make some kind of move. She picked up the smaller of the suitcases in both hands and slammed it in Pam's face. Then Nell ran to the back of the car. The gun went off, but the shot was wild.

"You'll pay for that," screamed Pam. "I'm gonna kill you slowly. And painfully. And your little dogs, too."

Nell crept next to the open driver's side door, reached in, and grabbed the garage door opener. She pulled an empty plastic recycling bin to her chest for protection and hustled to the big door, already out of breath.

Another shot rang out and this time the bullet hit the edge of the bin. Nell knew it was now or never. She hit the opener, which took its sweet time rising. She had positioned herself on the other side of the riding lawnmower and prayed someone had already heard the shots and called the police.

Nell was about to make a run to the door when she heard the loud roar of the vehicle's engine. She crouched down lower behind the lawnmower. Pam tore out of the garage, but not before getting one more shot off in Nell's direction.

The sound of the SUV could no longer be heard when Nell stood up. She saw flashing lights as a police cruiser pulled in the driveway and Officer Wunderlin jumped out of the car. He rushed toward Nell. "Have you been wounded? A call was made to 9-1-1 about hearing the sound of gunshots."

"No, I'm fine. The woman who killed three people in town is making her getaway. She's driving a red SUV. It's Pam Marshall. Go!"

The officer ran to his vehicle, and with sirens blaring, squealed his tires after the perpetrator.

Nell touched the hole in the recycle bin which had protected her and breathed a sigh of relief.

Neighbors came out of their houses and another squad car arrived on the scene. Chief Vance hurried over to Nell and put his arm around her. "Are you okay?"

"Yeah. It's Pam Marshall. She's the murderer, Chuck." Nell's fingers gripped Chuck's hand.

"Officer Wunderlin called it in and has her license number. Other officers are in pursuit. We'll apprehend her soon. I don't want you to worry."

"Of course, I'm going to worry. The woman is a psychopath. She told me she's been killing for years. She was planning to kill me. Slowly." Nell shivered and wiped away the mist that was forming in her eyes. "And painfully."

"You'll be under police protection until we have her in custody." Chuck gave her shoulders a squeeze and guided her towards his car.

"Police protection? You mean I have to stay at the station?" Nell asked.

"We'll take you down there now so you can make a statement. If we haven't located Marshall by then, I'll take you home and stay there with you." He took his arm away from her shoulders and held her hand. "I'm not going to let anything happen to you."

On the way to the police station, Nell's mind was going in several different directions as she thought about her day, or more specifically the time at Pam's house. She had been threatened with a slow and painful death. She'd been shot at three times. She was shocked Pam Marshall was the killer, and from her own words, had a history of psychotic behavior. Who else had she killed?

"Could we stop at my house before going to the station?" Nell asked. "I know my statement will take some time, and I'd like to let my boys out and give them fresh water and food."

"Of course." Chuck turned off Main and headed in the direction of Nell's street. "Anything you want." He used his radio to let the officer who was driving Nell's car know of the change of plans. He would drive it to her home instead of the station.

Then there was this whole thing with Chuck. Why was he acting downright solicitous? It was almost like he was treating her in a different way than with other witnesses. *Could he care about me in a romantic sense?* Chuck pulled in her driveway and stopped the car. Nell's head was spinning as she grabbed the handle to open the door. *Or is he trying to make up for not wanting my help?*

"Hang on. Let me get that for you." Chuck bounced out of the car and helped her out.

"Thanks." They walked to her front door, much to the surprise of George and Newman.

The yelping began in earnest as the two walked in the door. "Looks like your buddies here will warn you of any unwanted intruders. Especially the schnauzer."

"That's George. If, for some reason, he wasn't able to warn me, I know he'd help to ward them off." Nell bent to pet her boys. "The little Maltese is Newman. The three of us are good pals."

"I like dogs," Chuck said. He let them sniff his hand. "My wife and I had a bulldog named Fatman. He was quite a character."

"Bulldogs are great. My brother, Gary, has one, Roscoe." Nell let the dogs outside and prepared their water and food bowls. "How long do you think I'll be at the station?"

"Do you want to go to the hospital first and get checked out?"

"No. I wasn't hit. I'm fine."

Chuck gave her a serious look. "We have time. Maybe they could check your heart and blood pressure. You've had an experience that could be quite upsetting. You may not be aware of some side effects."

"No. I want to go down to the station and make my statement. Then I want to hear that Pam Marshall has been caught. Hearing that will allow me to have peaceful sleep." Nell tilted her head to the side. "She didn't have much of a head start. They should have caught her by now, don't you think?"

"Not necessarily. I don't want you to get your hopes up for a quick capture. Sometimes it takes days. I would have been notified if Marshall was apprehended. If you're ready, let's go and get the statement process started."

"I guess the sooner the better." Nell buttoned her coat.

Chuck's radio went off and he walked into the dining room to answer in private. When he walked back in the living room he announced, "Our suspect, Pam Marshall, was taken into custody heading toward Rhinelander." He reached over and held Nell's hand. "You don't need to worry about her sneaking back and killing you. She's coming back, but in a police car and with no options."

"Oh, thank God." Nell sighed. "I was more nervous than I wanted to admit."

"I know." Chuck nodded and put his arm around her. "Don't think about it anymore tonight. We'll put off your statement until tomorrow so you don't have to go downtown now. No need for a confrontation with that woman. Just try to relax."

"I think that's going to be easier said than done." Nell leaned over and gave Chuck a big hug. "Thank you for taking such good care of me. I feel safe and secure when you're with me." She could feel color rising to her cheeks as she walked him to the door.

Nell tossed and turned in bed, her head full of conflicting thoughts. She still had feelings for Sam, but so far it looked like his feelings for her had dissipated. Or was he being obstinate? She knew him well enough to know it was a possibility. Then again, did she want to spend time with someone who behaved in that manner? What about Chuck? Are the friendly words he's speaking more than professional politeness? Is romance with Chuck a possibility? Nell had no answers.

The true cause of her restlessness was Pam Marshall. Nell realized if Pam didn't give a confession to the police and the case went to trial, she'd have to testify. The thought of sitting on the witness stand and telling her story of what Pam did was terrifying for Nell, even if it was true. Whenever she closed her eyes, the vision of the murderer's cold, penetrating eyes frightened her and wouldn't allow sleep to come. What if there wasn't enough evidence to convict her? Nell rolled over and the sound of a demented voice haunted her. *Slowly. Painfully.*

Nell must have fallen asleep because the classic ringtone of her cell going off startled her awake. She reached over to the nightstand and saw the time was 2:47 a.m.

"Nell, are you okay?" Chuck asked as she answered.

"What? Why wouldn't I be okay? I'm in bed. You're making me nervous."

"Don't get upset. I'm in the car, driving to your house." He turned down the blaring police radio. "Pam Marshall has escaped."

"No!" Nell jumped out of bed and grabbed some clothes. "How long ago?"

George and Newman stretched themselves out on the bed and watched Nell move around the bedroom as she dressed.

"We're not sure. Don't open any doors or let your dogs go outside," Chuck cautioned. "I'm almost there."

"What makes you think she's coming here?" Nell's hands were shaking as she hustled to the kitchen and found a butcher knife for protection. The boys were soon at her feet and went to the front door as their ears picked up the sound of the siren coming in their direction.

The police cruiser came up the drive with lights flashing and Bayshore's chief of police stepped out. He walked to the front door as another squad car arrived.

The door opened enough to allow Chuck to enter and then closed. George and Newmie barked and jumped around him, but the boys didn't hold the chief back. He set the knife aside and put his arms around Nell and said, "You're safe now. I'm here."

She fell into his arms and started to fall apart. "What happened?"

"One of our jailers was found unconscious, locked in Pam Marshall's cell with a huge bump on her head. Marshall was gone. We know it couldn't be any longer than two hours ago. The last scheduled check was completed at one o'clock." He paused. "The female jailer was wearing only her underwear and the inmate attire was on the floor. In other words, our perpetrator wore the proper clothing needed for her escape."

"Does she have a gun?"

"No. Our jailers aren't issued firearms, only batons."

"Two hours ago," Nell whispered, looking at the clock. "Why do you think she'd come here? Did she make threats against me?" Nell rubbed her left eyebrow.

"No. She was a model prisoner for the hours she was held in our facility." Chuck patted her back. "We came here because I wanted to be sure you were safe. I *needed* to be sure. You live close enough to the jail she could easily walk here in twenty minutes. Even less time if the roads and sidewalks weren't so slick. She's probably headed in a different direction."

"She doesn't have a car, does she?"

"All official cars are present, as are the cars of nightshift workers at the police station and jail. She won't get far on foot, Nell."

"She could hide somewhere. She could be in the woods behind my house right now."

"That's why my officers are here checking it out."

The sound of Chuck's radio increased Nell's heart rate. He walked into another room for privacy. She sent up a prayer Pam was again in custody.

He returned in a couple minutes. "The unit that went to the Marshall house found a broken window and the sports car gone. They also found the computer. Dottie Dumpling's Dell was dumped in a dresser drawer."

"Nice alliteration, Chuck."

At the chief's raised eyebrows, Nell reminded, "I'm a retired teacher. I can't help myself."

"If you must. I'd imagine she's long gone from Bayshore by now."

"I don't think I'll be able to sleep until that woman is once again behind bars," Nell said. "She's the embodiment of evil."

"If it's any comfort to you, I'm inclined to think she would head as far from town as possible. She's not worried about you any longer. She wants to save her own skin."

"I hope you're right," Nell said.

"Yesterday she took off, rather than stay and turn out your lights."

"That's an interesting way of putting it." Nell managed a thin smile.

"I need to go back downtown, but I'll assign one of my officers to stay with you when he comes in from his search."

"No. You don't need to have anyone stay with me. I think you're right about Pam leaving town. I'll stay here for a few hours and come down early to make my statement. Maybe she'll be caught by then, or you'll at least have a report her car was spotted."

"I'll be in my office so come down as early as you want."

The officers returned to the house with no evidence Pam was in the woods. Nell and Chuck walked out on the patio and let the boys take care of their early morning business. "Are you sure about staying here alone?" Chuck asked.

"I'll be down in your office before you know it. Then things will be back to usual, and you'll want me to get out of the station and leave you alone."

"I'm not so sure about that."

Officer Wunderlin joined them on the patio. "Chief, is it all right if we take off?"

"Yeah, go over and take the jailer's statement. I'll be down there soon."

Nell, Chuck, and the boys walked back in the house and over to the front door. "There's something I want to say before you leave." Nell put her hand on his forearm. "Thank you for all you've done for me. I'm not sure I could have handled it without your support."

"I'm a public servant. I go where I'm needed." Chuck opened the door. "Pam Marshall will get her just reward. You can rest assured of that. See you in a few hours."

Nell closed the door behind him. She thought about his statement 'I'm a public servant. I go where I'm needed.' Was she nothing more to him than a member of the public? She had started to think there was more between them. He put himself out there, and then pulled back. Maybe he doesn't know what he wants, either. Or is it all her imagination? Had she misconstrued his words to mean something other than what was intended?

Nell hopped in the shower to wash away thoughts of Pam and clean her body as she cleared her mind. Her thoughts roamed from Sam to Chuck and back again. Life was so much simpler when she was still grieving for Drew and had no desire for any other man. She longed for that simplicity again, but never the grief.

As she thought back to the good times she had with Sam and also how much fun Elena and Herb were having, she knew she was ready for the complexities of a relationship. It was time she accept the bad times and know they'd be interwoven in the good.

She found an old red Christmas sweater to wear. It could have won an ugly sweater contest, hands down. The giant head of Rudolph had a nose that lit up. Her students loved it. Nell paired it with blue jeans that had a hole in the knee. She wasn't looking to impress anyone.

It wasn't much past seven when Nell pulled her car in the parking lot of the police station. Chuck came out to the lobby to greet her and escorted her into his office.

"I just received news that will be of interest to you." Chuck held the chair out for her. "I was about to call you, but here you are."

"Please tell me Pam has been captured."

"Not exactly, but she won't bother anyone again. The state police identified the Crossfire sports car with Marshall's license plates fifty miles north of Eagle River. They attempted to pull her over, but she took off. There was a high-speed chase on Highway 45 and Pam Marshall couldn't navigate a turn clocking ninety-seven miles an hour. She ran off the road, and she and her vehicle were consumed in a giant fireball."

"Oh, goodness. I wasn't expecting that." Nell's hands shook. "I've never been relieved to know someone has died before. It's a strange feeling."

"I know. Can I get you some coffee?" Chuck started to stand. "I made a fresh pot when I got here."

"No. I need a minute to compose myself."

"You don't need to worry any longer, Nell. This nightmare is over."

"Are the police sure it's Pam in the car?" Nell asked.

"They haven't been able to get close enough to the flames to check on it yet. Who else would have been driving?" Chuck shook his head. "Bodies being switched only happens in the movies. Once they put out the fire, they'll identify the body. Either by a DNA test or they'll compare dental records to give us our answer. Now for something you'll appreciate. Your statement doesn't need to be as detailed as if you were going to trial."

"That's a relief. I wasn't looking forward to facing her probing eyes in a courtroom. They were hate-filled and cruel. I've never seen eyes like those before."

"You'll never have to see them again."

Chuck walked her to the door where she thanked him again. She was only out a few steps on the sidewalk when he opened the door and called to her.

"By the way, love the Christmas sweater."

The rest of the morning was a blur. It was Christmas Eve day and Nell received calls from many friends and members of her family. Judy made an interesting call. She was ill at home the day Nell arrived with the platter of treats. Her husband had thanked Nell and she had gone on her way to her next friend. After speaking of her shock about Pam, Judy thanked her profusely for inviting her over to her house and for the treats. She hinted at a connection between Nell and Chief Vance. *Good grief, is it that obvious?*

One of the first calls Nell made was to Hazel, who was so looking forward to receiving word about the truth of the murderer and appreciated being one of the first to know. Nell reached out to those who didn't contact her. She repeated the Pam Marshall saga more times than she could count. Most knew parts of the story, but it took a long time to fill everyone in on the ending. Nell included Zane, who was happy to be personally informed.

In the afternoon she halfheartedly watched Christmas movies and tried to take stock of her life. Pam Marshall was not coming after her. She'd been given another chance.

Nell went to the Christmas Eve service in the evening and thanked the Lord for his continued blessing. She knew she had a purpose here on earth, but wasn't sure she was doing all she could to serve yet.

Then it was home and to bed. Nell anticipated falling asleep as soon as her head touched the pillow. She was awake most of the night before. Tomorrow would be a wonderful day. Christmas at Leigh and Ed's was always full of warmth and love. She knew of at least one invited guest who wouldn't be there—Pam Marshall.

Chapter 33

George and Newman were picture perfect in their festive sweaters as Nell fastened the leashes to their collars. The three stepped down the driveway and around the neighborhood with care. There were no clear sidewalks and the roads were slick. She didn't want a three-body pileup in the road on Christmas morning.

They returned without incident. After giving the boys food and water, Nell turned on some holiday music and prepared the dish she was making to take to Leigh's. Once it was cooling in the fridge, she gathered the boys by the tree to hand out presents. Both were delighted with the generous assortment of tennis balls, squeaky toys, and treats they received. George and Newman watched as Nell opened their present to her. The way they huddled around her, you'd think they thought it was for them. Didn't they remember purchasing it? Nell smiled at the thought and tore open the packaging of the new Cuisinart food processor she had purchased a month ago and set aside. Then she picked up the present that had arrived a few days ago from Jud. There was a medium-sized envelope wrapped inside and a card. She tore open the card in her zeal to read what he wrote. The picture and wording was humorous, but his handwritten sentiment brought tears to her eyes.

Dearest Mom,

Happy holidays from Alaska! Let me take this opportunity to share with you how much you mean to me. We've had some difficulties in the past, but I've come to realize they were of my own making. I guess I can say I've matured and understand more about life, love, and the importance of family. I see now that I made your life more difficult after Dad died when I should have tried to make it easier. I've made a host of mistakes, but I won't go into them all now. (This card doesn't have enough space.) You have made me a better man, and I'm so grateful and proud to have you for my mother. I think you'll be happy to know I'm making arrangements to come home for a visit at the end of January. I'm looking forward to spending some serious time catching up with you.

The merriest of Christmases to the Greatest Mom in the World!

Love, Jud

Nell read the letter over and over, tears streaming down her cheeks. He understood...and was grateful...and proud! She had to read it again. He thought she'd be *happy* for him to come home and spend some time with her? How about *ecstatic*?

She wiped away the tears and unwrapped the package. There was no need for any present. Her gift was the lovely card. She took her time pulling the top off the flat box. The boys were impatient, crawling all over her, but she held them at bay. A sparkling emerald bracelet and matching earrings gleamed up at her. A little note was tucked in the box.

> *Dad no longer can give you jewels, but you still deserve to have them.*

A whole new flood of tears threatened to deprive her body of all moisture. She looked at the clock. It was still too early to call Alaska. She'd take care of some chores around the house, shower, and give Jud a call before she left for Leigh's.

As she cut and plated her fudge, Nell realized she didn't feel the addiction to sugar which had long held her in its grip. Her clothes were loose enough she needed to go on a shopping spree. How much fun shopping in a smaller size would be! She acknowledged she wasn't perfect, and would still make poor choices at times. Like today—Ed was known for his luscious eggnog and she planned to enjoy it. But little by little her relationship to food and drink had been changing. As each year passed, Nell appreciated every aspect of her life and the choices she'd made. Even the bad ones were learning experiences. She then thought about the different relationships in her life. She made a spur of the moment decision, took a deep breath, and picked up the phone.

Walking in to Leigh and Ed's second-floor residence over the warehouse which housed Metallic Dreams was similar to seeing Christmas in a museum. A number of trees were decorated and displayed around the house, while others were perched up high in the upper windows of the warehouse. Nell recognized decorations from past years and also marveled at new frills and flourishes. Leigh's huge assortment of nutcrackers was only outdone by her Santa collection. The smell of the wood burning and the crackling of the fire enveloped Nell in a blanket of warmth. Friends and relatives were engaged in conversations throughout the open living area, but the three wise cats were nowhere to be seen. Nell knew they'd make an appearance before long and demand everyone's attention.

Leigh was circulating among her guests, but soon approached her friend with the offer of a mug of eggnog. The frothy concoction lingered in her mouth before gliding smoothly down Nell's throat. Ed had outdone himself this year. After a few moments of liquid bliss, she shared the wonderful news of Jud's card and the emerald bracelet and earrings she wore, paired with her fluffy crimson sweater.

"They're beautiful," Leigh said as she touched the bracelet. "So he no longer thinks his mom is the Wicked Witch of the West?"

Nell shook her head to rid the memory of Pam threatening to get 'your little dogs, too' and answered. "I called him before I left the house and we had such a great chat. He's back to being the Jud I remember."

"I'm so happy for you," Leigh said. "It's been a couple long and difficult years."

"Don't I know it? It's been more like *five* long and painful years. I'm so elated I could burst."

Leigh's daughter, Erin, a younger version of her mother, walked by at that moment. "Did you say Jud was coming home?"

"I did. He said he hoped to be here at the end of January. It'll be great to have him home for a while."

"If he does, we'll have to all get together like old times. Right, Mom?" Erin tossed her head of auburn hair in the same manner as Leigh.

"Of course." Leigh smiled at her.

"Kip, did you hear?" Erin called to her husband. "Jud is coming back for a visit soon."

"Maybe we'll have a chance to go ice fishing," Kip said.

They all heard the doorbell ring from downstairs. "It must be someone who hasn't been up here before and know the trick to entering the living quarters," Nell said. "I'll go downstairs, because I think it's probably Chuck. He's working today, so I called at the last minute and asked if he wanted to come over during his break."

Nell noticed Leigh glance at her daughter with raised eyebrows.

"It's okay I asked him, isn't it?" Nell asked Leigh.

"Of course."

"This is the perfect day. He's going to love my fudge." Nell beamed as she talked to herself going down the steps. "He has such a sweet tooth." She giggled like a schoolgirl in anticipation of seeing Chuck in a social situation having nothing to do with murder.

Nell opened the door with a big smile, but her heart skipped a beat as she greeted the man at the door. "Sam!" She stepped aside to let him in the entryway and closed the door.

"I see Leigh didn't tell you she asked me over for her Christmas celebration. I hesitated in making the decision of whether or not to come today." Sam took her hand in both of his. "Honey, I owe you a gigantic apology. I'm sorry I've behaved so poorly. This isn't an excuse, but the night you didn't show up, I slipped getting out of my car at home and was laid up. I was too proud to let you see me with a crutch and then a cane. This boot is still with me, though." He raised his foot an inch before he enveloped Nell in a big hug. "I should have called. I missed you so much."

"Sam, I don't know what to say," Nell blustered as Sam released her. "Those are the words I needed to hear, but we should talk about where we go from here."

"I know where I want to go." Sam smiled.

The doorbell rang and Nell's blood went cold. *Chuck.* How was she going to handle this situation? She took a deep breath, pasted on a smile, and faced the music.

Nell's hand gripped the upstairs doorknob hard as she inhaled, and pushed it open. She said in a loud clear voice, "Everyone, I need to make some introductions."

Amid the chorus of Merry Christmas and Happy Holidays, Nell walked in with the two new guests.

Leigh rushed over to the doorway to welcome first Sam, and then Chuck as they followed Nell into the room. "I'm delighted each of you could make it."

Ed stepped in to lighten the moment by occupying the two men with handshakes and including them in conversations with some of the other guests in the room.

Nell grabbed Leigh and whispered, "So much for my perfect day."

"This makes it even better," Leigh said. "You have two good-looking, single, sixtyish men interested in you. What more could you ask for?"

"Another mug of eggnog and a way out of this mess." Nell laughed and knew she was in for an unforgettable day.

Recipes

Nell's Jambalaya

Ingredients:

1 tablespoon olive oil

1 medium chopped yellow pepper

1 medium chopped orange or red pepper

1 medium chopped onion

1 (14.5 ounce) can of undrained diced tomatoes

1 cup water

1 (8 ounce) package of jambalaya mix

1 (12 ounce) package of andouille sausage sliced

1 pound uncooked shrimp, peeled and deveined

Optional

1 cup regular rice and add Cajun seasoning instead of mix

1 can of black beans (drained)

1 bunch of sliced green onions

Directions:

In a large skillet with a snug fitting lid, heat oil over medium heat. Saute the shrimp two minutes on each side, remove from pan, and set aside.

You may need to add more oil before you cook the onion and peppers. Stir until they start to soften, six to eight minutes depending on the size of the chop.

Stir in tomatoes, water, Jambalaya mix, and black beans if using. Bring to a boil. Reduce the heat to medium low, cover, and simmer 15 minutes.

Stir in the sausage. Cover and cook for eight minutes. Stir to mix well. Add the shrimp and heat until they get hot, about three minutes. Stir occasionally. Take the pan off the heat and let cool for four or five minutes. The optional green onions could be sprinkled on the top.

Shrimp with Artichokes

Ingredients:

¼ cup butter

¼ cup olive oil

1 juiced lemon

3 cloves garlic, minced

1 tablespoon capers

½ tablespoon crushed red pepper (or to your taste)

1 tablespoon parmesan cheese

¼ cup seasoned bread crumbs

1 (14 ounce) can quartered artichoke hearts in water, drained

1 pound uncooked large shrimp, peeled and deveined

Chopped green onions or parsley, optional

Directions:

Lightly grease a 9x13 inch baking dish and preheat the oven to 375 degrees.

Arrange the shrimp in the baking dish. Squeeze any liquid from the artichokes and set in spaces between the shrimp. Sprinkle in the capers. Top with bread crumbs, crushed red pepper, and onions or parsley, if desired. Then sprinkle the lemon juice on the top.

Melt the butter and garlic in the microwave for twenty seconds or until melted. Add in the olive oil. Drizzle over the bread crumbs and then add the cheese.

Bake for ten minutes or until the shrimp are pink.

This shrimp dish goes well over penne pasta or rice. When I'm watching carbs, I saute a package of chopped cabbage instead.

This is one of my favorite recipes.

Nell's Killer Fudge

Ingredients:

2/3 cup milk

1 ½ cups sugar

½ teaspoon salt

16 medium marshmallows

1 ½ cups chocolate chips

½ cup chopped walnuts

Directions:

Mix milk with sugar and salt in pan over low heat. Bring to a boil and cook for five minutes, stirring constantly. Add the marshmallows and chocolate chips. Then stir in the walnuts. Pour in buttered 9 inch pan and cool.

This is an old recipe that was easy enough for me to make as a child. At home we had a gas stove and I think I remember cooking it for longer than five minutes. At Christmas we used to add ½ teaspoon peppermint extract for some yuletide fare. This fudge brings back happy memories of Mom and home.

Easy Beef Stew

Ingredients:

2 pounds stew meat

1 small can peas with juice

1 cup diced carrots

1 cup sliced celery

1 large chopped onion

2 diced potatoes

1 can cream of mushroom soup

1 can tomato soup

½ soup can water

Directions:

Preheat oven to 275 degrees.

Put in a covered casserole and bake for 3 ½ to 4 hours.

*I like to make this warm and comforting stew in cold weather.
It was my late cousin's recipe and is easy to make. Thanks,
Kay.*

Christmas Cranberry Spread

Ingredients:

1 (16 ounce) whole berry cranberry sauce

1 (4 ounce) can green chilies

2 tablespoons sliced green onions

½ teaspoons each of chili powder, garlic powder, and cayenne pepper

1 tablespoon lime juice

Combine these ingredients.

2 (8 ounce) packages cream cheese at room temperature

2 packages crackers

Directions:

The cream cheese can also be microwaved for thirty seconds or so. Watch carefully. Spread cream cheese on two separate plates. Top with the cranberry mixture. Serve with your favorite crackers.

I've taken this to gatherings during the holiday season, but it is tasty anytime.

An excerpt from Mary Grace Murphy's new mystery...

Town Talk Terror

A Morning Star Mystery

"Your grandfather must be spinning in his grave."

Kyra turned, coffee pot in hand, to the smirking city council member at the nearest table. "What do you mean, Rob?" She bent to fill up his cup.

Before Robert Harris had a chance to respond, the door of the Morning Star Café flew open and Hayley Marsh burst in, marched over to the counter, and barked, "Are there any papers left?"

Kyra's heart jumped in her throat as she scanned her restaurant. Customers were chatting and texting, but it was obvious the conversations were based on the Morning Star Journal at each table. The expressions on their faces ran the gamut from amused to horrified. She leaned over Rob's table with fingers crossed to see what was so intriguing. *Talk of the Town? What could be in that little article to stir up such a ruckus?*

With a stiff smile in response to questions, Kyra circled the tables filling up coffee cups. She hustled to the counter, grabbed a newspaper, and headed to the kitchen.

TALK OF THE TOWN
aka Lucy's Loose Lips

Total Rumor! Vicious Gossip!
Don't Believe a Word of It!

Several years ago, there was a book about the gruesome murder of a man in a small town. The story never became famous or even sold many copies, but it was an interesting tale. There was a well-known secret in the area acknowledging the deceased, Joe Doe, had a history of abusing women. His wife, Jane, refused to press charges against him even though she was seen about town on many occasions with bruises, black eyes, and one time a broken arm. Doe was an unpleasant man, disagreeable to his neighbors, and quick to take offense. Bar fights and petty crimes were also in his repertoire. The local constabulary knew Joe Doe well as they'd had the opportunity to spend quality time with him.

Processing of the murder was beginning when Jane Doe disappeared. Perhaps *disappeared* isn't the correct term.

178

Escaped may be more accurate. Took off, hightailed it out of there, or made a run for it could also be used. According to the book, the police and residents in this particular small town grew suspicious of Jane.

Would this be the Talk of *Your* Town?

Kyra stood in the corner of the kitchen trying to compose herself as the cooks dunked French fries in oil and fried burgers on the griddle. She wanted to sit, but there was too much to do. First on her agenda? Walking to the other part of the ancient building to her mother's office and having a word with Lucy.

***

A hard knot formed in Kyra's gut as she stood outside the office door and knocked. Whenever she knew she was going to challenge her mom, the pounding of her heart increased and a wave of nausea overtook her. Thirty-five years and regular disagreements still hadn't released her of her prefight anxiety.

"Sweetheart, come on in and have a seat." Lucy Calloway popped up from behind her desk and put an arm around her daughter's waist. "What's the matter? You look a little pale."

"You have to ask? What's your explanation for that hideous column?" Kyra didn't take her eyes off her mother as she sat in the visitor chair.

"Isn't it great? Papers are flying out of here and businesses all over town are calling and asking for more copies." Lucy bounced her petite body up on the desk and hugged herself with a delighted little shake. "We're going to break a record."

"Mom, who told you Linda Norman left town?"

"Why would you ask? You know you told me yesterday."

Kyra threw both hands in the air. "I heard it yesterday at the café. I'm not sure it's true."

"It's true," Lucy announced. "I called her house last night and there was no answer. She's gone."

"Not answering the phone doesn't mean she's skipped town." Kyra combed her fingers through her dark hair and paused. "Even if she is gone, you can't print it in the paper. You're accusing her of murder!"

"Don't be such a worry wart. I wrote it as a synopsis of a book inside of a heavily marked gossip sheet. Remember, baby girl, I'm the newspaper woman."

"Yes, you are and you should know better. What would Grandpa say?"

"Your grandfather didn't have much of a sense of humor as far as his newspaper was concerned. And it was *his newspaper*. He owned it." Lucy sighed. "But now I own it and I'm making some changes."

Acknowledgements

I am grateful to the following people for their help and encouragement:

Al, Denise, and Lily as members of the small Oconto Writing Group who made the idea of actually writing a book take shape in my mind.

The Green Bay members of the Wisconsin Romance Writers of America. I have learned so much from the conferences, chapter meetings, and just listening to other authors. You've all helped me grow as a writer.

My wonderful friends and family who have listened to my ups and downs while writing and continued to keep my spirits high.

Joette S. and Sue S. for dispensing pharmaceutical expertise and advice. It's great to have lifelong friends.

Debi Schroeder whose attention to detail and thoughtful suggestions are appreciated more than she knows. You picked up on an overused word *that* I didn't realize I used so often.

Finally, Brittiany Koren and Written Dreams for putting it all together. Her vast knowledge and professionalism made the process run smoothly.

Many thanks to all.

About the Author

Mary Grace Murphy's penchant for reading has been a delight, both personally and professionally. She not only devoured books on her own, but encouraged her students to find their own joy of reading during her thirty-four years as a middle school teacher. Another thread running through Mary Grace's life has been her quest for intriguing eating establishments and interesting recipes. Solving mysteries and discovering scrumptious food set Mary Grace on the path to create her culinary mystery series, Noshes Up North.

Mary Grace resides in Oconto, Wisconsin, a community not unlike her fictional town of Bayshore, where she appreciates the varied food and events which symbolize Northeast Wisconsin.

Forthcoming from Written Dreams Publishing

A legal mystery, *Freewheel* by Katharine M. Nohr

A mystery thriller, *Picture of Lies* by C.C. Harrison

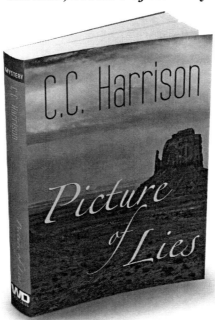